I0557596

STRAWBERRY GOLD

CHRIS GERRIB

This is a work of fiction. Names, characters, places, and incidents are products of the author's imagination or are used fictitiously and are not to be construed as real. Any resemblance to actual events, locations, organizations, or persons, living or dead, is entirely coincidental.

World Castle Publishing, LLC

Pensacola, Florida
Copyright © 2024 Chris Gerrib
Hardback ISBN: 9798341019058
Paperback ISBN: 9798891262881
eBook ISBN: 9798891262898
First Edition World Castle Publishing, LLC, December 16, 2024
http://www.worldcastlepublishing.com

Licensing Notes

All rights reserved. No part of this book may be used or reproduced in any manner whatsoever without written permission, except in the case of brief quotations embodied in articles and reviews.

Cover: Cover Designs by Karen
Cover-designs-by-karen.com
Editor: Karen Fuller

CHAPTER 1

Patrick Kowalski

I hate the smell of nursing homes. It's the smell of piss, dust, and death. Friday January 17, 1986, my eighteenth birthday, found me visiting a nursing home. It was a Friday and the start of the most important two months of my life.

The day had started shitty and had not improved. I honestly think my mom forgot it was my birthday. Hard to imagine since she was there, but things were going seriously south in our life. So, no cake, no card, and definitely no gifts. My dad was in the hospital, sick with something we'd just found out was called Goodpasture's syndrome. They were bringing in a machine from a big hospital in Indy the next day, Saturday, to try and cure him. He'd been in and out of hospitals enough for me to know they only did shit like that on a Saturday. If they thought that otherwise, you might not make it to Monday.

I'd also found out that the bank was foreclosing on our house. Dad had been in and out of hospitals for two years now, first when he lost his leg and now this not-so-goodpasture stuff. The only way we'd had food for Christmas dinner was that the IGA where Mom worked had given us a ham and let her take some dinged and dented cans home. But when you're eighteen, you still have to go to school – or at least I did, until I graduated in May or dropped out to live under a bridge, whichever came first. So I was at a nursing home, interviewing my great-grandmother for my Senior project – an oral history of Eastville.

At the time, I thought the project, let alone school, was a stupid idea. Later, when, because of the project, I found myself staring down the barrel of a gun, I was sure it was stupid. I was wrong.

Oral History Project

Oral History Project by Patrick Kowalski, Eastville High School, May 2, 1986. I started this project by asking my oldest living relative, Barbara Pikus, who we in the family called Great Barb, what her earliest memory was. This interview was conducted on January 17, 1986. Here's what she said.

———————

My oldest memory is of the day when the man with the good boots showed up. He was the first person I ever saw die.

I must have been four or five, so that meant I was speaking only Lithuanian. It was a cool day and dry. I remember that the trains weren't running. They usually roared by our house, belching big clouds of black smoke. I later learned this was during the big railroad strike. Anyway, my very first memory of that day was seeing some men walk down the road in front of our house.

House. Big word for a shack with an outhouse in the back and a pump well by the barn. But I was little, and it was all I knew.

Anyway, I saw some men walking by. They were waving black flags, and I waved at them. My mom came out, and I asked her if we could join them. Mom said something

I didn't understand and took me by the hand into the house. She probably called them anarchists because that's what they were. Besides the flags, they were carrying big wooden beams to block the railroad tracks.

No, now I remember. It was the day before my fourth birthday, so that would have been May 21. May 21, 1894. I remember being excited about my birthday. We made church mice look rich, so I wasn't expecting anything. But thanks to the man with the good boots, I got a rag doll and a piece of candy.

I don't know if Mom sent me out to pick strawberries or I just did. My brother Luidas, your great-great uncle, was just starting to crawl and always underfoot, so Mom wouldn't get upset if I wasn't around. There were wild strawberries in patches along the dusty road which ran parallel to the creek. I went to one of my usual spots, carrying a wicker basket. It's the little one over the fireplace. [Note: interview held in her room in the nursing home. I have no idea what basket she was talking about.] I remember back then thinking it was so big.

Anyway, I found some strawberries. I picked a few and ate a few, working my way into the patch. I came to a little clearing where a storm had claimed a big tree. From there, I could see the men standing on the tracks behind the pile of wood they were carrying. One of them, Robby Cee, we called him, waved at me.

At the time, I really liked Robby – he was friendly. My mom wasn't so fond of him. As I got older, I realized he was, well, you'd now say retarded. Back then, we weren't so nice. Anyway, he waved, and I saw one of the men he was with had an ancient gun he was holding. Even I knew it was old, and I think it was a muzzle-loader, which was obsolete even then. But it was probably all he had.

I waved back at Robby Cee and went back to picking

strawberries. When I got my basket and tummy full, I went back to the house. Mom thanked me and said we'd have a pie.

I got to the muddy patch just before the creek when I saw him. The man with the good boots, I mean. He had a funny look on his face, like he'd eaten something that didn't agree with him, and he was walking down the road faster than my little legs could carry me.

I picked my way carefully through the muddy area, which Dad told me was caused by an underground river coming up to meet the creek. I'm still not sure if he was serious or just telling tales.

I didn't know how, but I beat the man to our house. Well, I eventually figured it out, but I'm getting ahead of myself. I think I had just given Mom the strawberries when we heard footsteps on the bit of gravel in front of our house. I remember running out, followed by Mom carrying Luidas. I saw the man, swaying, pale and sweaty, standing in front of our house.

Dad walked out front from the garden, hoe in hand. The man said something which I didn't understand. Like I said, I didn't speak English back then. The man swayed again, then went face-down in the dirt.

Dad walked up to the man and said something I also didn't understand. For Mom and my benefit, he repeated it in Lithuanian. "Good boots."

Mom handed me Luidas and ran over to the man in the dirt. With Dad's help, she rolled him face up. Curious, I walked over, carrying Luidas as best as I could. The man's face was frozen in pain.

"He's dead," Mom said to Dad.

"You sure?" Dad asked. Mom glared at him. "Okay. So what do we do?"

My memory cuts out there. The next thing I remember

was Mister Calabro rolling up in a wagon. It was dark, and the only light was a lantern on Calabro's wagon.

Dad and Mister Calabro talked a bit, and then the two of them got the dead man into the wagon. It wasn't done particularly gracefully, more like tossing a sack of potatoes. Once they got the body situated on the wagon, Mister Calabro climbed up, took the reins, and rolled out. Dad came walking back in.

"What's he going to do?" I asked Dad.

"Bury the man, I suppose," Dad replied, settling heavily into a chair.

"What about his people?" I asked. "He's got a mommy and a daddy."

Dad chuckled. "I suppose he does," he replied. "But we couldn't find anything on him with his name. Just a train ticket to Chicago."

Back then, Chicago might as well as been the moon. "He's from there?"

Dad shrugged. "Don't know." Dad looked at Mom. "And?"

Mom smiled and lifted up a blanket. Underneath it was three big gold coins and a gun. The revolver I keep in my bedstand, in fact. [Note: I'm pretty sure they don't let 96-year-olds keep revolvers in their rooms in the nursing home.] "There were four in his pocket," Mom said, pointing at the coins, "and some paper money and change."

"Need to leave the man enough money to get buried," Dad replied. "Besides, Calabro might look funny at us if a well-dressed man like that had no money at all." I remember he ruffled my hair. "Looks like you get to pick out something at the store tomorrow. Happy birthday, Barbara."

CHAPTER 2

Monday, May 21, 1894

"Why isn't this damn train moving?" Dan Forrest asked the conductor. As he did, he winced from the sharp pain in his chest. *Heartburn. That's what I get from eating at backcountry train station restaurants.*

"Strikers have blocked the tracks," the conductor replied. A frown flickered across his pinched face.

"Strikers?" Dan asked.

The conductor shrugged, his too-tight jacket bunching up. "That's what I said."

"Damn anarchists," Dan replied, trying to ignore another sharp pain in his chest. "They should be shot."

"The National Guard's got some men on a train behind us," the conductor replied. "I expect that's what they're going to do."

"When's the Guard getting here?"

Another shrug. "As soon as they can, I suppose. They might be having trouble getting an engineer to move the locomotive. Some of the engineers went on strike, too."

Anarchists. Reds and anarchists. All of them should be shot. Dan reached under his coat and fingered the revolver he kept there. It was one of the new-fangled Colt Army .38 revolvers. He'd finally retired the .45 – damn thing was getting too heavy to lug around. "Are the trains running north of the blockage?" he asked.

"As far as I know, yes."

"And how far are we from a station?"

"Not far," the conductor replied. "Five miles."

Dan looked out the window, glad the wind was blowing the coal smoke from the engine away from the train. He could see a dirt road running parallel to the tracks, and it looked like there might be some houses just off in the distance. "Think I could get a horse?"

Yet another shrug. Did this damn man know anything? "Probably. Or at least somebody to give you a ride."

Dan looked at the sturdy leather pouch at his feet. *That gold needs to be in Chicago by morning. It ain't gonna get there at this rate.* He stood up, ignoring the sudden dizziness he felt. "Get me off of this train."

"I can't issue a refund..." the conductor said, backing away from Dan.

"Hang the refund," Dan growled. "Ain't my money anyway." Dan traveled light. Everything he had was either on his back or in the bag, which he picked up. It felt a lot heavier than it had that morning in Nashville. He glared at the conductor. "Well?"

"Follow me."

The pair went to the rear of the car, ignoring the curious looks of the handful of other people on the train. The conductor stepped out onto the car platform and produced a metal folding set of stairs from somewhere. He put them from the steps of the railcar to the ground and clambered down. "You'll want to go north," the conductor said, pointing in the direction they were traveling. "Nearest station is Eastville."

"Thanks," Dan growled. He stepped off, grateful for the light and cooling breeze. He shifted the revolver into a coat pocket for easier access.

As Dan drew even with the locomotive on the road, one of the strikers, more of a boy than a man, saw him and waved from their barricade on the single set of tracks. The boy didn't look quite right in the head. One of the other strikers, a Dago by the complexion and holding an antique musket, had followed the boy's eyes. He glared and said something to his companions, too quiet for Dan to hear.

Probably talking Dago, and I wouldn't understand anyway. Dan fingered the revolver in his pocket. *Six beats one any day of the week.* After a quick conference with his fellow anarchists, the Dago contemptuously waved Dan on. *Apparently, the blackguards are still okay with shanks' mare.* Dan walked on, half-sad there hadn't been any trouble.

The farmhouse he had seen from the tracks was just past the barricade. There was a black flag, really just a cheap strip of cloth, flying by the door. Anarchists, Dan thought, and probably not of a mind to help a train passenger. He kept walking.

As he walked, he pulled a rag from his pocket to wipe the sweat from his brow. *Getting soft in my old age*, he thought. *Hell, I've carried heavier loads in hotter weather than this without breaking a sweat.*

The road curved to the right, aiming to avoid a small creek which the railroad had tressled over. He came out of sight of the anarchist's nest and into a tree-lined road. It didn't look like it had rained, but this bit of road was still muddy. *Must be the shade and the creek*, Dan thought.

After about a hundred yards or so, the road finally crossed the creek via a bridge made of a few logs, bark still clinging to them, laid over the creek. *Man could have waded the creek*, Dan thought, then got a whiff of the creek. Somebody was dumping sewage into it from the smell.

Good thing the bridge is here, Dan thought, glancing at his new boots. He wiped his brow again and inhaled deeply, trying and failing to catch his breath. *Gotta lay off the pie*, he thought, patting his gut.

The road straightened out north of the bridge. It was lined on both sides by trees and uninhabited. The tracks had to be to Dan's left, but with the trees in leaf, there was no way he could see it. He kept walking. *Something was moving around in the bushes. Small, by the sound of it.* He patted the revolver again. *Probably a squirrel or maybe a fox looking for a squirrel dinner.*

About a half-mile down the deserted road, Dan came by a freshly cut tree stump just on the right of the road. He sat down on it heavily, putting the bag at his feet. The pain in his chest had gone from occasional to continuous, and he just couldn't catch his breath. Despite the cool May air, he was sweating, his shirt clinging to his back. He looked down at the bag.

"$24,000 worth of double eagles is damn heavy," he said, his voice startling a squirrel. It was ten times what he'd make in a year, and he was comfortable.

He looked around. The light was fading, and the only creature in sight was the squirrel busily chewing on a nut.

"Damnation." He said it again, the squirrel too busy with his nut to even look up. "This gold is not going to get to Chicago tonight." *Not at this pace, at any rate.*

The squirrel dashed away, running into the forest. "You're supposed to take the nut with you," Dan said to it. He looked down at the bag again. "I'll hide the bag," he said. *I'll hide the bag. Without the bag, I can move faster. I'll walk into town, hire a horse, come back for the bag, and then move on.*

He got up and put thought into action. Just a few steps deeper into the woods, and even with the stump, he came to a tree that had grown up next to a big exposed rock. Rain had gotten at the tree, creating a gap between the rock and the tree. A brown leather suitcase-sized gap.

It took longer than he'd liked – hell, everything was taking longer than he'd liked today – but he got the bag in the gap. Covered with a few leaves, the brown bag was well-hidden. Since it was a few feet from the stump, Dan could easily find it. He stepped back into the road. *Maybe I'll get a hotel room in town tonight. Sleep this off. Telegraph ahead. Not like I can control a herd of damn anarchists.*

Another half-mile down the road, he walked over a tiny stream bridged by a few planks. Probably the same damn stream, meandering its way off to find the Mississippi. To his right, the stream was flowing out of the wall of the valley and had cut an arch through some rock. The arch looked just barely high enough for Dan to walk through. He stopped for a second on the tiny bridge to catch his breath, then continued. No more than a hundred yards down the road, he came to a tiny, unpainted shack. A girl, no more than five, peeked out at him from the open door of the shack.

"Do you have a horse?" Dan asked, stopping in the road. *Probably not. Probably don't have a pot to piss in.*

The girl stared at him.

Dan suddenly felt very dizzy. He tried to steady himself but lost his balance on the road and crumpled to the ground. The fall somehow knocked the wind out of him. He struggled to breathe, his mouth kicking up dust on the road. The pain in his chest went from strong to shooting. He let out an involuntary scream, but all that came out was a croak.

Dan lay on the dirt, unable to move. The last thing he heard was a man's voice saying in a heavy Russian accent, "Nice boots."

CHAPTER 3

Amy Burton, Land of Lincoln Legal Aid, Champaign, IL

I glared at my wristwatch again. The Kings were late. I let out a sigh. What did I expect? Maybe if they came in soon I could still get out to happy hour at Houlihan's.

Fortunately for my temper my phone rang, the two short rings that signaled an internal call. I picked it up, and Lisa, our receptionist, told me that the Kings were in the waiting room. I went to collect them and led them back to my tiny office.

"What seems to be the problem?" I said as soon as my ass hit the chair. I decided not to add 'this time' to my question.

"Damn bank is screwing us," Mr. King said.

I glanced at him. He was a white dude, short and wiry, sporting long black hair and a mustache. His t-shirt had seen better days. "How so?"

He tapped his wife's arm. "Show them."

Mrs. King, a mousy little woman with strawberry blonde hair, handed me an envelope that had been ripped open by hand. I extracted the letter and read it.

The letter was from a local bank claiming that they were two months behind on their house payment. Why any bank had given the Kings the time of day, let alone a loan, was beyond me, but mine was not to judge. "Did you make the payments?" I asked.

"Of course," Mr. King replied.

"Then all we need to do is pull a cancelled check," I started.

"Not check," Mr. King said. "Cash. I took it into the bank myself."

"Then let's find the receipt..."

"I looked," Mrs. King said, her voice barely above a whisper. "I couldn't find it."

"She must have thrown it out when she was cleaning," Mr. King said.

I've had the misfortune to be in the King's house on several occasions. Not much cleaning got done. If Mr. King had actually come into the $449.56 monthly payment in cash, it was highly likely said cash went into booze, maybe drugs, and probably the services of some entrepreneuring woman he'd met at the bar.

"Without a receipt," I said, spreading my hands, "there's not much I can do."

Mr. King glared at me. I'd seen that same glare used on his wife, and the woman just melted. I was made of sterner stuff, so I just sat there and waited. After a minute in which it finally sank into Mr. King that glaring at me would do nothing, he softened and said, "So, what do we do?"

"Ideally," I replied, "you pay them what you owe. And get a receipt."

"Like I've got that kind of money lying around."

Surprise, surprise. "In that case, I'll call the bank Monday and see if I can make other arrangements."

"Couldn't you call now?" Mrs. King asked.

I gestured at my watch. "It's five 'til five on a Friday. I doubt anybody with the power to make a decision is still at their desk." And if they were, the chances they'd be willing to delay their departure to cut a favor for a crappy customer like the Kings was slim to none.

"I'm just so worried," Mrs. King said.

I screwed on a smile. "I'll handle this," I said. I held up the letter. "I'll keep this so I have the details for Monday."

"Thank you," Mrs. King gushed.

I stood up. "If that's all, I have an appointment to get to."

The Kings stood up, and Mrs. King said something about how she was sure my appointment was important. It was – happy hour ended at six.

John B. Hood, Dallas, Texas

"You want me to go where?" John Hood said. He looked past his boss to the window outside. Another rainstorm was brewing. He hoped it had gotten above freezing outside. The city of Dallas, not to say the whole state of Texas, shut down when any freezing precipitation hit the ground. As it was, the dark clouds fit his mood. Nothing good ever came out of a Friday afternoon meeting.

"Chicago," his boss, Brian Wells, said. "Actually, a suburb of. Downer's something." Brian looked down at a paper on his desk. "Downer's Grove."

"Why?"

"We build motels, John," Brian replied. "And we got a contract to build one there."

I've only worked for this company for ten years. I know we build motels. "For who?"

"SleepTight."

Oh, Christ on a stick, Hood thought. SleepTight was the biggest pain in the ass client they had. Tighter than bark on a tree, slow to write a check, and acted like the cookie-cutter bargain-bin motels they ran were the fucking Ritz. Other than that, they were great people to deal with.

"Why me?" Hood asked.

"It's a demo and a tight lot," Brian replied. "It needs your expertise."

"And this couldn't be done when the weather breaks?" Hood asked. "I mean, Chicago in January..."

"They were supposed to start three months ago. The former owner of the property put up some last-minute roadblocks."

"Great. Go up to Siberia to get behind the eight ball."

"Would a five-grand bonus make you happy?"

Well yes. "Ten would make me even happier."

"We seem to have settled on seven-and-a-half. Marge will book your tickets when she gets in on Monday."

CHAPTER 4

Patrick

Saturday, January 18th, dawned gray and cold. Mom had me drive to the hospital. It was a quiet ride. Once we got to the ICU, Dad's doctor, Doctor Thing, met us. He's an Indian guy (Asia, not American) and was wearing a lab coat over jeans and a knit pullover. I think 'Thing' was short for a longer Indian name, but I really don't know.

"Doctor Hansen is getting the plasmapheresis machine ready," he said. I assumed that meant the blood-filtering doohickey.

"Can we see Mike?" Mom asked.

"He's pretty out of it," Thing said, "but yes."

We both went into the ICU. A gray-haired white guy and a younger man were hooking something up to Dad's right arm. He had more tubes in him than I thought was possible. We both went to Dad's left. He looked at us, smiled, and said hi.

"We love you," Mom said to him.

"I know," he replied. He waved a feeble hand at me. "Take care of her."

"You'll be out of here in no time," I said. "They got the box to fix you."

He just smiled at me. To Mom, he said, "I'm sorry."

"Sorry for what?" she said.

"The money. Leaving you alone."

"You'll pull through this," she said.

He gave her another wan smile.

The younger medical guy said to the older, "We're ready, doctor."

"Will it hurt?" Mom asked them.

"No," the older guy said. He pushed a button on the machine, which started to make a low whirring sound. Blood came out of a clear tube from Dad's arm into it, and after a few ticks, blood came back via another clear tube. "Looks good," the younger man said.

The older man turned to us. "We should step outside," he said.

Once we were in the hallway outside Dad's room, watching him from the window, the older man introduced himself as Doctor Hansen.

"Will this work?" Mom asked.

Hansen stood there gravely for a long pause. "I'll be honest," he finally said, "this is a Hail Mary."

Thing walked up to us. "I'm still trying to figure out how he got this."

"When he lost his leg," Hansen said, "did he get a blood transfusion?"

He'd lost the leg a few years ago. He was cutting trees one weekend with a chainsaw, and it got away from him. It got his leg so badly they had to take it off. Still, he's a tough old man – he used his belt for a tourniquet and got to the road where he flagged down a car.

"Two liters," Thing said. "Barely had time to type him."

Hansen shook his head. "I've been seeing an uptick in these cases. Most of them are tied to blood transfusions."

"How long will this take?" Mom asked, gesturing at Dad.

"Six to eight hours," Hansen replied. "We need to take all the blood out we can, filter it, and put it back."

"You should go home," Thing said. "We'll call you with updates."

———————

"How was your great-grandma?" my mom asked as we drove home from the hospital.

"She was having one of her better days," I said, wondering why the health of her grandmother was important enough for her to ask about it. In truth, for Great Barb, a better day was one in which she remembered to talk in English.

"Good," she replied.

"So that's it?" I asked.

"About Great Barb?"

"Well, no. About Dad. About the house."

"What about the house?"

"The bank's foreclosing."

She gave me a surprised look. "Who told you that?"

"I saw the damned letters, Mom. I'm not a kid." I didn't have to ask why we weren't paying the bank. When Dad lost his leg, he was out of work for a year. You can't be an auto mechanic at Brown Chevrolet if you can't stand. He finally got back on his feet, as it were, but Brown had hired somebody else, so Dad went to an independent shop. They didn't pay nearly as well.

She sighed. "I'll handle it."

"How much do we owe?"

"I'll handle it."

"Mom!"

Another heavy sigh. "Around fifty thousand," she replied. "Plus, we're still on a payment plan with the hospital for the leg."

Plus this round of hospitals, I thought. I'd been to the hospital in Indy – that was too nice of a place to be cheap, and the doohickey they were bringing over probably wasn't cheap either. I didn't think Dad had real good health insurance. I felt my face flush – damn greedy hospitals!

It wasn't a long ride from the hospital to our house. I parked in front, and we walked into the house to find my grandma, Mom's mom, Mary Balthus, sitting at the kitchen table.

"One of these days," Grandma said, pointing at the door.

"Some crazed drug addict is going to bust in," Mom finished for her. We'd heard it before. Nobody locked their doors in Eastville. Well, except Grandma Mary.

"I hear the bank is foreclosing on this house," Grandma said.

"Did Pat tell you that?" Mom asked sharply.

"He did not," Grandma replied. "I heard it from somebody at my euchre club, who probably shouldn't be spreading gossip. Is it true, Ruth?"

Mom just nodded a yes.

"So he's worth more to you dead than alive?" Grandma said.

"Mother!" my mom exclaimed.

"It's a fact, right?"

"My husband, the father of your only grandson, is sick, and you're worried about money?"

Grandma glared at her. "Hell, yes." Her face softened. "I don't want you to end up like me."

My grandfather, her husband, had died when I was in grade school. The details were never explained to me, but he didn't leave her much, if any, money. What she had was mostly what she'd earned from Social Security.

"I love him!" Mom said.

"And I loved Ollie," she replied. "Look what it got me." She shook her head. "I told you..."

"Not now," Mom said, a dangerous tone in her voice.

I got up to head to my room.

"Where are you going?" Mom asked.

"I don't know," I replied.

"You're on break, right?" Grandma asked. "From school."

"No," I said."

"Darn," she replied. "We could get you a job."

"I can drop out."

"The hell you can," Mom said. To Grandma, she said, "He's got one semester left to graduate."

"Then he should finish it," Grandma replied. "You are going to graduate, right?"

"Of course," I said. "My last major thing is finishing my senior project."

"What's that?"

"An oral history of Eastville," I said. "Mr. Olsen assigned it to us just before the break."

"The teacher thought they'd have a chance to meet with their relatives over the holidays," Mom said.

"I picked Great Barb as my subject," I said, "and she had some interesting memories."

"Great Barb?" Grandma said with a scoff. "Anything she tells you is more like fiction than history."

"Mom," my Mom said.

"She's senile," Grandma said. "And Ruth, you didn't answer my question."

"What question?" she said.

"How much more is he worth to you dead?"

I sat down reluctantly, not wanting to listen to the two of them argue. My Mom, who I love dearly, would let her Mom chew her out over the phone. It got worse in person.

"Actually, no, he's not worth more to me dead," Mom said, much louder than needed.

"You don't have life insurance on him?"

"Dave's doesn't offer it," Mom said, referring to Dave's Auto Repair, where Dad worked. "And we couldn't afford it."

"What about all those ads on the TV?" Grandma offered. "The ones with life insurance and no medical questions."

Mom turned and glared at her. "I called them. Every. Single. One. Of them."

"They all say you don't need to answer any health questions."

"And what they all don't say until you call is that they don't pay jack if you die within twelve months of paying the first premium!" Mom said, frustration in her voice. Dad had gone into the hospital for the first time just before Halloween. "So no, he's not worth more to me dead." She waved her hands around the house. "We might have to move in with you!" Mom stormed out, heading to her room.

Grandma sat there like a fish just landed on a hook. Grandma had a one-bedroom apartment at the old Wolfburg Hotel. The hotel had closed before I was born, and the county had bought the building and turned it into subsidized housing for senior citizens. Moving in with her was not really an option.

I guess Grandma didn't know what to do when her daughter didn't take her shit, and I wasn't in a mood to help her. She got up and left without saying a word. I cleaned up and went to my room to start typing up my interview with Great Barb.

———————

We went back to have dinner with Dad. My grandfather and namesake, Pat Kowalski, met us there. He didn't say much, mostly complaining that they wouldn't let him smoke. As far as I was concerned, if he needed nicotine, he could get some from licking his clothing.

Grandma Mary met us in the hospital just as we were finishing. She patted my dad's pillow. "You look great," she told him. He did, in fact, look better after the treatment. That wasn't saying much – when I saw him that morning, I kept watching his chest to see if he was breathing. Mom, Grandma, and I all told him he was going to beat this.

Dad knew better. He smiled at our lies and told us he loved us, even saying that to Grandma Mary. (They never seemed to get along.) We left after an hour or so and went home.

The next day, Sunday, we visited again. He looked better and seemed happy.

The next morning, Monday, January 20, the hospital called. He'd passed around two in the morning. They said it was quiet and quick.

It felt like I'd been punched in the gut. I mean, my gut literally hurt. I cried for the first time in years, as did Mom. We sat on the bed for a while, still in our nightclothes, until the tears stopped.

"I'll call the relatives," Mom said. "Why don't you get showered and dressed?"

She'd finished calling everybody who needed to be called by the time I got out, so we ate breakfast. Cereal for me, toast for her, coffee for the both of us. We finished in silence, and then Mom asked me if I wanted to go with her to the funeral home.

I really didn't. "Are they open? It's a holiday," I said.

"Only for schools and banks. The rest of the world is

open."

It didn't seem like I had a choice. "Sure. I'll go brush my teeth."

———————

There are two funeral homes in Eastville – Calabro's and Mroz's. We've always gone to Mroz's, and that's where we ended up. Mister Mroz's daughter, Stephanie, met us at the side door. She'd been a senior and cheerleader when I was a freshman and a klutz.

"I thought you'd be back at college?" Mom said to her as we stood in the foyer, taking off our coats.

"Well," she said, looking bashful, "school *is* in session. But I've got a light load, and Mom and Dad got a deal on a trip to Hawaii, so here I am."

"And you graduate this year?" Mom asked.

"Yes, ma'am," Stephanie replied.

"What kind of degree do you get to be a funeral director?" Mom asked. She was asking for me – I hadn't thought much about college, even though I was graduating in May.

Stephanie, who was leading us back through the parlor area, replied over her shoulder. "You can get a two-year degree in mortuary science, but Southern offers a four-year program. It combines mortuary science with business."

"How nice," Mom said.

Yeah. Four years of school so you can work with stiffs. Sounds like fun to me.

We had passed through the front parlor of Mroz's, which was decorated with a lot of light-colored prints of flowers and old-style looking chairs, to arrive at a more plainly-decorated office. There was a big wooden desk, but Stephanie put us on a small pale pink couch with a coffee table in front of it. She brought out a big binder and sat it on the coffee table, then moved to take a seat in a matching armchair. "I'm sorry," she said, stopping mid-sit, "do you want anything? Coffee, water?"

"Any more coffee, and I'll bounce off the walls," Mom said. "I'm good."

I waved Stephanie off, and she took her seat.

"When does your dad come back?" I asked, more to make conversation than because I cared.

"They just left," she replied. "Not for almost two weeks."

"So you'll run the funeral?" Mom asked, a note of concern in her voice.

"Unless you want to wait until they return, yes," she replied. "I should ask before we get started – will there be an autopsy?"

"I have no idea," Mom replied. "Are they required?"

"Usually not," Stephanie said. She bent over to the coffee table and opened the binder to remove a thin letter-sized pamphlet. "Here's a little guide we provide to our families," she said, handing it to Mom. "It gives you a starting point to organize Mister Kowalski's affairs." She reached behind her and took a clipboard from the desk. "In the meantime, I'll need a couple of things. I assume he was at Riverview?"

Mom nodded yes. Stephanie asked who his doctor, or more accurately who his 'primary care physician' was and his phone number. "I'll call Monday and find out about the autopsy. Usually, when somebody dies after a long illness, there isn't one. But Mrs. Balthus said he died of a rare disease, so they may request one."

"Would I have to pay for it?" Mom asked.

The critical question, I thought to myself.

"If the doctor wants one, no. You only have to pay if you want one."

We discussed burial versus cremation and church service versus at the funeral home (burial, no church service. The last time Dad was in church was for his wedding.)

"Then we should look at caskets," Stephanie said.

"What about flowers?" Mom asked.

"You may want to coordinate flowers with the caskets," Stephanie said. She stood up. "Would you like to follow me?"

No, I thought, but we really didn't have a choice, did we? She led us back even further to a more-or-less heated garage with a slab floor. There were eight coffins sitting on shelves along the back wall.

"These are what we have in stock," Stephanie said. "We can order just about anything from Batesville and have it here by Tuesday. The factory is just the other side of Indianapolis."

"Ah, Stephanie," Mom began. "We need to discuss something." Mom stopped, clearly trying to figure out what to say.

"We're broke," I blurted out, feeling my face blush. "I mean really broke. What's cheapest?"

"Son!" Mom said.

"It's true!" I said.

"I'm sorry to hear that," Stephanie said. "But I appreciate the honesty." She sat her clipboard down on top of a coffin. "So I'll be honest. Cremations are much less expensive."

"How much less?" I asked while Mom stood there with her mouth open like a fish out of water.

"With a burial, we offer a package deal for $3,000," Stephanie said. "That's a casket, hearse, visitation, graveyard, and a small flower package. You still need to pay the priest or minister and cover the funeral lunch, plus buy a plot if you don't have one."

"That's a lot."

Stephanie gave me a wan smile. "I did one Friday that

went for double that."

"Cremation?"

"Assuming you don't buy a casket, fifteen hundred."

"So we just lay Dad out on a slab?" I asked. I felt weird like I was watching myself.

"No, I rent a casket for viewing," she said. "Actually, I'll let you use that one for free." She pointed at a coffin off to one side of the display area.

"Why that one?" I asked.

"It got dropped when they took it off the truck," she said. "The other side's got a ding. But I put the dinged side against the wall, and nobody knows."

"Or cares," I said.

"Son!" from Mom.

"Mom," I said. "We're broke. Do you have three grand under your mattress?" She didn't say anything, so I turned to Stephanie. "So, how's this cremation work?"

"The remains are in a box designed for cremation, which we set inside the display casket," She said. "We do a visitation like normal. When the visitation's over, I close the casket, and you leave. I take the remains and the cremation box out, drive to Urbana, and we cremate the remains. You can come and watch if you want or not. I recommend not. We put the ashes in a very nice urn and give them to you. You can scatter them or keep them on a shelf."

"We may not have a house to keep them in," I said, getting another glare from Mom. "And I'd like to have someplace to go visit later." My voice broke on that.

"Do you have a plot?" Stephanie asked Mom. She nodded no. "Hillside cemetery offers columbarium niches."

"A column-what?" I asked.

"It's a wall," Stephanie said. "You buy a little slot, we put the remains in the slot, brick it up and put a plaque on the outside. I've got pictures in the office."

"Let's go look," I said. "And I do think I'd like some water."

An hour later and a phone call to Hillside, we had our prices. Cremation with the hole in the wall was $2,000. Burial was $4,000 (to include buying a plot) plus the tombstone which Stephanie didn't sell. (Hillside did the nameplate as part of the wall, so they were 'stylistically consistent,' which meant that all the nameplates matched.)

"I'm not sure it matters," Mom said in the car. "We don't have even two thousand."

CHAPTER 5

Patrick

Tuesday, we had school. Dad's body was sitting in the freezer in the hospital while Stephanie was figuring out when we could get it. I went to school, not that I particularly wanted to, but what else does one do on a cold January day? At least it was clear, and the wind wasn't howling.

The day was mostly a blur – everybody in town had heard about my dad and wanted to know 'the arrangements.' Saying, "We're too broke to afford a funeral – I'm going to put the body in the garage until the thaw and bury him in the yard" didn't seem real nice, so I just said, "We're making the arrangements."

At lunch, I sat in my usual spot. Three-Sticks ambled over, carrying a loaded tray of food. No, that's not his real name. It's Vincent Bisceglie III, hence 'three sticks.' By the way, I know what that name looks like, but it's pronounced bee-SHEL-yeh.

I had a complicated relationship with Three Sticks. I don't really like him and we don't hang out together after school or anything. But I'm a senior, and there are 78 of us at Eastville High School, including Three Sticks. Neither of us are stoners or jocks, and we're in the school band. (The two of us are the entire saxophone section.) That and two other classes in common mean we get tossed together a lot, pretty much whether we like it or not. So sometimes we end up together at lunch.

"Sorry about your dad," Three Sticks said, sliding next to me. "You gonna eat that pie?"

"Hell yes, Oh Large One." Three Sticks had a bit of a weight problem on account of his lack of exercise and tendency to inhale any edible substance in reach.

"Ouch," he replied. "So, when's the funeral?"

I gave him the slightly longer version. "Dad died of some rare disease, so we need to see if the docs want to do an autopsy for science or stuff."

"Oh."

At that, the other dude named Vincent in my class, Vincent Gigante, plopped down on the bench across the table from us. He's tall, but so skinny I sometimes wonder how his pants stay up. He's a jock – runs cross-country and the mile and two mile in track. "Hey, Three Sticks. What's with the furniture store?" For the record, VG, as we called him, had already asked about my Dad.

"Going out of business," Three Sticks said.

"So I see," VG replied. "Why?"

Because they sell crappy furniture at inflated prices, I thought. Only reason anybody ever bought from them was because you could put furniture on layaway. Nobody did that anymore – you just charged it on a credit card.

"Ever since Furniture Barn opened up in Maple Corners," Three Sticks said, "we've been struggling." Furniture Barn also sold crappy furniture, but the prices were "more popular," as their TV commercial said. "More popular" meant "cheap." He shrugged. "So we cut our losses."

I thought not for the first time that it must be nice to be rich. Three Stick's dad, Vinnie Junior, owned the furniture store. His mother, Three Stick's grandmother, still showed up there most days to work. They also owned B-Friendly Savings and Loan, also known as the place that would soon own our house. That wasn't why I didn't like him, but it didn't help either.

"Sucks. What's Grandma B gonna do?" VG asked.

Three Sticks shrugged and talked around a mouthful of cafeteria fried chicken, which was actually pretty good. "Don't know. Dad's been after her to take it easy after her fall."

Grandma B had fallen earlier in the year, hard enough to merit a call-out of the town's volunteer Fire and Rescue service. Supposedly, she had slipped on the ice going into the Senior Citizen's Center to drink coffee and play euchre.

I had my doubts. I'm on the Fire and Rescue squad. Well, technically, I'm not 'on' it – you have to be a high school graduate – but they need the help, and our house is half a block from the fire station. So I go out on calls occasionally, for which I get a hearty handshake and a free dinner at the VFW post once a month.

Anyway, it was right after school the day of the first good freeze, and I was walking by the fire station on the way home when my beeper goes off. Jack Cross, our lead paramedic, was getting out of his pickup at the station. He jumps out, says "rescue call" and I follow him in. My job on the team was to fetch and carry.

A third guy shows up so we roll out to the call, which was in the alley behind the Senior Citizen's Center. They have a back door which opens up to the back door of Paisano's, one of the twelve taverns of Eastville. (No, I can't legally drink, but as part of the Fire and Rescue Squad, I've been to all of them. It's amazing how often drunks get hurt on Friday and Saturday nights.)

Anyway, we pulled into the Senior Citizen's Center parking lot (the alley was too narrow for the ambulance) to find the center's director, an old codger, waiting for us. We jump out carrying our first-aid bags, and he tells us to be careful about the ice in the alley. Except there was no ice. The alley was as dry as a bone. We walk down the alley, which, unlike most Eastville alleys, was gravel the entire width, to find Mrs. B. sitting up on her ass on the ground.

She was semi-coherent at best, and her face was flushed. Her coat wasn't buttoned up right – she'd gotten the top button into the second-from-the-top buttonhole. We helped her to her feet, but I had to catch her as she fell.

"I'll hold her," I said to Jack. She was a small woman and not very heavy. "Go get the stretcher."

"Don't need a stretcher," she said. "Just coffee."

"Mrs. B," Jack had said. "We're taking you to the hospital just to get you looked at." He nodded at me and went to get the stretcher.

To make a long story short, we got her on the stretcher and to the hospital. She had apparently managed not to break anything except her dignity.

Back at the cafeteria, the conversation went to other topics. I think the big discussion was around whether or not Michael Jordan would recover from his injury and get back to playing for the Bulls or was his career over. How anybody at the table had any hard information on the matter was beyond me.

Vincent Bisceglie III

Vincent Bisceglie III hated the nickname "Three Sticks." He hated it with a passion, and stress made him eat. Eating made him fat, and he didn't like being fat, which stressed him. It was a shitty cycle, he thought.

His name was Vincent, and you could shorten it to Vince, his preferred name, Vinnie, or even Vin, but not Three Sticks. Unfortunately, pretty much everybody except his family called him Three Sticks, and there was nothing he could do about it.

But as he walked to class after lunch, he smiled. There was hope. Washington University in St. Louis had accepted him for their architecture program. St. Louis, a good four-hour drive, was far enough away that few people from Eastville would just drop by. Even better, nobody from Eastville was attending or planning to attend the school.

I can be my own man. When I get to St. Louis, nobody will even know about "three sticks." He mentally practiced introducing himself. "Hi, I'm Vince. Vince Bisceglie. Yes, St. Louis is lovely. My family owns a bank, and we come here every November for a banking convention. It's a great town, isn't it?" College was so close he could taste it.

Patrick

After lunch, I went to Mr. Olsen's room for my independent study session. He had an office on the one-and-a-half floor of the high school. There were two flights of stairs separating the first and the second floors of the school, broken up by a landing. His office opened up to that landing, putting it right between floors. There were some windows in his office which opened into the auditorium, so I think it was originally meant as the place to put lights for stage shows and stuff.

"Sorry about your dad," he said when I walked in. Olsen was tall, bald, and amazingly calm. I never saw him lose his cool.

"Thanks. And not to cut you off, but we haven't

finished the funeral arrangements yet."

"I understand." He patted me on the shoulder. "How's your oral history project going?"

"Funny, that," I said. "Great Barb's earliest memory was of a man coming to her house and dropping dead."

Mr. Olsen made a face at that. "Sad. When did this happen?"

"1894, she thinks. The day before her fourth birthday."

"Oh. Well, you should ask her about her first plane ride."

"I doubt she's ever been in one," I said. "I mean, I've never been in a plane."

Mr. Olsen smiled. "Well, she has. Let me show you what I found."

The faculty was finding all sorts of old stuff that year. The district had just finished a new addition to the high school, and the building we were in, built in 1915, was scheduled to be torn down over the summer and made into a parking lot. (We really needed the space – all the students had to park at the football field, which was a long walk on cold or rainy days.) As a result, there was a lot of cleaning out of old file cabinets and other storage spaces.

"Isn't that your Great Barb?" he asked, handing me a framed black-and-white picture.

I took it from him. It was a group of six people, five men, and one woman, standing in front of a box-kite-like contraption with a propeller in the back. Somebody had hand-written the names of the people on the side, and the woman was identified as "Miss B. Vidas."

"I'll be darned," I said. She must have had guts – no way in hell would I have taken a ride on it. You could probably rip off a wing with your bare hands.

He then handed me a photocopy of an article from a

newspaper, the *Eastville Bugle*, dated May 1912. "A new-model aeroplane, made by the Curtis Company, arrived in town today. Local residents, including Miss B. Vidas of Strawberry Creek, were given rides. Our Correspondent reports Vidas was the first passenger."

Vidas was Great Barb's maiden name, something I had just recently discovered. "I'll have to ask her about it," I said. It would make a nice addition to the oral history project.

———————

I called home from the pay phone in the school lobby and left a message for Mom on her answering machine. She normally worked until seven at the IGA on the checkout line, but I had no idea what the plan was for today.

I was driving Dad's car, which was handy for a high school kid. Alas, it was a puke-green 1977 Chevy Vega with no air conditioning, which wasn't a problem in January. It was an automatic, on account of Dad's foot, but it had the larger of the two engine options, so it could almost get out of its own way.

Grandma Mary was walking in the same time I pulled up, so she waited for me at the door.

"What brings you here?" I asked.

She shrugged. "The home doesn't get a lot of visitors on Mondays. Besides, families of residents eat free."

I love my Grandma, but she's a lousy cook. I think she could burn water.

"Here to tell my mom about Mike?" she asked me.

"No. I was going to let Mom or you do it. Unless you think I should."

"I'll tell her," Grandma said. So, what brings you here?"

"I was going to ask her about her first airplane ride."

"Why?" Mom said. "As far as I know, she's only been

on a plane once. 1960, when she flew to see my brother in San Diego."

"She was a passenger on the first plane to arrive at Eastville. This was in 1912. She didn't tell you?"

"She did," Grandma said. "I figured she was full of it."

"I saw the newspaper article. It even had her picture."

"Huh." We started walking down the tiled hallway to her room, me trying to ignore the smells of old people and industrial cleaning products. "On second thought, let's hold off telling her about Mike. We can do it after we figure out the funeral arrangements."

Our arrival at her room prevented me from telling Grandma about the cost of a funeral and our lack of cash to cover it. When we walked in, Great Barb greeted her daughter in Lithuanian, and Grandma replied in the same language. I can say hello and goodbye in Lithuanian, so I tuned it out.

After they chatted for a bit in the old language, Grandma said in English, "So, Patrick here wants to ask about your first plane ride."

Great Barb smiled, reminding me that she still had most of her teeth. "I think the pilot was trying to get into my pants," she said.

"Mom!" Grandma said.

"I used to have sex, too, you know," Great Barb said with a wink. "That's how I got you."

"Did he?" I asked. "Get into your pants, I mean."

She laughed, and Grandma glared at me. "A woman has to have some secrets." She looked at the white-tiled ceiling. "It was before the war. The first war, I mean. I was working at the Eastville Hotel, making box lunches for miners at a penny a box. Late spring, right about when the strawberries started ripening, we heard this terrible clatter overhead. Everybody rushed out to see us getting buzzed by the plane."

"It landed in the field that's now the park, and by the time I got there a crowd had gathered. The pilot, a terribly young man, was offering to take people up for a ride."

"For free?" Grandma asked.

"Heavens no," Great Barb said. "Fifty cents, which was a day's wages for me." She waved her hand feebly. "But nobody wanted to pay. Finally, he said he'd take one person up for free to prove it was safe." She smiled again. "I volunteered. I was the only one."

I waved for her to go on. "So I climbed up onto this contraption. The seat was just two pieces of wood attached to the wing, and my feet dangled out in the air. He offered me a leather helmet, which I declined. I didn't want to mess up my hair, and besides, what good was that going to do? I did take the goggles."

"After a bit of fussing with the engine, which was behind us, he got it running. Heavens, was it loud! Then we were off."

"What was it like?" I asked.

"Windy," Great Barb replied. "Once we were in the air, it wasn't as loud. Really weird looking down on the town from height." She laughed again. "Not that we ever got very high. Probably about cruising altitude for a fat goose and not any faster."

She sighed. "After a quick circle over town, we landed. And then the floodgates opened. 'If a woman could do it, every man had to.' After he was done, the pilot even gave me two whole dollars. Said it was a 'commission' for getting people to go up."

"That's cool," I said. I had seen the picture of the plane – it looked like a box kite with delusions of grandeur. You'd never have gotten me up in it. "And that was the last flight until 1960?"

"No," Great Barb said. "I flew to see my brother Matis when his ship was in New York. That was the second war."

"Matis?" I asked.

"Matthew in American," Grandma said. "He was born in 1901 and ended up in the Merchant Marine."

"Submarine got him in '42, or was it '43?" Great Barb said.

"42, Mom. And I thought you took a train?"

"Train to Chicago, dear, then plane to New York."

"Out of O'Hare?" I asked.

"It wasn't there yet, I don't think," Great Barb said. "Municipal. I think they call it Midway now."

I gave Grandma a 'you didn't know' look, and she shrugged.

Great Barb looked at me. "He had a wife in New York, and they had a son. The son died in a car wreck in the early fifties."

I didn't know what to say, so I said nothing. Then Great Barb said, "So, when were you going to tell me that Mike was dead?" She said something in Lithuanian, and Grandma made a face. Great Barb and Grandma never really liked my Dad. The feeling was mutual.

"Apparently, we don't have to tell you, Mom," Grandma said.

"Before you ask, one of the nurses heard," Great Barb said. "When's the funeral?"

"Hasn't been planned yet, Mom."

"Well, I'd like to go if they'll let me out of jail."

"Mom, you're not in jail."

"Just try and leave and see if you think that," she replied, raising a bony finger. "By the way, don't forget that I have a pre-paid funeral with Mister Mroz. And don't let that cheap Serbian SOB try to up-charge you. I get what I paid for and nothing more." She smiled. "Unless, of course, he wants to toss in something for free."

"Yes, Mom," Grandma said.

"Speaking of free," she replied. "I'm hungry. Pat, I hear they'll let family eat for free. Care to join us?"

"Sure, why not?" I replied. "Where's your wheelchair?"

"I'll show you," Grandma said. "It's outside."

We stepped out into the hallway to get a wheelchair.

"For the record," Grandma said, "when I go, I also have a prepaid funeral at Mroz's."

"About Dad's funeral..." I started.

"Let me guess," Grandma said. "You can't pay." She sighed heavily. "How much?"

"Four grand for a burial plus headstone, two grand all-in for cremation."

"Which funeral home?"

"Mroz's."

"Hell, for the amount of business we're going to throw at them, you'd think they'd comp us."

"When I told Stephanie we were broke, she was very helpful," I said.

"Stephanie? Oh, you mean Jack's daughter."

"The four grand is a lot lower than the initial number."

"Well, that's good of her."

I had grabbed a wheelchair. "She's been helpful, but comping was not offered."

"Did you talk to Pat?"

She meant my grandfather Pat Kowalski. "Yes."

"And?"

"He hemmed and hawed."

"The cheap bastard." The man lived in a trailer, so I didn't think he had a lot of money either, but I didn't say anything. Grandma sighed heavily. "Let me talk to my banker."

"Thanks."

"To be clear," she said, "this is for your mother and you. Not Mike."

That was hurtful, but I wasn't in a position to take offense. "I understand."

"I'll get Mom into it," she said, pointing at the wheelchair, "and you drive."

CHAPTER 6

Patrick

When I got home, Mom was staring blankly at the TV. I kissed her on the head. She liked it, and nobody was looking.

"How's Great Barb?" she asked.

"Feisty as usual," I replied. "Did you know Great Barb flew in an airplane in 1912?"

"She told you that?" Mom asked. "I suppose she was the pilot, too."

"There's a newspaper article with a picture of her, the pilot, and the plane."

"I'll be darned," Mom said. "Great Barb had a lot of stories. Most of them baloney."

"No baloney in this one. Maybe some ham."

Mom smiled wanly. "Stephanie called. No autopsy needed. We can pick up the body..."

Whenever we found the money to do something with it. "I know."

———————

We had a late start at school on Wednesday for some teachers' meeting, so I was just putting my coffee cup in the sink when the phone rang. It was a yellow wall-mounted rotary phone. I picked it up on the third ring. "Kowalski residence?"

"Is your mother there?"

"She just jumped into the shower, Grandma. Can I have her call you back?"

"Tell her to meet me at Mroz's in thirty minutes. I got the money."

"How?"

She sighed. "I sold my rings. It will be a cremation."

———

I decided to blow off school and join the group. I'm glad I did – Mom was almost useless. Grandma, on the other hand, acted like one of those people in the movies who was buying a rug in some Third-World back alley. We went line-by-line through the funeral expenses. She made Stephanie show us the 'display casket' that Dad would be laid out in. Truthfully, the nick Stephanie was worried about was tiny – a scratch maybe two inches long. If you weren't looking for it, you'd never find it.

After the bargaining was done, we settled on Thursday from 3 to 6 for a visitation and 6 to 7 for a service at the funeral home. Some retired preacher who lived in Grandma's complex would say the words. He was Protestant and allowed to have sex, and I think he thought he was going to get some from Grandma. (Yeah, just thinking about them bumping ugly made me throw up in my mouth a little.)

As a result, no school for me on Thursday. My one-and-only suit still fit, if a bit tight around the shoulders. I couldn't find my tie, so I wore one of Dad's.

The visitation sucked. I knew about half of the people who came. The other half, mostly Dad's coworkers, I had no idea who they were. Mom was catatonic, and no help. Not sure why I expected otherwise.

I found myself getting pissed as the event wore on. Pissed at Mom for being useless, pissed at Grandma for her looking down at Dad and his family, and pissed at Grandma's minister/boyfriend, who I saw nipping on a hip-flask when he thought he wasn't being watched.

In truth, I was also pissed at Dad. It wasn't fair to be mad at him, but I was. He'd gone off and died and left us in the lurch.

One of the many things that amazed me was how many people looked at Dad's body and said 'he looks good.' The fact that people felt the need to lie about him made me embarrassed.

He didn't look good. He looked like a dead man spray-painted with flesh-toned paint. Stephanie had put him in his one suit, a cheap-ass brown polyester number. It was his 'go-to-funeral' suit, as he called it. He'd lost a lot of weight, and so he looked like a kid playing dress-up. God help me, but I found myself thinking, couldn't we at least afford a damned decent suit.

So when the visitation was over, and the family had a private moment alone with 'the remains' as Stephanie kept saying, I was angry, hurt, and ready to hit somebody. Fortunately, Stephanie knew what to say.

"It's okay to be upset," she said, her hand on my back.

"I'm not upset," I said, biting off my words.

"Whatever you're feeling is okay."

I glared at her. "What if I'm mad?"

"That's okay," she said. She looked at the coffin. "He was taken from you. It's not fair, and you're not happy with it."

That's when I lost it. She handed me a Kleenex and led me to a chair. I cried like a little kid for a bit. When I got my shit together, I found myself alone with Stephanie and my dad's body.

"Mrs. Balthus took your mother home," Stephanie said. "I had Fred take Mrs. Pikus back to the nursing home.

It's on his way."

"I should have done that," I said.

"Bullshit," she replied. She must have seen the shocked look on my face. "Pardon my French, but you deserve a minute to grieve."

"Thanks." It was like in the movies where somebody gets slapped in the face and suddenly stops being hysterical. The only difference was she hadn't slapped me.

We sat there for a minute, then I said, "I really should be going."

"No rush on my account."

"Don't you have to go home?"

She smiled. "I stay in the same house with the remains until they go to their final resting place."

"Does it bother you?" I asked, pointing at the coffin. "I mean..."

"Working with dead bodies?" she replied. "Can I tell you something?"

"Sure."

"When I was a kid, I used to play in the caskets."

"Wouldn't you get locked into one? I mean, if the lid closed?"

She shook her head no and took something out of the pocket of her dress. "It takes a key to lock them closed," she said, holding up a piece of metal the size of a small screwdriver.

"Oh."

We sat quietly for a minute. "So, the crematorium is in Urbana. Sometimes, the family wants to escort the remains."

I thought about that for a minute. "Great Barb doesn't get out much." I left unsaid that Grandma didn't like my dad and that Mom was a basket-case.

"If you or they don't want to, that's fine."

"Truthfully, I'd like to go, but my car's getting new

tires tomorrow." Dad's boss was giving me a set for free. It was literally the least he could do.

"If you don't mind, you could ride with me in the hearse."

I looked at Dad's coffin. I felt I owed it to him. "Okay. What time and do I need to wear this monkey-suit?"

She laughed. "Wear what you're comfortable in. We can be as formal or informal as you want."

Stephanie was one of those morning people, so we left before the sun was up. The 'remains coffin' she'd put Dad in was just a glorified cardboard box. The crematorium was a small building in the back of a funeral home in Urbana and had all the charm of an auto-body shop. We were met there by a man Stephanie's age. The two of them rolled Dad's body out of the hearse onto a metal contraption and wheeled it into the building.

I hadn't slept much that night and was tired and cried out. The two of them seemed to understand my desire to just get this done, so they did their thing with respect but with a minimum of ceremony. Once they rolled Dad in and hit the button, it was a couple of hours of, well, sitting in front of a furnace.

I was offered the nicest of a collection of mismatched and worn-out chairs and settled in with a book. Stephanie had suggested that I bring one. She planted herself at a table and took out a textbook, which she attacked with a pink highlighter. The guy running the cremation machine, a man Stephanie's age, parked on the same table, situated so he could glance at the furnace. He fiddled with some paperwork, then after a while, went into the main building.

He returned a few minutes later with a thermos of coffee, some Styrofoam cups, and a small plastic container with sugar packets and creamer. We all three took cups and he settled down in a chair next to me.

The book I'd brought wasn't holding my attention, so I said to him, "You know, when they said crematory, I was thinking of the one in the James Bond movie."

He nodded somberly. I was thinking that part of Undertaker's College was a class on how to do that. "Display crematories, we call them." He took a sip of his coffee, steam rolling off of it. The room was chilly – I think the only source of heat was the cremation furnace. "And we recommend not using a nice wooden casket like in the movie."

"It does seem wasteful," I said.

"This is much more environmentally friendly."

And cheaper, which was the key factor for us. "So, how do you know Stephanie?"

"We went to SIU together," he said. "I was a year ahead." He pointed at the furnace. "I talked Dad into getting that. Where are you going to college at?"

The School of I Ain't Got No Money, where I'd major in Being Poor. "Haven't decided."

"You should check out SIU," he said. "Good programs, and cheaper than here." He meant the University of Illinois, the local college. "Cost of living's lower down there as well."

"I will." Given our finances, unless they paid me, there was no way I could afford anything.

———

A little while later, Stephanie and I left for lunch. We ate at the Courier Café, a trendy little place in downtown Urbana. After a leisurely lunch – I couldn't tell you what I ate but Stephanie picked up the check – we went back to the crematorium.

Instead of going into the back building, we went into the main funeral home. The guy there escorted us into a small side room where we sat on a pair of newer armchairs. He slipped into the back and returned with a plain metal urn. He sat the urn on a tiny table and screwed a cap on it, then stepped aside.

"Now what?" I asked, feeling my face flush.

"If you'd like a moment," the guy said.

"I'm out of moments," I said.

"Whenever you're ready," Stephanie said. "We can leave. Do you want to carry the remains, or should I?"

"I'll do it." I went over and picked up the urn. It was surprisingly light and slightly warm. "Hard to believe..."

"I know," Stephanie said.

"Ashes to ashes, dust to dust," the other guy said.

That got me choked up, so I just nodded to Stephanie. She led me outside to the hearse. There was a little stand inside just behind the seats where we put the urn. It was a quiet ride home.

When I got to our house, Dad's ashes spent the night sitting on the kitchen table. Mom conspicuously avoided the kitchen, to the point of insisting we accept an invitation to one of our neighbor's houses to eat.

I couldn't sleep that night. Around one, I gave up and walked into the kitchen. I sat down at the table with a glass of water and looked at Dad's ashes. At some point, I finally did fall asleep, waking the next morning with my head resting on the table like I was a little kid at school naptime.

The next morning a small group of family met at Hillside Cemetery. There was a brief ceremony where we put Dad's ashes in the wall. The same preacher – Grandma's boyfriend of the moment – said a few words. We went back to the Wolfburg Hotel, now officially the Wolfburg Apartments, for the funeral lunch, which was KFC chicken on paper plates. Like I said, every penny counted.

Great Barb had obviously gone to the funeral home, but

nobody wanted to expose her to the cold at the wall, so she'd sat in her wheelchair at the Wolfburg with a volunteer from the nursing home. Great Barb had 'helped' set up the food, which I had assumed meant 'get in the way,' but apparently, she'd actually contributed a bit.

Mom had transitioned from her crying phase to her semi-catatonic phase. I found myself sitting across from Great Barb, picking at a piece of pie one of our neighbors had brought over.

"Nice service," she said, looking at the preacher, who was discreetly putting a move on Grandma. "And it looks like your grandmother has found a new friend."

"I noticed." Not wanting to talk about old people having sex with other old people, I asked, "Was your husband's funeral like this?" (Yes, I know it was insensitive. It just came out.)

"He didn't have a funeral," she said.

"Why not?"

"He just disappeared. I never knew what happened to him." She sighed. "Maybe Al had him whacked."

"Al?"

"Al. You know, Mister Capone." She pronounced it ca-PON-e, and it took me a second to figure it out. "Al Capone? Scarface?"

She smiled. "Nobody called him that. Least not to his face."

"How would Great-Pa run into Capone?"

"He worked for him, dear."

CHAPTER 7

Oral History

Oral History Project by Patrick Kowalski, Eastville High School, May 2, 1986. My oldest living relative, Great-Grandmother Barbara Pikus, told me this story the day we interred my father's ashes.

It was the evening before my birthday. My husband, Michael, had just gotten back from work. The kids were asleep, and it was just the two of us in the front room of our four-room house. Front room and kitchen, two bedrooms – one for us (also nice for a quick romp in the hay) and one for the kids.

The only downside was the outhouse. Cold on the tushy in winter, bugs and stink in summer. But it was what we had.

Anyway, it was the evening before my birthday and we were sitting in the front room by the light of a kerosene lamp.

"Happy birthday, Barbara," Michael said to me.

I remember smiling wanly. I was pregnant, big as a house with your mother. [Note: She means my grandmother. She has problems keeping the generations straight.] She was always a hot baby and moved around a lot. That day, I felt like she was playing football in my womb. It was 1924, and fortunately, my last pregnancy.

"Thank you, my love," I said, wiping sweat from my brow.

"I got you something," he said, smiling. He handed me a box. Small, like a shoebox, but fancy. I opened it, and inside, wrapped in a sinful amount of tissue paper, was a very nice hand mirror, comb and brush.

"Michael! How can we afford this?"

"Mister Capone gave me a bonus."

Oh, close your mouth. Yes, that "Mister Capone." Alphonse "Al" Capone.

To be clear, your great-grandfather didn't directly work for Mister Capone. We'd met him, or rather, I'd met him only once. It was when he'd come down to watch Red Grange play football. He'd rented a hotel ballroom and had a bunch of his people in for dinner after the game, and we shook his hand.

But Michael didn't talk to Capone on a regular basis. From day to day, he worked for Mister Big.

[I asked who Mister Big was.]

Some Dago [sorry – her words] who worked for Capone. Fat guy – we also called him Three Chins (but not to his face). Young man – barely in his twenties.

[I asked if she knew his real name.]

I did. It was a Dago name – hard to pronounce – so we didn't bother. He kind of liked being called Mister Big because he had an ego almost as big as his gut. Anyway, to get back to the story, I said, "You know I don't like you working for him." We were talking Lithuanian – your grandpa was born in the Old Country and was more comfortable in that language.

[Again, she routinely gets her generations mixed up. She also routinely cycles through the names of her descendants until she gets to the right one.]

"He pays," Michael said.

"For breaking the law!"

Michael waved a hand dismissively. "A law nobody follows. Not even you."

She winked at me as she talked. Yes, your grandmother drinks. I drank through both of my pregnancies, and everybody turned out fine. [she paused, and I had to prompt her to continue.]

"Not the point," I said to Michael. "You're smuggling." I waved a hand at him while I clutched my womb with the other. Your grandmother was playing bouncy on my kidneys. "And you carry cash."

Michael made wine for the mob. It was Prohibition, after all. Then he'd drive that wine to whatever speakeasy he was sent to, collect the money, and deliver it. He'd also pick up hooch from other people and deliver it. Errand boy.

He patted the pocket of his vest. "I have protection."

"That damn little peashooter of yours..."

"No, I'm not lugging around that hand cannon your dad gave you," Michael replied. "Nor am I your brother."

"It shoots," I said.

[I asked what her brother had to do with this.]

"My brother made whiskey for Capone." She waved her hand at me. "So he always carried a gun, too."

To get back to this story, Michael continued. "I have made my decision, Barbara, and that's final."

Yes, dear, Lithuanians are hard-headed. "If you say so, my husband." I leaned over and kissed him. "Thank you."

"You're welcome." He patted his vest again. "Speaking of that, I need to go to Chicago day after tomorrow. The wine is ready."

"The wine quit bubbling just yesterday." I was referring to a collection of jugs and vats full of grape juice we had fermenting in the barn. Not the one you remember, but the one that burnt down.

[I'd never seen her barn.]

"Which means it's ready," Michael replied. "We bottle tomorrow."

"You'll get champagne if you bottle tomorrow," I said. "It's still fermenting."

"Do you think the swells in Chicago will pay more for champagne?"

I rolled my eyes hard enough to see spots. "You are bad, my husband." I smiled. "And I love you."

"I know," he said. "And I bought a cake."

"You *bought* a cake?"

He smiled, and I giggled. Tony, your great-uncle, was four, and he loved store-bought anything. Mostly because it was different.

[She looked away, and I thought she was done talking. After a long pause, she continued.]

It was early morning on December 23, 1924. I remember the day because that was my brother Luidas' birthday. The phone rang – we'd just gotten one about a month ago, and I still wasn't used to it, so when it rang, it startled me.

It startled your grandmother, too – she was still in my arms and especially fussy that day.

Michael called me. He was in Chicago, or actually near it, in a town called Downers Grove. He'd gone up to deliver some booze.

"My love," he said.

"Why aren't you home?" I asked.

"I got asked to help out," he said. "One of the guys here stacked up his truck, and I had to run his route."

"So when are you coming home?"

"Tonight. I have to drive into town and make a green

delivery."

Cash. He had to turn in his cash.

"And then?"

"As soon as I do that, I'll head south. Be there for dinner."

[She had another long pause.]

He never showed up. I found out he picked up another errand boy, and both of them disappeared. With a lot of cash.

It was a crappy Christmas, then things got worse. We were living pretty much hand-to-mouth, and with him gone, there was no money. I had two kids, one still nursing, so it was hard to work. Luidas tried to help, but he had three of his own, and truth to be told, he only drank to excess. That's what killed him so young.

[At this point, my Mom and Grandmother came – Mom wanted to go home, and Grandmother wanted to take her mom, Great Barb, to the nursing home. We left.]

CHAPTER 8

Tuesday, December 23, 1924, Downers Grove, Illinois

Michael Pikus hung up the phone and lit a cigarette. Usually his Chicago runs were just to a warehouse that Capone controlled. There, he offloaded his stuff, as directed by the warehouse boss, a tall and excitable Italian named Gino. Another crew moved the booze from the warehouse to the customers.

But the week of Christmas and New Year was a busy one for the booze business, and Ivan, one of Gino's local drivers, had lost control of his truck on some ice and rammed a tree. With Ivan's truck in the shop, Michael and his truck had been pressed into service.

Ivan came out of the men's room at the train station as Michael finished lighting his cigarette. "All well at home?" Ivan asked in Russian. It was better than his English, and Michael understood it almost as well as his native Lithuanian.

"Yes," Michael replied. "She's a typical woman – worried."

"Well, let's get you home."

"Yes, let's," Michael replied. They both turned and walked out of the small train station to the parking lot. As they did, Michael thought about the day. Once they finished Ivan's route, they still had to turn in their money, and then

Michael had a good five-hour drive home in his Model T pickup truck. That was, if it didn't snow, something it looked like it could at any time.

"Where is home?" Ivan asked as they walked up to the truck in the parking lot.

"Eastville. Down by Urbana."

"Long way."

"Yes."

They got into the cab and Michael got it running, glad he'd paid extra for the electric starter. I should have also gotten the heater, he thought, as his breath fogged the window. They lurched into gear and clattered down the road.

It was late afternoon and getting dark under a slate-gray sky. They were out in the country south of town, driving through farm fields.

"Anybody live here?" Michael asked.

"Yeah," Ivan replied. "There's a cluster of houses around a crossroads." He waved vaguely. "Just up ahead. It's our last stop."

They were approaching a T in the road. "Which way?" Michael asked.

"Left," Ivan grunted.

"How far from this stop to the warehouse?"

"Not far. This place is on the way."

"Good," Michael said, glancing at the gray skies. "Maybe I can be out of here before the snow hits."

"Don't worry about it," Ivan said. "We'll be done soon."

A short time later, they arrived at a cluster of small houses, looking forlorn in the cold. Just past the intersection of two country lanes, there was a small roadside building. Ivan pointed at it. "That's the place."

"Looks like a gas station," Michael said.

"Owner's redoing it," Ivan said. "Going into the restaurant business."

Michael grunted. The sign out front read "Bell's Burger Barn."

"Stocking up early?" Michael asked, noting the painted wooden sign underneath that read "opening soon."

"I think this is for his personal use," Ivan said. "But I don't ask as long as the money is green. Pull around back."

Michael did as directed. When he shut the truck off, he said, "Place looks empty."

"Well, he said he'd be here," Ivan said, a note of irritation in his voice. "Why don't you go see if he's here?"

"Why don't you go see?" Michael asked. It was only marginally warmer in the truck than outside, but at least there was no wind. *My Christmas present to me is to buy a heater for this rig.*

"I got out the last two times," Ivan said. "Your turn."

This is your route, and I didn't wreck a vehicle. But since Ivan didn't seem willing to budge, Michael got out. *The sooner I make this delivery, the sooner I head south.*

The back door of the restaurant, which was really an enclosed two-car garage, was open, so Michael went in. He noted that the floor was still dirt, although it looked like they were almost ready to lay a slab. *Better get some heat in the joint first.*

"Anybody here?" Michael asked into the dim room. He took a couple of steps inside and heard somebody step out from around a corner. "Got a delivery," Michael said.

"So do I," came the reply. A Tommy gun burped, shooting hot pokers into Michael's chest. He grunted and collapsed to the ground.

"Damn, that was loud," Ivan said in almost unaccented English.

"Ain't nobody to hear it," said a fat man holding a Tommy gun. "Where's the money?"

"Here," Ivan said, pulling out a wad of bills from his coat. "Where can we count it?"

"Count it?"

"My split," Ivan said. He looked at the dead body and made a face. "Wow. What a smell."

"Bowels," the fat man said. "That all of it?"

"Yes," Ivan said, waving the money. "Your half and my half." He gestured at the body at his feet. "What about him?"

"Why do you care?"

"I don't want this to come back on me."

"He's going under the slab," the fat man said. "As are you." Ivan dropped the money and went for his pistol, but the Tommy gun cut him down.

"You can come out now," the fat man said.

Moses Rawlings, a tall and skinny black guy, stepped out of the kitchen. "That thing is loud, mister."

The fat man was bent down, picking up the money. "That's why we're out here in the middle of nowhere." He straightened up, a wad of cash in his free hand. "That and the floor."

"Pouring it Monday, sir," Moses said.

"Good." The fat man started to leave.

"They might have more money on them," Moses said.

"You can keep it. Consider it a tip."

Moses tipped his hat. "Thank you, sir."

After the fat man left, Moses said, "Cash and a truck.

Merry Christmas to me." A sour look crossed his face. "And a shit sandwich for y'all. I'm sorry for y'all. I really am. But my kids need to eat."

CHAPTER 9

John B. Hood – Willowbrook, IL Monday, January 20, 1986

John Hood pulled up the collar of his entirely inadequate coat. It hadn't been so bad last night when he'd gone from a warm airport to a warm hotel shuttle bus. But when he'd picked up the rental car at his hotel this morning, it had sat out all night and was an icebox.

He wondered if a seven-and-a-half grand bonus was really worth freezing his balls off in Chicago in January. Not to mention working for SleepTight, the tightest-with-a-buck motel chain in the world. He made a face at the thought as he rolled into the parking lot of the old restaurant. There was a sign announcing, "Coming Soon – A New SleepTight!" The sign was fading a bit.

In typical SleepTight fashion, they were calling this location "Downers Grove South." It was south alright – another suburb or two south. Apparently, Willowbrook didn't have the right marketing buzz for SleepTight. Hood put his car in park, shut it off, and, with an effort, climbed out into the arctic blast.

As he strode into the soon-to-be demolished restaurant, his breath swirling around his face, he reflected on the call he'd gotten just before heading to the airport. His ex-wife had initiated the call, telling him that his daughter had decided to go to Tulane.

That news hit him square in the wallet. He'd gone to UT Dallas, not only in-state but in-town, and gotten a solid education, which yielded a good job. Why his daughter had to go to a private school out of state was beyond him. He shook his head. The raising of their children had been one of the many factors leading to his divorce. And now his role in his kid's life was to write big checks on demand.

He stepped inside the abandoned restaurant. The place had gone to SleepTight lock stock and barrel, so today, they were going to auction off everything not securely nailed down. Even inside, he could faintly hear the roar of cars on the Interstate just out back. That visibility from the road was the only redeeming quality about this property, John thought. Otherwise, it was going to be a bitch shoehorning the motel in the small and awkwardly-sized lot.

This is going to be even harder than I was told in Dallas, he thought. I really should have stood my ground on ten thousand for this mess.

"You the project manager?" a tall, thin, and balding man asked, standing at a portable podium.

"I am," John said. He offered his hand. "John Hood."

"Gary McGlauchlin," the man replied. "I'm the 'M' in M & B Auctions."

"Glad to meet you," John said. "We expecting a crowd?"

"Never know," Gary replied. He looked down at his podium. "Looks like I left something in the truck."

"I'll hold the fort," John said as the man left.

A few ticks later, a short man with gray hair and a beard with a camera around his neck came out of the back room. "Your boss went to get something from his truck."

"Oh, I'm not with the auctioneer."

"Getting a run on bidding?" John asked.

"No." He held out his hand. "Rick Webster," he said in a smoker's gravelly voice. "I'm with the local historical society."

"Oh," John said as they shook hands. "Didn't think this place was historic."

"Well, given that it was here thirty years before the first subdivision went in, it was."

"I suppose so." John glanced at one of the restaurant tables piled high with cheap plastic plates. "Looks like some of these were here in the beginning."

"Actually, no," Rick replied. "When this place opened in 1925, he had white china with Bell's Burger Barn on them in blue."

Thus, the faded and rusted sign on a decrepit metal pole outside. Getting that thing down before it fell on somebody was high on his list of priorities. "The plates sound fancy. So the Bell family owned this?"

"Well, Campana," Rick replied, "which is Italian for bell."

"Why didn't he open a pizza joint?"

Rick smiled. "Being an Italian in 1924 was looked down upon. Besides, this was a roadside stop. In and out. That road out front is what's left of Route 66."

"Ah." John stamped his feet, deciding to go buy a warmer coat tonight. "So what happened?"

"The usual," Rick replied. "First generation had a passion, second felt duty-bound, third was too busy grab-assing the waitresses and buying drinks for 'friends' to run the place." He pointed at the bar, now lined with glassware for sale. "When the business started to fall off, the owner started running lingerie shows."

"Lingerie shows?"

"Models," Rick said, making air quotes, "Would 'model' lingerie which you could supposedly buy for your wife. Not much lingerie got sold, but a lot of other stuff happened in the back room."

"I can imagine," John said.

"Between that and late-night fights, the Village kept pulling his liquor license. The owner, I mean the former owner," Rick said, correcting himself, "ran out of money. Last I heard he's heading to Florida to find a bar there that needs running into the ground."

"At least he'll be warm," John said. At that, Gary returned, carrying a microphone.

"Almost ready," Gary said, plugging it into his gear.

"We golfing?" Rick asked.

"In this weather?" John said.

"A group of couples go down to Destin the last week in February," Rick said. "The guys golf, and the girls shop."

"Ah," John said.

"I think we're going," Gary said. "I'll check with my boss, I mean the wife, when I get home."

"Call me," Rick said. "We need to book the tickets before they go up."

"Will do," Gary said. Into the mic, he said, "Testing..."

CHAPTER 10

Patrick

The Tuesday after Dad's internment was supposed to be a day of infamy for me. My nemesis, Mr. Parker, who taught Senior English, had scheduled that week for oral presentations. I was scheduled to give mine that day – something I dreaded. But burying my dad had put little things like talking in front of the whole class in perspective.

I found I just didn't care what he thought. It was surprisingly liberating. When I rolled into the class, he offered a perfunctory I'm sorry then asked me if my homework was done.

Usually, I gave him a smart-ass answer. Like last month, I told him that the dog ate my homework, but we'd strained his poop and recovered it. Today, my priorities had shifted. A man had showed up at our door on Saturday after the interment and handed us a paper. We'd been served with an eviction notice. As a result, I really didn't give a damn, so I was able to sit back and watch the show.

We had been assigned to read a book from a list provided by Mr. Parker and deliver a written and oral report on it. Three Sticks had picked *Frankenstein*, because he thought he could just watch the movie on videotape and do the report. He was up at the front of the class, making a hash of it.

"Mister Bisceglie," Parker said running his hand over his massive bald spot, "you do realize that, in the book, the Monster does talk?"

There were a number of giggles over that one. Even I joined in. I had, after all, told Three Sticks that you couldn't *just* rely on the movie. At least get the Cliffs Notes, I told him.

"I do," Three Sticks lied, almost convincingly.

"Then press on, Mister Bisceglie."

Press on was a favorite phrase of Parker's. Three Sticks pressed on, generating more hilarity and getting more red-faced by the minute. He stumbled to an ending.

"Vincent," Parker said. "Be honest. Did you actually read *anything* of the book?"

"There was a bit at the beginning talking about the book that I read."

You probably read that bit this *weekend.*

Parker sighed heavily. "Well, congratulations. Since you failed this assignment, please pick another book and have something ready for next week."

"Next week?" Three Sticks squeaked.

"Did I suddenly stop speaking English?" Parker asked.

"No sir," Three Sticks said. He was sweating, given that we had had three weeks for the first book report. Still, I thought that Parker was bending over backward for him. It helped to be the son of the richest man in town.

"Given that we're just about out of time," Parker said, "we'll hold off on Mister Kowalski's report until tomorrow. Class dismissed."

Everybody jumped up and headed out, but Parker stopped me. "Is your report really ready?" he asked.

"Actually, yes," I said. I was doing *Heart of Darkness* and had read it while they were cremating Dad. It had fit my mood.

"And how's the college search going?"

"Slow," I lied, wondering why he even asked.

"Pat," Parker replied, "you will never make it as a professional poker player."

"We're broke."

"Did you talk to Mr. Sims? He should be able to get you some scholarships," Parker said. "You're smart, unlike that rock with lips who was just up here."

"I talked to him," I said. "He wants me to talk to somebody about ROTC."

"GI Jack rides again," Parker said.

It took me a minute to process what Parker had just said. "GI Jack" was the kids' nickname for the school's guidance counselor, and we only used it behind his back. We called him that because the walls of his admittedly small interior office were literally covered with certificates of appreciation from the local military recruiters. I thought he could get an overweight squirrel into some branch of the service.

Something in my face must have shown my surprise because Parker said, "Oh, come on. You've called Jack Sims GI Jack before."

"Well, yes, I have," I said. "I'm just surprised that a teacher would say that."

"Teachers are people, too, you know."

It dawned on me that Parker was probably of draft age for the Vietnam War. He might not be a fan of the military. Also, Parker was black, and what hair he had was in a short Afro. I had a vision of him in a tie-dyed shirt and bell bottoms, smoking a doobie.

"Apparently," I said.

"Tell you what. Let me make a few calls."

"You don't understand," I said, louder than needed. Parker gave me a sharp look. "I'm probably going to have to drop out."

"Until your Dad's insurance pays?"

"We don't have insurance," I said, a whine creeping into my voice. A whine that was pissing me off. "Grandma had to sell her rings to pay for the funeral."

"Your mom has a job."

Yeah. Checkout clerk at the IGA. "They're foreclosing on the house."

"That's bad. Relatives?"

I gave him the short answer. "The best we can hope for is Grandpa Kowalski's trailer." A falling-down and cockroach-infested crapsack that smelled of piss, booze, and cigarettes. Everybody else either had no room at all or was way out of town. Although, personally, I'd take out of town over Grandpa K's. I might even take an underpass over Grandpa K's.

"When do you have to move out?"

"Don't know. We've got some kind of hearing tomorrow."

"I'm guessing you don't have a lawyer."

"What good would that do?" I said, waving my hand dismissively. "We haven't paid." My eyes started to water, and I got really mad. "But don't worry, I'll be here tomorrow."

"Like hell you will, Mister," Parker said.

"You're kicking me out?"

"No, I'm telling you to go to the hearing. Actually, I'll go with you if you want."

"To do what?"

Parker sighed. "To at least make sure the judge hears both sides of the case."

"Which will do what?"

"Buy time."

"How?"

"Pat, back when I had hair, I spent some time down south working for an anti-poverty group. One of the things I found out was that, even in hellhole Southern states, if you fight foreclosure, you can buy a lot of time."

"Again, how?" The bell for the next class rang. "Never mind. Hearing's at 9 at the county courthouse."

"I'll be there."

"Okay," I said. I walked out of there, not believing I'd invited 'Press On' Parker to what promised to be the second-worst day of my life.

CHAPTER 11

Patrick

Fourth period was science with Mrs. Vostik. When I came into class, there was a TV on a stand in the front of the room. CNN was on, and somebody was intoning technical gibberish. Mrs. Vostik, a rather round and short woman, was glued to the set and waving us in distractedly. "They're almost ready to launch," she said, not taking her eyes off the screen. "*Challenger*. What a great name for a spaceship."

"Teacher in space," VG said with a wink. "Mrs. V. thinks she should be there."

NASA would need an extra rocket to get Mrs. V. into space. One of the other kids shushed us, so we both settled into our usual seats. Watching a rocket go up, beat the hell out of actually working.

After a bit of the usual technobabble punctuated by inanities from the talking heads on the TV, NASA lit the candles. Even the sound from what had to be the cheapest TV the school district could find, the roar was loud. I got a bit of goosebumps thinking how loud it must be down in Florida.

That triggered a thought about Dad. Mom and Dad got along pretty well, but one of the few sources of arguments was over space, of all things. Any time NASA sent a rocket up, Mom wanted to be in front of the TV. She'd taken time off of work once to watch a shuttle launch.

Dad, well, he was just okay with rockets. If a rocket was going up and he was in front of a TV, he'd watch it unless the Cardinals were playing. That had been an argument – the Cardinals were playing – a rare day game – and Dad wanted to watch that. But NASA was launching a rocket at the same time and Mom wanted to watch that. I think it had been "settled" by Dad going to a local bar to watch the game.

Well, I thought, now you get to watch whatever you want. I felt my eyes water. Hell, maybe the Cardinals will even win the Series this time.

I looked away from the TV for a second to clear my eyes. There was a collective gasp in the room. Wondering why, I looked back at the TV. There was a massive cloud of smoke in the middle of the screen where the Shuttle should have been. I remember the TV announcer saying something inane about altitude. I guess he was looking at a different screen. Then he said, "Obviously, a major malfunction." Three Sticks, sitting in his usual place in the back, said, "No shit." This got him several glares and a book tossed at him from the center of our basketball team.

"I was talking about the announcer!" Three Sticks said.

"Nobody gives a damn!" VG growled at him.

The rest of us sat there for a long moment, stunned, until somebody realized Mrs. V. was weeping. A couple of the girls went up to comfort her, and I decided that watching the talking heads on TV was no good. So I went up and turned off the TV.

After that, I figured Mom might be shook up as well, so I mumbled something about needing to use the restroom and left, taking my books with me. The word was spreading throughout the high school even though it was in the middle of the class period. As I left, I heard the principal get on the

PA system.

———————

Mom was at work at the IGA. When I got there, she hadn't been watching the launch live – she'd been on a checkout lane. I found her in the break room, glued to a TV, which was alternating between instant replays of the blow-up and random people speculating wildly about stuff they didn't know about.

The manager came up to me. "I'm sorry," I said to him. "I'll get her calmed down and back to work."

"Don't," he said, his bald head bobbing. "She's fine."

"But."

"But nothing," the man said more emphatically. "We're not busy. She can sit here and get paid for a while. It won't break the bank." He patted me on the shoulder. "Do you like ham?"

My confusion must have been obvious. "I was going to send her home with a ham," he continued. "And some fixings. But if you don't like it..."

"Ham is fine," I said. I gestured at Mom. "She likes the maple-flavored baked beans."

"Good," he said, nodding firmly. "We'll send her home with a package." He glanced at Mom. "After she gets a full shift of pay."

"Thanks," I said. There was a lump in my throat. I wasn't really in favor of taking charity, but damn it, we needed it. "If there's anything I can do..."

"Just take care of her," the manager said. "She's good people."

"I will," I said. My eyes were getting watery, so I thanked the manager. Then I went to Mom.

"How you doing?" I asked, taking a seat next to her. I laid my hand on her shoulder.

"The hits just keep on coming," she replied, waving a hand with a Kleenex in it at the TV.

"I know."

"You should go see Great Barb."

"Why?"

She waved at the TV again. "I'm sure she saw this."

"Okay," I said. I decided not to remind her it was a school day. *What the hell? I might be homeless in a month.* Missing school was the least of my worries.

When I got to the nursing home, I found Great Barb in her room. She was sitting in her bed, eating lunch from a tray on a hospital table. A small black-and-white TV was at the foot of her bed, playing CNN. "I miss Walter Cronkite," she said as I walked in. "These new idiots just talk to hear themselves talk."

I kind of thought that talking to hear oneself talk was a job requirement of a TV anchorman, but I didn't say that, merely saying something noncommittal. Great Barb gestured at the TV. "Turn it off. They're just repeating the repeats."

I did so. "How are you?"

"Okay. Not my first disaster. How's your Mom?"

"Shook up. Sitting in the breakroom of the IGA watching TV."

"She always was a space nut," Great Barb said. She took a small bite of her lunch, made a face, and pushed the tray back an inch or so. "Not exactly Huey Sam's."

"Huey Sam's?"

"Chinese place. That wasn't the name on the door, but that's what we called it." She sighed in remembered pleasure. "Great food. Any time I went to Chicago, we had to stop there. Haven't been there in years."

I pulled up a chair. It was metal and vinyl, cheap and

uncomfortable. "I didn't know you liked Chinese food."

She shrugged. "Back when I was young, it was exotic." She chuckled. "I'm sure what they fed us white people wasn't nearly what real Chinese folk ate, but it was way different than a steak and a potato."

I kind of nodded at that. It didn't seem to require a comment, so I didn't offer one. After a long minute or two, unbidden, Great Barb started up again. "I remember the first moon landing."

"A long time ago," I said.

"For you, yes," she said, a smile on her thin old lips. "We were watching it at my house. You were much more interested in banging blocks together than in what was on TV."

"I was at your house?" I said. "I don't think I remember your house."

"I got moved into here when you were four," she replied. "For a while, I was in the other wing."

The other wing was 'assisted living' which meant the residents mostly fended for themselves. Great Barb was no longer able to do so. "Why were we there?" I asked.

"Besides it being a really big deal?" she asked, a smile on her face. "I had a great big color TV." She nodded as if agreeing with herself. "Bought it a month before. I think that was the last time I used the Good Boots Fund."

"The what fund?"

She looked startled. "Never mind," she said. She took another bite of her food and chewed it carefully. Finally, she continued. "Yep. We had a big color TV, so your mom came over and brought you."

She waved her hand at the black-and-white set at the foot of her bed. "Not that my color TV mattered – the feed from NASA was grainy black and white."

I thought of my dad again and wondered if he'd been dragged in to watch. I asked that question more diplomatically.

"Your dad had gotten some overtime at the factory, so he was working. Your mom had quit her job to take care of you, so she was free. I asked her over for dinner." She chuckled. "We actually ate TV dinners. You didn't – I think you were still on bottled food."

"Everybody's got to start somewhere," I said weakly.

"Yep," she replied. "Anyway, we watched the landing and the moonwalk. You took a nap on the couch." She chuckled. "Actually, your mother did too. There were a couple of hours between the landing and them actually walking on the moon. You were still keeping your mother up at night."

"Not deliberately, I'm sure," I said. I did a bit of mental calculation. "Where were you when the Wright Brothers flew?"

"Darned if I know," she said. "There was a long time between when they flew and when anybody knew about it. Years, I think. I vaguely remember reading about it in the papers, and they were talking as if they weren't sure if it was real or a hoax."

"So it wasn't a big deal?" I asked.

"Not at the time," she said. She pointed at the TV. "But if you'd told me then I'd be looking at teachers flying into space now. I'd have been looking for a guy in a white outfit with a butterfly net to take you to a soft, padded room."

I chuckled at that. When Great Barb was all there, she was a pretty sharp cookie. There was a knock at the door, followed by the entry of a girl not much older than me but dressed in a uniform.

"Are you done with lunch, Mrs. Pikus?" she asked.

"Very much so," Great Barb said.

"It's not Huey Sam's," I offered with a smile. Great

Barb smiled too. The aide or whatever she was smiled but was clearly bewildered.

"Let me take your tray," the aide said. She started to do so and looked at the TV. "Is the news upsetting you?"

"Less so than Pearl Harbor," Great Barb said. She looked at me and winked. "Now that was a shock."

"You remember that?" I asked.

"Like it was yesterday," she said. "I was cooking a big Sunday dinner. We had boarders at the house, and I did dinner at 1 on Sunday." She looked at the orderly. "I was just finishing up cooking, and I had the radio on. Chicken, I think. While it was cooking, I had on a musical broadcast from New York City. The announcer broke in, telling us of the attack." She waved a bony finger. "He made a point of telling us that he had the program sponsor's permission to cut in with news updates."

The idea that you'd need somebody's permission to cut in for a news update boggled my mind. Times had changed. "What was it like?"

She waved at the TV. "Like now. Shock, surprise, pain. A little fear. They'd started the draft in '40, I think, but now that the war was on, everybody figured they'd expand it." She clucked. "Oh boy, they did. By the end of January, two of my boarders were in the Army, and the third was working at a factory in Detroit. Making bombers of all things."

"He didn't join the Army?" I asked.

"She. I think she would have if they'd let her. A tough bird. Can't call her old, or at least she wasn't then, but tough."

"It's time for her nap," the orderly said.

"The hell with naps," Great Barb replied. "I'm not five years old."

"I'll wait with her," I said.

The orderly just nodded. We sat for a few minutes in

quiet until Great Barb drifted off. I checked to make sure she was still breathing, and when I was satisfied she was I tucked her in and left. I left, wondering if the Good Boots Fund would be good for an oral history session. Assuming I was still in school, that is.

CHAPTER 12

Patrick

I got to the courthouse in Maple Corners at 8:45, dressed in my funeral suit. Mom was supposed to come but said she was sick. I was not surprised.

The courthouse was an old gray stone building in an L-shape, with the main entrance at the crook of the L. The heyday of Maple Corners had been right around World War I when their local Congressman was Speaker of the House. The courthouse, like a lot of the business district, dated from around then. At least the county had found the money to keep up on the maintenance.

When I got inside I found Mr. Parker, also in a suit, standing there along with Grandma Mary.

"I was just talking to your nice teacher," she said to me.

"How'd you know he was with me?" I asked.

"I didn't," she replied. "I thought he worked here and asked him where we were supposed to be."

"Room 202," I said.

We walked to a rickety-looking elevator with a black latticework door and rode up to the second floor. The courthouse wasn't that big, so finding the room took no time at all. We sat on three chairs behind a wooden railing facing the bench. It was just us, a graying man with a dark suit up at a table in front of the railing and a bored-looking sheriff's deputy.

At 9:01, the judge, a woman about Grandma's age, strode in, and the deputy told us to rise. We did, then sat down when told, and the judge said, "Call the first case."

The bailiff read off a name, not ours, and Dark Suit said, "Tom Ford for the plaintiff."

"Anybody for the defense?" the judge asked. Nobody answered. The judge waved Tom Ford on. He rattled off some mumbo-jumbo, and when he finished, the judge said, "Motion granted."

They repeated this for somebody else, and then the bailiff called "Michael and Ruth Kowalski." All three of us stood up and said, "Here."

This took the judge aback. "Well, come on down," she finally said. "I can guess who's Mary, but which one of you is Michael?"

"Neither, Your Honor," Parker said. "I'm Trevon Parker here with Patrick Kowalski, Michael's son, and Mary Pikus, mother to Mary."

"Are you a lawyer?" Ford growled.

"No, I'm not," Parker replied. "Due to the death of Michael, the family can't afford a lawyer. I was hoping the court would appoint somebody *pro bono*."

The judge made a face, then looked harder at Grandma. "Are you the Pikus that used to work at Maple Corners Tent and Awning?"

"I am," she replied. "Is your son still there?"

"Yes, he is," the judge replied. "Mister Parker, I'm reluctant to spend the taxpayers' dollars on a civil matter."

"Never hurts to ask, your Honor," Parker said. Under his breath, he added, "Didn't think she would."

"Since Mister Parker here admits he's not a lawyer..."

Ford said.

"I'll keep him out of trouble with the bar association," the judge replied. "Proceed."

Ford pulled out a paper and started to hand it to the judge. "Your Honor," Parker said, "we haven't seen any documentation."

"You were sent letters," Ford growled.

"So you claim," the judge replied. "Give him a copy."

"This is my only copy, Your Honor," Ford said.

"Then let Parker read it first," the judge replied.

Ford handed the document to Parker with ill grace. He skimmed it and handed it back. "We object to this document."

"On what grounds?" both the judge and Ford asked.

"It's just a computer printout that says a loan number is delinquent," Parker said.

"And what more do I need?" Ford asked.

"You claim that a foreclosure notice was sent," Parker said. "Was it filed with the Recorder of Deeds?"

"You're here, aren't you?" Ford said. "You know we're foreclosing."

"Did you provide 30 days' notice of this proceeding?" Parker asked. "And can you prove it?"

"Your Honor, this is a patent attempt to delay these proceedings!" Ford shouted.

"It may be," the judge replied. "however, the legislature has been very clear – they don't want people getting the bum's rush in these proceedings." She looked at Parker. "The court would favorably consider a motion to delay these proceedings for thirty days in order to allow the homeowners time to prepare their defense."

"Your Honor!" Ford said. "You're helping them!"

"We move for a 30-day delay to prepare our defense," Parker said.

"Granted," the judge said, banging down her gavel. She looked at Ford. "What's next?"

I had been expecting to get told to move out that day, so I took our experience so far as a win. We left.

"Now what?" Grandma asked when we were in the hallway.

"Do you have all the paperwork they sent you?" Parker asked.

"No. Mom has it at home."

"Then you're going to your house, collecting everything, and taking a drive to Champaign."

"What's in Champaign?" Grandma asked.

"The Land of Lincoln Legal Assistance Foundation," Parker said. "They provide free legal assistance to people who don't have money."

"You get what you pay for," Grandma said.

"Free legal help is better than none," Parker replied.

"But what about school?" I asked.

"Worry about a roof over your head first," Parker replied. He patted me on the shoulder. "My next stop is getting GI Jack on the scholarship hunt."

"I hate camping," I said. "Tell him that when he tries to ship me to the Army."

"I'll keep that in mind," Parker replied.

"And sir?" I said, my voice quavering. "Thanks for your help."

"My pleasure."

———————

I was expecting the offices of Land of Lincoln Legal Foundation to be some kind of dump. It wasn't but rather was a nice office on the second floor of a new office building in downtown Champaign. I had a brief wait, then I was walked back into a small office and introduced to Amy Burton, a woman who looked to be just out of college.

"Please, Mister Kowalski, have a seat."

"Thanks," I said, settling into a green plastic chair with chrome legs. "But call me Pat."

"Okay, Pat, what can I do for you today?"

"Mister Parker suggested you could help. The bank is foreclosing on our house."

"Would that be Trey Parker?"

"I think his first name is Trevon."

She nodded. "My dad called him Trey. They went back a ways." She settled back in her chair. "Tell me your story."

I gave her the Readers' Digest version of events, ending with Mr. Parker getting us the thirty-day delay.

"Wait," she said. "He went into court with you?" She seemed both surprised and impressed.

"Yes ma'am, he did."

She nodded her head. "Well, then that means he thinks highly of you. The man hates courts."

"I wasn't really happy to be there," I said.

"Yeah, well, him and my dad did some work down south back in the day. Trey damn near got beat to death in a court in some flea-bitten Southern town."

"Didn't know that," I said. Apparently Press-On *was* a bit of a hippy back in the day.

"Yeah, they tend to give him flashbacks. That's why he got into education."

"You still friends with him?"

She shrugged. "Not really. He was more my dad's friend, and since dad retired to Arizona, I don't see him very often." She sat there reflecting for a minute, then gathered herself. "So, it sounds like we've got a ticking clock here. I'll see what I can do, but you're going to have to do some work."

She gave me some booklets and told me to find some

papers, including Dad's will (which I doubted he had), and we set up a meeting for next week.

I got back into Eastville at around one and made an executive decision to blow off the rest of the day at school. If Press-on Parker was okay with me missing his class, then everybody else should be. I decided to stop by Great Barb's nursing home.

She was in her room, staring at a TV with the sound off. "Isn't this a school day?" she asked when I walked in. "The Phil Donahue Show was just on."

"It's a school day," I said. "I had to go find a lawyer."

"Why?"

"The bank is foreclosing on the house."

"Why?"

"We're too broke to pay the mortgage," I said, my eyes watering again. "Grandma had to sell her rings to cover the funeral."

"I didn't know," she said. She glanced around the room. "People don't tell me things."

"We didn't want you to worry. The stress..."

"I can handle stress," she said, forcefully. "And I know how you feel. About the house."

I made a face. "How?"

"When my husband Michael disappeared. I was in the same boat."

CHAPTER 13

Amy Burton, Land of Lincoln Legal Aid

I have to say I found the Kowalski kid a refreshing change of pace. I got into the law to help people. Call me an idealist.

Unfortunately, too many of my clients were like the Kings. Mr. King was a drunk ne'er-do-well, spending his life lurching from one self-induced crisis to another. His wife was a limp, dead fish. I sometimes wondered how she managed to get herself dressed in the morning.

But Kowalski seemed like he had a good head on his shoulders. Also, if Trevon Parker liked the kid well enough to step in personally, well, that spoke a lot.

When I told Kowalski that Trey didn't like courts, I didn't tell him why he'd ended up in one. My dad and Trey had been registering voters, the black kind, in Mississippi back when what passed for the law down there didn't like that. The beatdown administered to Trey and my dad in court was just the beginning of their trouble.

Fortunately, this was Illinois in 1986, not Mississippi in 1962. Unfortunately, I didn't have a lot to work on. Trevon was a good guy but not a lawyer, and apparently, Mrs. Kowalski had gone to the same school of adulting as Mrs. King. All I really had in hand was the foreclosure notices that had been sent to the family.

But something felt fishy about this deal. I mean, I got that with them not paying the bank had to do something. But most banks really didn't want to be "in" the collateral. They weren't in the business of selling houses. They were in the business of selling money.

I had a busy day, so it wasn't until late in the afternoon that I got a chance to do more than glance at the letters the Kowalski kid had given me. That's when it hit me. The letter was on B-Friendly letterhead but signed by somebody who was listed as Chief Collection Officer, Fifth Street Mortgage.

I smiled to myself. Stopping a foreclosure is a matter of picking at details. Here the detail to pick at was simple. Who actually held the mortgage – Fifth Street or B-Friendly? If, as appeared here, B-Friendly was working on behalf of Fifth Street, did the two entities have all the signed agreements they needed to legally foreclose? Had they assigned the deeds and notes through the county like they were supposed to? Just making them jump through the hoops to show that all of this was done (assuming it *had* been done) would run a lot of time off the clock.

Vincent Bisceglie III

Vince was not fond of his school nickname of Three Sticks. He was even less fond of his family's preferred name for him. They called him BV, short for "Baby Vincent." Nor was it very original since a lot of old-timers called his dad VJ, short for Vincent Junior. That was really odd since his grandpa had gone missing in 1954. The Old Man had gone to Chicago to meet some friends and never came back.

Mrs. Donato wasn't exactly family. She had, however, worked for the family at the bank since its founding in 1949. As she was fond of telling everybody, she had been the first teller and only the third employee hired. So, to her, Vince was "Mister BV" when she wanted something done.

What she wanted on this afternoon was for him to copy files. Dozens of them. And Vince couldn't just dump the file into the copy machine and press the green button. No, each file had multiple sections, bound onto thin cardboard dividers with metal tabs, which had to be unfolded, copied, the copies hole-punched and then both original and copy reassembled. It was tedious as hell.

When I get my architecture degree, instead of making copies, I'll have somebody make copies for me. He looked up from his files at the decidedly dumpy Mrs. Donato, clad in a shapeless blue dress. *And she'll look a hell of a lot nicer than that walking potato.*

The files had been sorted out in some order that made no sense to Vince, but nobody seemed to care what he thought. He got to the last of the pile and popped it open. Kowalski. He glanced at the address. Looked like it was Pat's place. He did his thing and put the original back and the copy in the box, then went to go punch out and go home. He wondered, not for the first time, why the son of the president had to punch in and out. Hell, why did the son of the president have to work at all?

"Did you get those foreclosures copied, Mister BV?" Mrs. Donato asked.

"What foreclosures?"

She pointed at the box he'd been working on. "All those loans are foreclosures."

He glanced at the box. "I got them all done. What's a foreclosure?"

Mrs. Donato made a sad face. "That's what we do when people don't pay back their mortgages. We take their houses. It's very sad."

"So we're going to take Pat Kowalski's house?"

"We're foreclosing on a house owned by Mike and Ruth Kowalski. I think Pat's their son."

"He is." Vince nodded. "Thanks."

"See you tomorrow?"

"No, ma'am. Basketball game. I'm in the band."

"Oh, that sounds fun. When I was your age..."

After a mercifully short albeit pointless story, Vince was able to make his escape. Since he hadn't been able to punch out before storytime, he at least got paid to listen to her.

CHAPTER 14

Oral History Project

Oral History Project by Patrick Kowalski, Eastville High School, May 2, 1986. My oldest living relative, Great-Grandmother Barbara Pikus, told me this story the day I was first in court about the foreclosure on the house.

So I told you that Michael called and said he was coming home. He never made it, and I never saw him again. Mister Big, his mobster boss, had no idea where he was. Suggested that he'd 'traded me in on a newer model.' He also told me that Michael owed Capone a lot of money and that the Capone organization was looking for him.

That may have been true, but I had two kids to feed and a house to heat. Michael had left me a little cash, but he'd just bought a new truck, which was also missing, and we were counting on his cut of the latest booze run to catch us up.

Come the end of January, right after a big blizzard, I walked into town. I see that look, young man. Yes, I walked. Didn't have a car, and if I'd had a horse we'd have eaten it by then.

Mister Big was in Eastville. He had a set of rooms on the third floor of the Eastville Hotel. When it burnt down, they put the CVS store on that lot.

I marched up those stairs and marched right into his hotel room. He was sitting on a big leather armchair, his fat gut spilling everywhere. One of his torpedoes was seated in a wooden chair just inside the door, reading a newspaper.

"Mister Big," I said. "Sir. I need help. I've got two kids..."

"Times are tough all over," he cut me off. "You should have done a better job with your husband in the bedroom. Maybe he wouldn't have run off."

"How dare you!"

He got up with a grunt. "Lady, you don't seem to understand. I'm the boss, and your deadbeat husband ran off with my money. Him and some floozy are probably down in Florida sipping those drinks with the umbrellas in them."

"That's not my fault! It's not the fault of those little kids!"

"Don't you take that tone with me!" He reared back his hand as if to hit me. That's when I pulled Dad's revolver out of my purse and stepped toward him, shoving the barrel of the gun into his gut.

The torpedo shoved a .45 into my ear. I heard the hammer click back, and I thumbed the hammer back of my gun.

"Mister," I said, "I haven't eaten for three days, and I gave the kids the last of the food this morning. I've got nothing to lose."

"Let's all just calm down," Big said, his face sweaty. "Nobody needs to do nothing that they might regret."

"She'll be dead before she hits the floor," the torpedo said.

"And he'll have a hole in his gut," I said.

"I said," Big said with emphasis, "let's all just take a moment here."

"Not too many moments," I said. "I'm hungry and getting light-headed."

"Look, Missus Pikus," Big said, "I really owe you nothing. Your husband owes you and me big-time." His open hand, still frozen mid-slap, changed to holding one finger up. "But I'm not entirely without sympathy. I got a mother too, and back in the Old Country, sometimes the gravy on the macaroni was thin, you know."

"I'm sure I don't," I said.

"In any event," Big replied, "out of the goodness of my heart, I'm prepared to offer you a one-time interest-free loan. When your husband finds his way home, he can catch me up."

"I'm listening," I said.

"A hundred dollars," he said.

"Not even close," I replied. I gave his gut a little poke with the gun.

"Fine. I have three hundred dollars in my pocket. You can have it. All. As a gift." He waved his finger. "But that's a one-time only deal. And nobody needs to know about this day."

I really was hungry, and I had no faith that his torpedo wouldn't shoot me. "Okay. But call off your dog here."

"Bruno put the gun away."

Bruno did so reluctantly.

"Your turn, sweetheart."

"Money."

"I'm reaching for it now," he said, "Don't shoot."

He handed over a wad of bills. "Thank you."

"Don't mention it. Literally."

I walked backwards out of the room and ran down the stairs.

Patrick

"Now, three hundred dollars was a lot back then, right?"

"Not as much as you think," Great Barb replied. "We were out of cash again by early April, and that was with me cutting every corner."

"And Mister Big?"

"Glared daggers at me when he saw me in town."

"So then what?"

"I got lucky," she said. "I decided to go squirrel hunting."

"To steal their nuts?"

"No, silly, to eat them. Squirrels are tasty!" She sighed. "I actually wish they served them here."

"So you hunted squirrels?"

"I hunted squirrels. I found gold."

"Gold?"

"I was out in the woods by our house. The one in Strawberry Creek. I watched a squirrel run up a tree – shot it with my slingshot and missed. I got right up under the tree to see if I could take another shot, and my foot slipped."

"On what?"

"Leather," she said. "A piece of leather from a rotted-out satchel. A satchel monogrammed DF – same as the monogram on the shirt Mister Good Boots wore."

"The guy who died at your doorstep," I said.

"Yep. Inside the bag were gold coins. Twenty-four thousand dollars in coins."

"You lived off of that, then?" Twenty grand was a lot of money, even now. Back then, it must have been a fortune.

"For a bit. We used some for food, then some more to buy a house in town. Cost us two thousand dollars."

It hit Pat. "The TV you bought for the moon landing. That was from the Good Boots Fund."

Great Barb smiled. "Yep. I occasionally tapped into it over the years."

"What did you tell everybody? Back then, I mean. You're poor, and all of a sudden, you had money."

Great Barb smiled. "Well, it wasn't like I was flashing it around."

"But the house?"

She shrugged. "Nobody asked, so I didn't tell."

I kind of questioned that, but apparently, I wasn't going to get any other answer. "So why in town?"

"I could get a job, or so I thought," she said. "Ended up taking in boarders and laundry. Wasn't until the second war that I got a job at Maple Corners Tent and Awning. With the war on, they needed everybody they could get to make tents for the Army. By then, the kids were old enough to fend for themselves."

We sat in silence for a minute. I was stunned. My great-grandpa ran booze for Capone, and now this little old lady tells me she stuck a gun in a gangster's belly? *Although she did have the guts to fly in that box kite with delusions of grandeur. Next she's going to tell me finding the gold got us wrapped up in some ancient curse.*

"Question?" I finally said.

"Yes?"

"You moved into town. What about Mister Big?"

"What about him?"

"Wouldn't he, I don't know, want his money back?"

She smiled. "Oh, I took care of that."

"How?"

"Once I got the gold situated and before I moved, I dressed in my most threadbare outfit and went to church."

"Church?"

"Saint Elizabeth. The old church, not the one you went to. The fat man went every Sunday. I went, and when he came out I grabbed him on the front steps in front of the priest and everybody. Hugged him. Kissed his hand. Then asked him exactly how much my husband and I owed him."

"And?"

"And he looked at the priest and all the other people and said thirteen hundred dollars." She laughed. "His face was red, and the priest was glaring at him."

I held up a hand. "Wait a second. He only gave you three hundred."

"But he claimed my husband owed him money, too. That included Michael's share."

"Wow. Cheap bastard." I was expecting to get corrected for the language but was not. "Then what?"

"Then next Sunday, I went to church again, and as he was leaving, I gave him the money. Made him count it in front of the priest. Oh, he was so mad."

"Why was he mad?"

"Because he wanted all the non-gangsters in town to think he was a generous man. He wanted all his gangsters to think he'd take care of their families if they got pinched. Seeing me pay him off made him look bad. It made his people wonder just how well he'd take care of them if they took a fall for him."

"But he was off your back."

She shrugged. "Officially. I think he did a lot of snooping around after I bought the house."

We sat there for a bit, silent. Then she finally said, "There's still some left, you know."

"Really?" I asked.

"Half. Twelve thousand dollars."

That might help get a real lawyer. As I thought that, one of the nurses walked in.

"Are you eating with Barbara tonight?" she asked me.

"No, thanks." I looked at Great Barb. "Can we have a minute?"

"Sure. I'll be outside."

When she left, I asked Great Barb, "Where is it?"

"Where's what?" she asked.

"The gold. From the Good Boots Fund."

"What gold?" She started to sing to herself in Lithuanian. I waited for a bit, hoping she'd switch back to English. She didn't, which was typical. The nurse came back in, and I left. *Probably never was a dime of gold.*

Grandma Mary came over that night to eat some of the leftovers. A lot of people had brought food over, and with just Mom and I, we had plenty.

"Great Barb said you were a hot baby," I said to Grandma.

"When she tell you that?" Grandma asked.

"At Dad's funeral lunch. We were talking about when her husband disappeared. She said you had just been born."

"No, not me," Grandma replied. "I was born in 1920, and my first memory is the Christmas daddy didn't show up."

I wondered how much of anything Great Barb was telling me was the truth.

CHAPTER 15

Patrick

"I missed you yesterday," VG said. We were in the library for study hall and were sitting at a table in the back.

"I was in court."

"For?"

I sighed. "They're taking our house. The bank."

"Why?"

"Because that's what they do when you don't pay the mortgage."

"That sucks," VG said.

"Yeah, no shit," I replied.

"So what are you doing about it?"

"Mr. Parker helped us get a lawyer."

"Press-on Parker helped?" VG said, incredulous.

"Back in the day, he was some kind of hippy. He's also talking to GI Jack about scholarships for me."

"I thought Sims and him didn't get along."

"They don't – Parker called Sims 'GI Jack' to my face."

"Wow," VG said. "I bet that makes for some testy conversations in the teacher's lounge."

"I'm sure the two of them put on their smiley faces for each other, or at least just don't talk. I mean, look at you and Boom Boom." Boom Boom was the nickname for another kid in our class. VG and Boom Boom were at each other all Freshman year, including at least two fistfights. Finally, a pair of seniors had brokered a truce. The only thing flying between the two of them now were dirty looks.

"Point."

"How's your oral history project for Mr. Olsen going?" I asked to change the subject.

He was talking to his grandmother, who'd been born in Italy and still had a strong accent. We chatted a bit, and then I asked, "Why do Italians put gravy on pasta?"

VG laughed. "Dude, we don't. What you call spaghetti sauce, we call gravy. At least that's what the old-timers call it."

"Oh."

"Why do you ask?"

"Great Barb told a story about when she was talking to an Italian, and he said that back in the Old Country, sometimes the gravy on the macaroni was thin."

"Yeah, for my grandma, the generic term for spaghetti sauce is gravy. In Italian, 'salsa' and 'ragu' are types of sauce."

"You mean salsa like the stuff you get in Mexican restaurants?"

"Well, her salsa is thinner and is just tomatoes," VG said. "You know, Spanish and Italian are very similar languages."

I did not know that and said so. The only foreign language we offered at Eastville High was Spanish. VG, who was trying to get into college, had taken two years of it and gone on a trip with his class to Mexico last summer. The longest trip I had ever taken was the summer of my eighth-grade year to Florida with the parents. We'd been back a week when Dad cut his leg off, putting an end to our traveling.

"So, how's your project going?" VG asked.

"Well, she talks a lot," I said, "but I don't know how much of what she says is true or not."

"Such as?"

"So the first airplane to come to Eastville flew here in 1912. She got a ride in it – Mr. Olsen showed me a newspaper article. I asked, and she told me a story about it. Even told me the pilot was putting the moves on her."

"Gross."

"Well, she'd have been," I did the mental math, "22 then, so presumably she was a decent-looking woman."

"So maybe the pilot did put a move on her."

"Maybe. But she told me a story about being pregnant with one of her kids and being always hot. Yet she got the wrong kid."

"I've heard of hot mammas..." VG said.

"Oh, stuff it," I replied.

"Well, one of her kids was hot."

"Maybe," I said. "That's it. I have no idea when she's here on Earth or out on Mars. And that's when she remembers to speak English."

VG laughed. "At least my grandma only speaks Italian when she's pissed at my dad."

"That happen a lot?"

"Occasionally," VG said with a shrug. "So what's the biggest whopper she's told you?"

"Well, either when she was four years old, she saw a man from a train die in front of her or that she found twenty grand in gold." I shrugged. "Either or both could be total bullshit."

"It would sure be nice if the gold was real and you had some," VG said.

"She says half of it is left," I replied.

"Really? That would be a nice college fund."

I laughed but with no humor. "If it were real? Maybe. If she remembered where it was? If somebody else hasn't stolen it before we were born?"

"Did you ask her?"

"Of course, dummy."

"What did she say?"

"She started singing in Lithuanian."

"Well, that sucks."

I waved him off. "It doesn't matter. We need a lot more than ten grand to get out of this shit."

"Still, dude, ten grand is better than a sharp stick in the eye."

———————

I was back in study hall the next day when VG plopped down in the chair in front of me, a book in his hand.

"Question," he said. "Your great-grandma said she had ten thousand dollars of gold left."

"She did."

"How did she know how much gold she had?"

I shrugged. "How would I know?"

VG opened up the book to a page he'd marked with a strip of notebook paper. "See this?" he said, pointing to a picture in a book. It was a color picture of a gold coin. The coin had an image of a woman with flowing robes and a spear in her hand walking towards you.

"What's this?"

"That is a double eagle," VG said. Specifically a Saint-Gaudens."

"Okay. And?"

"And, in 1924..."

"1925," I corrected.

"Same difference. Before 1935, it was worth twenty bucks. Said so on the back."

"Great."

VG smiled. "As of yesterday morning's Wall Street Journal, which this library gets a copy of, just the gold in one coin is worth 354 dollars."

"Oh, shit."

"Yeah, oh shit is right, my broke-ass friend," VG said, smiling. "So let's do the math."

"It was my understanding that there would be no math."

"You'll like this math," VG said. "So, 10,000 dollars divided by twenty means five hundred coins. Five hundred coins times 354 per coin equals 177,000 dollars."

"Wow," I said.

"I was expecting a bit more than 'wow.' Would that solve your money troubles?"

"Hell, yes," I said. That would cover the house, college, maybe a not-puke-green car, and, well, it was a dizzying amount of money. Literally, I felt dizzy.

Then I got over it. "But that's if it's real. If she remembers where it is. We had to sell her house, so if she hid it there, we're screwed."

"Hold on there, partner," VG said. "One thing at a time. We've decided that it's well worth our time to seriously dig, right?"

"Yes. And what's this *we*?"

VG patted himself on the chest. "If it hadn't been for me, you'd have blown this off."

"And so what do you want for that, Oh Wise One?"

"A mere finder's fee. Twenty percent."

"The hell! I was thinking I'd buy dinner."

VG shrugged. "Dude, I really do not want to go to Jag-off U."

Jag-off U was our nickname for the local community

college on account of its less-than-stellar educational reputation.

"Fine. A finders' fee. Ten percent."

"We seem to have agreed on fifteen," he said, offering his hand.

I looked at his hand and finally decided that fifteen percent of nothing was still nothing. I reached over and shook on it. "You know, fifteen percent of zero is still zero."

"Now you're the math expert," he replied with a smile. "But what else do we have to do?"

"Good point."

CHAPTER 16

Patrick

Grandma took us out to dinner that night. It was the last Friday of the month, which meant the VFW was having a fish fry. Five bucks a plate, which included pop or iced tea, so even Grandma could afford it. I decided to approach the gold question from an angle.

We were eating in the bar area. It was a wood-paneled room, high-ceilinged and smoky. Around the walls just below the ceiling were a bunch of large black-and-white photos from WWII. The TV over the bar was on, tuned to the local news. "When you put Great Barb in the nursing home, how well did you clean out her house?" I asked.

"Really well," Grandma replied. "Why?"

"I was just curious," I said. "I mean, what happened to all of her stuff?"

"Why all of this curiosity?" Grandma asked. "That was a long time ago."

"I'm doing this oral history project," I said. "It got me thinking about my oldest memory, which I think was in her house."

"She went into the nursing home in 1972," Grandma said. "You were four."

"And her first memory happened when she was four,"

I said. "Ironic, huh?"

"Let me guess," Grandma said. "She told you the story of Mister Good Boots."

"The guy that died in front of her."

Grandma shook her head. "Never happened."

Mom, who had gone to the ladies' room, returned and said, "What never happened?"

"Supposedly," Grandma said, "some man off of a train walked up to their old house and croaked." She waved dismissively. "Mom always said we should be grateful for his arrival."

"So you've heard the story?" I said.

"More than once."

"Did you hear the story about her finding something in the woods?" I asked.

"In the woods?" Grandma said. "No. And until we moved into town, us kids were always in the woods."

"Playing?" I said.

"Hell no," Grandma replied. "Picking strawberries, gathering nuts, finding branches for firewood, no, we worked."

One hundred and fifty thousand dollars, the amount of gold in question, even minus VG's cut, was not something I wanted to let go of. "Not to be a pest," I said, "but how do you know that the Mister Good Boots story was bogus?"

"They gave him to Calabro to bury, right?" Grandma said. "So, where's the grave?" She shrugged. "Shouldn't there be a grave marked 'unknown man with good boots' in the cemetery?"

"I guess so," I said.

Mom looked at me. "You ready to go?"

"Yep."

———————

That following Monday, I had my regular session with Mr. Olsen about the oral history project. He started by asking about things at home. He meant how was I handling my dad's death. I lied and said things were fine. He offered to help, but I shrugged him off.

After we got that out of the way, I said to him, "My problem, Mr. Olsen, is I don't know how much of what Great Barb is telling me is true or not."

He smiled. "Ah, but that's the challenge of oral histories. You get what they remember and what they want to tell you. But what makes you think she's not telling the truth?"

"Well, she got stuff wrong. I mean, she told me my grandmother as a baby was always hot, but it turns out she was talking about another of her kids."

"That's not uncommon."

"According to my grandma, another story she told me was flat wrong."

"Was that about the airplane ride?" Mr. Olsen asked with a smile.

"Well, I had to show Grandma a copy of the article to get her to believe it."

Mr. Olsen nodded. "Sometimes, with oral history, we can't tell if what they remember is true or not. That may not even be the point – the point is what they remember. But sometimes we can prove at least part of the story is true."

"Like the article about the plane."

"Exactly. We can prove she rode in it. We can't prove that the pilot flirted with her or that he paid her a fee, but at least part of the story is for sure real."

I pondered what Mr. Olsen had said for the rest of the day. I decided that, after school, I'd do a little detective work. There are two funeral homes in Eastville – Mroz's, where our family went – and Calabro's, which I assumed was the same 'Calabro' as in Great Barb's story. I decided to go to the source, as it were, and stopped by Calabro's.

Mroz's was an old two-story brick house. Calabro's, by contrast, was a one-story building, more like a bank branch than a house. I walked into the lobby, and immediately to my right was an office with a glass window looking into the lobby. An old guy, balding with a prominent nose, was sitting at the desk, looking through a newspaper.

I went in and introduced myself.

"Sorry about your father," he said in a deep and gravelly voice. "Did John do a good job?"

"Actually, his daughter Stephanie did most of the work," I said. "I was happy, well..."

"I understand. It's never a happy time." He had a grave manner about him. "So what can I do for you?"

"Well, I have a weird question, if you've got a few minutes to talk, that is."

He held his hands out. "At the moment, I've got nothing but time."

"So I'm doing a history project at the high school, and my great-grandmother was telling me about somebody who died when she was a little kid. I had some questions about how a funeral was done back then."

"When was 'back then?'"

"1894."

He smiled. "I'm old, but not that old." He pointed at a black-and-white picture on the wall. "Now, my dad got into the business around then."

"May I?" I asked, noting that the picture had a brass nameplate on it. He nodded, and I got up to read the plate. "Emil Calabro."

"Emil Senior," Calabro said. "I'm Emil Junior, but I go

by Bud."

"Emil is a funny name."

"Old one. Comes from Latin."

"So Senior was doing burials back then?" I returned to the seat in front of his desk.

"Yes," Calabro said. "Obviously not here. The old funeral home burnt down in the early 60s. We built this – Dad and I."

"So you wouldn't have any records of a funeral from the 1890s."

"I'm afraid not," he said.

"Would there be a death certificate?" Thanks to Dad's passing, I was getting an education in things about death.

"There was supposed to be," Calabro said. "But back then, people were kind of lax about such things." He shrugged. "So maybe yes, maybe no. I have to say, these are really specific questions."

"So here's the scoop," I said. "My great-grandmother, Great Barb, we call her..."

"I do remember her," Calabro said.

"Well, she's half-senile." Calabro nodded encouragingly. "And she told me a story about a death that happened in 1894. Supposedly, your dad picked up the body. But my grandma says that because there is no tombstone in the cemetery, the death didn't happen."

"And you're trying to find out one way or the other?" Calabro asked.

"Yes."

"Got a tough history teacher? Making you dig?"

"Not really," I said. "More for my own curiosity."

"Well," he said, stroking his chin, "not having a tombstone is not at all uncommon. Back then, tombstones were hand-carved and very expensive. Some people made tombstones out of concrete, which deteriorated over time. Poor people used wooden crosses, which, of course, fell apart even faster." Calabro pointed at his dad's picture. "But Dad was a stickler for paperwork. If he handled the body, the certificate was filed."

"Would it still exist?"

"Probably. In this county, they're pretty good about keeping those records."

"And can anybody get a certificate?"

"If you need a certificate from back then, it costs a couple of bucks because they have to print one up from microfilm. If you just want to see if somebody died and when they'll usually let you look at the book."

"The book?"

"Back then, they'd write the name and date in a book which told them the filing cabinet to pull the paper from. Now it tells them what roll of film to look at."

"But there should be a record?"

"If Dad did the burial, he turned it in. After that, who knows what happened."

"Well, thanks, Mr. Calabro," I said. "That helps."

"Call me Bud, and you're welcome," he replied, offering me his hand.

CHAPTER 17

Vincent Bisceglie III

"That's Sofia's job," Vince said. He was standing in the kitchen, his coat on, having just gotten back from his after-school job at the bank.

"She's got cheerleading practice tonight," his mom replied.

"How much practice does it take to say, 'Go fight go?'"

"I don't know. Just do it. And we're in the dining room tonight."

"Fancy."

"Bud's coming over."

She meant Bud Calabro. He was Vince's great-uncle, having married Grandma's youngest sister.

The back door opened, and Bud walked in. He looked at Vince's mom. "What's for dinner?"

"Macaroni and ragu," she replied. "We're eating in the dining room."

"What's the occasion?" Uncle Bud asked, taking off his hat and hanging it on a hook mounted on the wall by the door.

"Tom Ford's coming over, too," she replied. "So we don't have enough seats at the table."

"Okay," Uncle Bud replied. "Where's VJ?"

"In the front room," she said.

Bud, who had gotten his coat off, walked in that direction. *It didn't even occur to him to offer to help.* Vince shook his head. *Why would it? When Aunt C. was home, she stirred his coffee for him.*

Aunt C. was not home – she was down in St. Louis with their daughter, who had just had a baby. Since the limit of Bud's cooking skills were making a sandwich or pouring cereal into a bowl, he was eating dinner with them until she got back. Vince sighed and went to set the table.

They had just all sat down for dinner when Tom Ford, Dad's lawyer, breezed in. "Sorry I'm late," he said, tossing his coat on the couch as he walked through the living room. Vince thought the man would be late to his own funeral.

"Hi, Tom," Bud said. "I was getting ready to eat your portion, too."

"Well, get un-ready," Tom said. "Debbie, thanks for inviting me," he added, nodding at Vince's mom.

As the noodles were being passed around, Uncle Bud said, "So, BV, are you in this oral history project too?"

"What project?" Vince asked.

"I guess that's a no," Uncle Bud replied. "I'll take the garlic bread, please."

After the bread was passed, Uncle Bud said, "That Kowalski kid was at the shop today." By 'shop,' he meant the funeral home. "Wanted to know about old-time funerals. Supposedly, ones my dad did."

"And this was for the oral history project?" Dad said.

"Yep. Said it was something for the high school."

"Why aren't you doing it?" Mom asked.

"Because I took a different elective," Vince replied.

"Yes, art of all things," Vince's Dad said.

"You need to be able to draw to be an architect," Vince replied.

"And being an architect is a respected profession," Mom said.

"Which takes five years of college," Dad replied.

"You picked a school yet?" Ford asked, talking around a piece of garlic bread.

"Yes," Dad replied. "An expensive one. Private and out-of-state." From his dad's tone, you'd have thought Vince was getting a law degree and M.D. from Harvard or something.

"What's wrong with the U of I?" Ford asked. He'd gotten his undergraduate and law degrees from there and made sure everybody knew it.

"Washington University is one of the best schools in the country," Vince said.

"U of I's not shabby," Ford said. "And cheaper."

And way too close to home, Vince thought. Everybody would be dropping in to 'visit.' He'd considered SIU, but if he was going to go that far south, he might as well get a name school. Not that Vince was opposed to partying, but he figured there'd be parties at Washington U., too. Fortunately Sofia wanted to talk about her band concert next week, so the conversation shifted to her.

Immediately after dinner, Vince's dad invited Tom Ford and Vince to his office – an unusual event. Not that the 'office' was anything special. VJ had finished off a room in the basement with plain drywall and all-weather carpet. Some old furniture from God-knows-where had been plopped in.

The three of them trooped downstairs. "BV, turn on the electric," Dad said, settling into his brown leather high-back armchair. The electric was a small battleship-gray space heater, needed to knock some of the chill out of the room. Vince turned it on and took one of the wooden side chairs.

"Tom," Dad said, "tell BV what you told me yesterday."

"Are you sure he's ready for it?" Ford said.

"I wasn't much older when my dad disappeared. Besides, he needs to know."

"If you say so, VJ," Ford replied. He looked at Vince. "I think we're going to lose the S and L."

"Lose how?" Vince said.

"The government's gonna seize it," Ford replied.

"They can't do that!" Vince said. "It's ours! We own it!"

"Actually, they can," Ford replied. "We're technically bankrupt already."

"By law," Dad said, a sour look on his face, "we have to buy insurance for all our depositors. From the government. A condition of that insurance is that if we look like we're going belly-up, the government can take the institution from us."

"They'll pay us, right?" Vince asked. He felt like he was standing next to himself as this conversation was going on.

"No," Ford replied. "They'll probably sue us for whatever it cost them to seize the institution."

"Sue us? And why would it cost them money to take us?"

It was a long explanation and had to do with things like 'negative bids' and 'reserve risk-based capital' and 'delinquency rates.' Vince understood very little of it, but at the end of the explanation, his dad made the impact very clear.

"We've been trying to funnel assets to another organization," Dad said, "but there's a limit to what we can move. We're not going to be on the streets, but money is going to be tight."

"Going to U of I tight?" Vince asked.

"I was thinking more like Maple Corners Community

College," Dad said. "At least for a year to get some of the general ed crap out of the way."

"A fucking junior college?" Vince said.

"Language, young man," Dad snapped. "And yes, a junior college – unless you've got thirty grand stashed under your mattress."

Vince had maybe thirty bucks in his pocket, which was the sum total of his savings. "How did we manage – how did *you* manage to faltz this up?"

"So now he's J. P. Morgan," Dad said.

"Who?" Vince replied.

"Never mind," Dad said, glaring at Ford's smirk. "To answer your question, Baby Vincent, we were participating in loans with an institution in Texas."

"Like buying," Ford said by way of explanation. Vince didn't exactly understand how or why one 'bought' a loan, but he let it slide.

"Yes," Dad said. "Oil exploration loans."

"And what the heck do we know about oil exploration?" Vince asked.

"You sound like your grandmother, at least before she's had her third drink of the day," Dad replied.

"She was a bit more emphatic," Ford said. Vince had a pretty good idea of what he meant by that. There were probably blue words in English and Italian at that discussion.

Dad waved the remark away. "That's why we worked with the Texas people."

"So what happened?" Vince asked.

"How much did it cost for you to fill up your car?" Ford asked.

"Fifteen bucks," Vince replied.

"Roughly a dollar a gallon," Ford said. "That's way down from a few years ago."

"So?" Vince said.

"So, Rockefeller," Ford replied testily, "with oil prices way down, a lot of those drillers we were giving loans to went bust."

"We've got collateral, right?" Vince asked.

"We got collateral coming out our ear," Ford replied. "We've got parking lots full of clapped-out oil drilling equipment that's barely worth its weight in scrap metal."

Vince sat there, stunned. *How stupid did you have to be to invest in something you didn't understand?*

They sat there for a minute, apparently to let Vince absorb the situation. Finally, Vince said, "Tell me about this 'other entity' we're moving stuff into."

"We created a mortgage company," Ford said. "Well, we are in the process of creating one."

"What's a mortgage company?" Vince asked.

"A company that writes mortgages," Ford replied testily.

"Great," Vince replied. "Why?"

"So," Ford said, "when the government goes looking, it's an asset they can't seize."

"And we can use it to hide money?" Vince asked.

"Exactly," his dad replied.

"But not enough for Washington U?" Vince said.

"There are limits to what we can move out," Ford replied. "Especially now that the government is watching us."

Vince felt like he'd just fallen into the *Godfather* movie. He looked around at the shitty, damp, and plain basement room and suppressed a hysterical laugh. At least the Corleones had nicer digs.

"Speaking of the new mortgage company," Dad said, changing the subject, "what's up with the asset move?"

"Mrs. Donato finished up the last transfers," Ford replied.

"Hey wait," Vince said. "Were those the papers I was copying?"

"Probably," Ford said. "Getting stuff signed over has been pretty much all she's been working on."

"So if we're trying to stash money," Vince said, "why are we moving a foreclosed loan to this other company?"

"Which foreclosed loan?" Dad asked.

"Kowalski," Vince replied. Ford made a sour face at the mention of the name. "I just happened to notice his name since I go to school with him and all."

"We couldn't move all good loans to the new company, or it would look suspicious. Besides, their house is worth way more than they owe on it." Vince's dad leaned back in his chair, a satisfied look on his face. "We'll come out like bandits on that deal." He apparently noticed the sour expression on Ford's face. "Problem?"

"Judge Hoffman gave them a thirty-day extension," Ford said.

"Why?" Dad asked.

Ford shot his dad a look. "The judge gave them an extension because some nosy parker came with them to help out and asked for one."

"How can they afford a lawyer?" Dad asked.

"They didn't. Some black dude with a big bald spot showed up to help."

"And Hoffman gave them an extension?"

"She even suggested one," Ford said.

"But we'll get the house, right?" Dad asked.

"They're poorer than church mice," Ford said. "We'll get it. It just might take a bit longer."

"Well, keep up the heat," Dad said. "that's a diamond in the rough."

"I am, don't worry," Ford said.

CHAPTER 18

John B. Hood

John Hood shivered in his coat as he walked briskly into the construction trailer. The coat was the heaviest thing he could find at the Target store near his hotel, and he was still cold. He opened the door to the trailer and was greeted by a blast of marginally warmer air.

"Close the damn door!" shouted the site superintendent, Joe Kelly.

"I am, damn it!" John shouted back, trying to sound good-natured.

"Sorry, boss," Kelly replied, not-at-all sorry-sounding. "I made a fresh pot of coffee."

"Sounds great," John said, grabbing a small Styrofoam cup and filling it. "How we doing?" John had eyes and could see that they had very nearly completed demolition and were down to the slab foundation, but he wanted to hear from Kelly.

"Tommy's gonna hit that slab with a 'dozer," Kelly replied. "Looks like it should come right up."

As if on cue, John heard the growl of a diesel engine. There's the 'dozer, he thought, taking a sip of coffee. He grabbed some paperwork from his inbox and took a seat at one of the three desks in the room. He had just finished his coffee and was going for a refill when a young man in a Carhart winter coverall came busting through the door.

"I found a body!" the man shouted.

"What kind of body, Tommy?" Kelly asked.

"The human kind!"

"Shit," John growled.

"Are you gonna call the cops?" Tommy asked.

"Let's go brave the tundra and take a look," John said.

"It ain't that cold, Tex," Kelly said with a chuckle.

"It's a body!" Tommy said.

"Let's just make sure it ain't a Halloween decoration first," Kelly said calmingly. "And if it is a body, it ain't going nowhere."

It was only a few steps to where the 'dozer had lifted up the slab. The rest of the demolition crew was standing around gawking. Hood walked over to the find. Tommy had most certainly not found a Halloween decoration. Somebody had dug a deliberate hole under the slab and dumped a body into it. Looked like it had been there a while – it was a skeleton with boots.

"Looks real to me," Kelly said.

"Unfortunately," John replied. *Christ on a stick. The schedule on this was tight enough without a problem like this.*

Kelly's daughter's car had pulled up, and she came walking up to them, leaving her car door on. She had her coat open, and just looking at her made John cold. The girl was a Chicago native fresh out of school and doing some typing and filing for them.

"What's going on?" she asked. "Somebody get hurt?"

"He did," Tommy said, pointing at the body in the hole.

"That body's been there for a long time," John said. "Nobody on the job site got hurt."

"Good," she said.

"Now, what do we do?" Kelly asked.

John turned and looked at the crew. He pointed at Kelly's daughter. "Go park your car, then get back out here with a clipboard. Cops are going to want a list of everybody who was on the site and their phone number."

She nodded and moved to comply. Kelly said, "Why phone numbers? They can talk to them here."

"Trust me," John said, "I've hit bodies in demolition before." He hadn't, but he knew people who had. "We're going be shut down for two or three days while the lab-coat crowd starts digging him out with toothbrushes. So Kelly, get this equipment parked and secured and help your daughter get that list together. I'm gonna make some calls."

Kelly nodded, then said in a loud voice, "You heard the man. Get your gear parked up."

"What about pay?" one of the guys said.

"You'll get eight hours for today," John said over his shoulder as he went to the trailer. "We'll call you when the job is back on."

Once inside, John called the cops. This suburb didn't have 911 yet, so he had to dial the regular number. Once he got them moving, he called the office in Dallas and told them briefly what had happened. His third call was to M & B Auctions.

"Gary McGlauchlin, please," he said to the woman who answered the phone. A few ticks later, Gary came on the line.

"I need to get hold of that history fellow," John said. "Webber."

"You mean Webster? Rick Webster?" Gary asked.

"Yeah," John said.

"Mind if I know why?"

"We found a body buried under the slab at the Burger Barn," John said. "When the cops get here, they're surely going to have questions about when things were built – questions I won't have answers to."

"Sounds interesting. Got a pen?"

"I do," John said. He took down the number.

Interesting was not the word I would have used, he thought as he hung up. More like a major pain in the ass.

————————

The sun was setting, and John's stomach was growling when the two detectives walked into the trailer. Lunch had been a sandwich he'd sent Kelly's daughter out to get. The cops had set up a tent over the bodies, and several people in white evidence suits were shuttling into and out of it from a white DuPage County sheriff's van.

"How's the digging going?" John asked. As he did, the Webster guy walked in.

"Slow," the stockier of the two detectives said, sitting heavily on a folding chair in the trailer. Webster nodded with his chin at the coffee pot. Hood waved his okay. The heavy cop continued. "It will be a couple of days."

The other detective, younger with the build of a runner, said, "We used to call this place Bell's Bimbos and Brawls. Now we'll have to call it Bell's Bodies, Bimbos and Brawls."

"Bodies?" Webster asked over his shoulder as he stirred creamer into his Styrofoam cup. "I thought there was just one."

"Well, unless the dude had two right feet," said Stocky Cop, "we got at least two bodies. Who are you?"

"Rick Webster. Like the dictionary."

"He's the guy who knows the history of the place," John said. "Like I told you earlier."

"Oh," Stocky Cop said.

"Mr. Webster," Runner Cop said.

"Call me Rick."

"Rick, when was that slab poured?"

"Late 1924 or very early in 1925," Rick replied. He took a sip of his coffee and, with his other hand, pulled up another folding chair. "The grand opening as a restaurant was in early February '25."

"As a restaurant?" Stocky Cop asked.

"That building was built in 1920 as a gas station," Rick said. He settled gently into the chair, making a face and holding his back as he did so. "What's now the bar area – where the bodies are - was originally the service area for car repairs. It had a dirt floor until they made it into a restaurant."

"How do you know that?" Stocky Cop asked. "The dirt floor?"

"I found a picture of the construction. The change to a restaurant made the local newspaper. Back then, this whole area was unincorporated farmland."

"What about the rest of the joint?" Runner Cop asked.

"The long room closest to this trailer was the main dining room. It was added on and opened in early 1947," Rick said. "The small room that tees off of it was the game room, and it opened in '54."

"Any work in the bar area?" Stocky Cop asked.

"Serious enough to tear up the slab?" Rick said. "Not to my knowledge. You might check and see if somebody pulled a permit."

"Campana had an allergy to doing things the right way," Runner Cop said. "The only reason he kept his liquor license current was because we'd shut him down otherwise."

"Well, if those bodies have been down there since 1925," Stocky Cop said, "we got one seriously cold case here."

"It's good weather for a cold case," John said. The two

cops did not seem amused. Stocky jerked a thumb toward their car, and the two cops left.

"You seem awful eager to help the cops," Kelly said after they were gone.

"The sooner they're gone, the sooner we're back to work," John replied. He looked at Rick. "Anyplace good to eat around here?"

Rick pointed down the block. "Tellio's Steakhouse is to die for. Assuming you've got an expense account, that is."

"I do, and a steak sounds great," John said, standing up.

CHAPTER 19

Patrick

On Wednesday, I blew off school again. I had given Mom the list of papers the legal aid attorney had needed, but she had been too busy to get them. She'd also been too busy to cook and too busy to even think about moving out of the house.

I love Mom, I really do. But she has a terrible habit of shutting down when there are problems. I'd seen it when Dad lost his leg, and now that he was gone, it was worse. To be fair, we had enough problems to make anybody want to shut down. So, if we were going to make any attempt to stay in the house, even if just long enough for me to finish high school, I was going to have to make the effort.

At the courthouse, I wandered around for a bit, finally finding the right office in the basement. Mindy Samuels, a girl a year ahead of me at Eastville High, was working the counter. I gave her the list of what I needed, and as she shuttled back and forth with the papers, we talked.

She was going to Maple Corners Community and working at the Clerk's office part-time. Her mother knew somebody there and got her the gig. When she was done, I thanked her, then said, "Two more questions."

"You're just full of questions today," she said, a smile on her face.

"I'm full of something," I said, trying to sound gallant. She was way out of my league, but a guy's got to try, right?

"Ask away."

"So, could you find a death certificate?"

Her smile faded. "I thought you'd gotten one for your dad?"

"I did. It's not for him. It's for a class."

"Sure. Name?"

"Unknown."

Her eyebrow arched. "That makes it interesting. What do you know?"

"May 1894, male, died in Strawberry Creek."

"Whoa. That's way back." She smiled again, showing a cute dimple. "But you're in luck. Mrs. Whipple's in here once a week doing her family tree, so I got good at those old records."

She went in the back and returned with a big and heavy-looking old book bound in leather. "Deaths listed chronologically. February – June 1894." She plopped it on the counter and opened it up.

After a bit of flipping, she found something and spun the book so I could see. In a thin ink, somebody had written in old-style cursive, "John Doe. May 22, 1894. Found at Vidas residence, East Creek Road, Strawberry Creek."

"That would be the right date," I said.

"You need the actual certificate?" she asked.

"Would it have any more detail than that?" I said.

"Just who filled it out."

"Then no, thanks." I looked at my watch. I could get these papers to Champaign and back in time for my afternoon classes.

"In a rush?"

"Kinda," I said. "Just out of curiosity, could you tell if

somebody bought a house? And how they paid for it?"

"Of course," she said. "Who and when?"

"Barbara Pikus, 1925."

She smiled again. It was getting infectious. "You are so lucky."

"How?"

"So I work the counter here on Wednesdays. On Thursdays, I'm in the back, computerizing the records. I just finished 1925."

"Computerizing?" I asked.

"Yeah." She pointed at the book. "Taking old stuff like this and keying it into a computer." She pointed to a CRT on the counter. "So, who are we looking for again?"

"Barbara Pikus, in Eastville. I don't remember the address – we had to sell it when I was four."

"Give me a minute," she said, going to the computer. After typing a few things in and making a note on a piece of scratch paper, she said, "Got it."

"Cool."

She spun the CRT around so we could both see it. There was a lot of green text on a black background. "Looks like Greek to me."

"It's in codes," she said. "What do you need to know?"

"How she paid for the house?"

"That's easy," Mindy said. She pointed at a blank line. "Cash."

"That doesn't say cash," I said.

"No. But if she didn't pay cash, there'd be a mortgagee recorded here." She reached over and took the pile of papers she'd given me for the lawyer. "See," she said, pointing at a line in a computer printout. "Your house is mortgaged to Fifth Street Mortgage."

"We're supposed to be with B-Friendly," I said.

She shrugged. "They probably sold it. Banks do that all the time."

"Well, thanks again for your help," I said.

"No problem. Hey, drop by the college Friday. We've got a great volleyball team."

"You play?"

"Of course. Heck, I'm the short girl for once."

If she's the short girl, then the rest of the team must be giants. "I'll try. What time?"

"Seven."

"Cool," I said, collecting my papers. "I'll check my calendar. Oh, can I write down the address?"

She wrote it down for me on a piece of scrap paper and I tucked it in my pocket.

As I was driving to Champaign, I thought the gold hunt was looking a little bit more promising. Mister Good Boots had definitely been real, and a few months after her husband vanished, she came into enough money to pay cash for a house. Either she'd hit the lottery or found a leprechaun's stash. Now the questions were, was there any of it left, and if so, where?

Vincent Bisceglie III

Vince had not slept at all well the night after his dad's news about being broke. Vince just couldn't go to Jag-off U, one of several nicknames for Maple Corners Area Junior College. *Now calling itself a community college, as if that made a bit of difference.*

He'd *told* people he was going to Washington University. He'd *been* car shopping – there was a red '86 Pontiac Sunbird that fit his ass just fine. The space bar on his word processor was sticky, and a PC would be *much* more suitable. He just could not be broke!

It hit him in the shower Wednesday morning. He wasn't completely broke. He had a coin collection, and some of the coins were from his grandfather. Maybe they were worth something? Probably not, he thought, but at least he should check.

At the high school library that afternoon, he checked out a book on coin collecting and values. It was printed in 1981, so it was a little dated, but it would give him some idea of what, if anything, was worth a closer look. That night in his room, he cracked the book open and took down the shoebox he was keeping the collection in.

When he opened the book, a piece of paper fell out and onto the floor. He ignored the paper and started to work through his collection.

An hour later, he had his answer. Most of the coins weren't worth more than face value, and that wasn't much. The most valuable bunch of coins in his collection were some steel pennies from WWII, and they were only worth a nickel or so each. "It was worth a shot," he said.

Bored, he flipped through the book, idly looking at pictures of coins that were actually valuable. He noted that the page with the double eagle coins had been dog-eared. "Somebody else was dreaming."

He shut the book and tossed it at his unmade bed but missed. He went to retrieve the book, and while he did, he picked up the paper.

"A VG special," he said, looking at the paper. The other Vince, Vince Gigante, was notorious for using both sides of any sheet of paper he got his hands on. This one was half of an 8 by 11. On one side was a mimeographed biology handout with VG's name scrawled on it. The other side was some math calculations.

Rather specific math calculations, Vince noted. "Double Eagle = 20." "Gold = $354 / ounce."

"Hey," Vince said. "Double eagle." He grabbed the book. The page with the double eagle coins had been dog-eared. And a double eagle had a face value of 20 bucks. He went back to the sheet.

"What are you up to?" Vince asked. Because it looked to him like VG thought he had 500 double eagles worth over one hundred and fifty thousand dollars. "Maybe I can go to Washington U after all."

CHAPTER 20

Patrick

"She paid cash for the house," I said to VG during study hall. "Six months after her husband disappears, she's paying cash for a house."

"Insurance settlement?" VG asked.

"I thought you wanted to find this?" I said.

"I do. I also just want to be realistic about this."

"Well, would insurance pay off that quickly?" I said. "I mean, there's no body."

"True." VG stretched. "Where's the house?"

"221 Garfield. I had to look it up at the courthouse."

"You didn't know where it was?"

"I was four when Grandma went into the nursing home," I replied. "I wasn't paying attention to addresses back then."

"You've been in it?"

"That I remember, once." I thought back to that early memory. "It was hot and dim."

"Not useful."

I shrugged. "Sorry. If I'd known what gold was back then, I'd have asked."

"I guess we need to go take a drive tonight."

———

221 Garfield was in the middle of the block on the north side of the street. It had snowed last night, not enough to cancel school. Eastville only had one snowplow, so most side streets didn't get so much plowed as snowpacked by cars driving on them. Fortunately, the Vega had good tires, so I wasn't slipping around too much.

Like most houses in town, there was a strip of gravel between the street and the sidewalk that everybody parked on. I pulled in behind a Chrysler minivan. Somebody had made a half-assed job of sweeping the snow off of it.

"Now what?" I said to VG in the passenger side of the car.

"You got your camera?" he asked.

"I do." It was an Instamatic pocket camera with a built-in flash and I even had some film in it.

"You go and ask to take pictures," VG said.

"You coming with?" I asked, my mouth dry.

"No."

"So what exactly is my 15% getting me?"

"My ass in the car. Now, if we bump that..."

"I'll leave it running," I said, cutting him off as I got out into the cold. As I walked up the freshly shoveled driveway to the front door, the door opened, and a woman, maybe a bit younger than Mom, came out. She was wearing a bulky coat over a pair of hospital scrubs.

"We don't want whatever you're selling," she said as she walked up to me.

"I'm not selling anything," I said. "I'm doing an oral history project..."

"Also not interested," she said. "I'll be late for my shift at the hospital."

I held up my camera. "Could I take some pictures?"

"It's a public sidewalk," she said. "Now, if you'll

excuse me." She pointed to her car.

I stepped aside and took out my camera. Might as well play along, I thought.

The house was a two-story wood building, white with brown shingles. It had that barn-style roof where the side of the second floor was at a steep slope and shingled. There was nothing remarkable about the place.

As soon as she left, I got back in my car and drove around the back and up the alley, managing not to get stuck in the snow. From the back, the house had a deck, snow-covered, and a little green and white shed just big enough for a lawnmower.

"You know what I don't see?" I asked VG.

"What?"

"A big black X with an arrow and the words 'here there be gold.'"

"You didn't think it be that easy, did you?" VG said.

"I didn't think it would be impossible."

"Now you need to go talk to Great Barb."

Vincent Bisceglie III

VG was about as subtle as a dog in heat, Vince thought to himself. He'd seen VG and Pat Kowalski hanging out in their study hall, thick as thieves. Then, after school, the two of them had made a beeline for Kowalski's puke-green junkmobile and rolled out.

Vince had climbed into his junkmobile, a 1981 VW Rabbit in faded piss-yellow, and followed. They'd rolled down the back streets to Garfield, then parked in front of a house. It had been so sudden that Vince had to drive past them.

He'd parked down the block and, facing them, situated

so that he could see one of them get out and take pictures of a house. It was Kowalski – he was wearing his letterman jacket, the big orange E visible like a beacon against the black coat. "Why is Kowalski taking the picture?" Vince said to himself. *It's VG's gold.*

Anyway, Kowalski took a couple of pictures, then climbed back into his car and headed up the alley. Vince drove by on the street, noting the address. The house was an older one, in decent shape, and good-sized, but Vince couldn't figure out why VG cared about it. "I wonder who owns it?"

Vince drove to the savings and loan, arriving there just before the lobby closed. He waved at the tellers and went to the back office, heading for Mr. White's desk. White was there, just packing up his briefcase. "Do you have a minute, Mister White?" Vince asked.

"Sure," White lied, his hand on his coat. He waved at the wooden guest chair in front of his desk. "What can I do for you?"

"How do you find out who owns a house?" Vince asked, ignoring the chair.

"Run a title search," White replied. "Why?"

"There's a house we might want to buy. Dad and I." It was a weak lie but the best Vince could come up with.

"Okay," White said, clearly not believing it but also apparently not coming up with a reason to tell the owner's son no. "It costs fifty bucks."

"No problem."

White opened up a drawer of his desk and took out a sheet of paper. "Fill out as much information as you know," he said, handing it to Vince, "and fax it to the number on the top. Where it says 'reason for search,' put 'purchase,' and where it says 'officer,' put your name. When the results come back, I'll call you."

"Great," Vince said. "Got a pen?"

White stood up. "In the cup," he said, pointing at a coffee cup with pens and pencils in it. "Use my desk. Fax machine is next to the copier."

Vince did, in fact, know where the fax machine was, but he decided to ignore that. "How long until I get a report?"

White paused in putting on his coat to shrug. "Depends on how complicated the title is and how backed up they are. This time of year, there isn't much real estate action, so I'm guessing Tuesday-ish."

"Cool," Vince said. "Thanks."

"Don't mention it," White said, finally putting on his coat.

As he walked out, Vince took White's seat and started to work on the form.

CHAPTER 21

Patrick

I walked into the nursing home. There was a little sitting area with some fussy-looking old people's chairs separated from the rest of the joint by a waist-high railing. The gate to the railing was guarded by a high desk where visitors signed in. There was nobody at the desk.

Just as I sat down in the least fussy of the chairs to wait for the attendant, my grandma walked in.

She scowled at the empty desk and then saw me. She walked over as I stood up. "Talk to any leprechauns?" She asked, a wicked grin on her face.

"You know," I said. "I have no idea why you don't believe her."

"Because she's full of it, and her mind's gone," Grandma said. She waved around, gesturing at the nursing home. "That's why we had to put her here. She damn near burnt down her house twice! Not to mention the St. Louis trip."

I had heard about the St. Louis trip where she'd run out of gas on the way back. But I was getting a bit pissed in that everything Great Barb had told me so far checked out. Why was her daughter so dismissive? "A house she bought for cash in 1925," I said, "six months after her husband disappeared."

"She tell you that?"

"No, the county courthouse records don't show a mortgage recorded against it." I leaned in. "And they also show that an unknown man died at their house in May 1894."

Grandma paused for a bit. "Maybe the mortgage wasn't recorded or got lost?"

"Who the hell is going to give a woman with no job and no prospects a mortgage to buy a nice big house?"

Grandma rolled her head, clearly processing the information. She glanced over at the still-empty desk, then pointed at the chair next to mine. We both sat down. Finally, she said, "Well, she never told us kids about any gold."

"And how old were you in 1925?"

"Five in May."

"Would you tell a five-year-old that you had a secret stash of gold somewhere? Especially if the local mob boss was pissed that your husband had run off with his cash?"

"But why wouldn't she tell us later?"

"Well, if every time she tells you something, you look at her like she's got two heads, maybe she got tired of talking to you."

Grandma glared at me. "That's no way to talk to me."

"Maybe it is," I said, glaring back. "Damn it. We're going to lose the house."

"I thought your hot-shot lawyer..."

"She can stall and make them jump through hoops," I said, but sooner or later, if we don't have the cash, we're out on the street."

She looked away. When she turned back, I could see a tear in her eye. "You are about to learn a lesson at a young age. A lesson I didn't finally learn until Ollie died."

Ollie was her husband, my grandfather. He'd died when I was in grade school. "What's that?"

"Hope is dangerous. Hope can get you hurt."

"How so?"

She rummaged around in her purse for a minute, finally coming up with a tissue that she used to wipe her eyes. "I loved your grandfather dearly."

She stopped there. I waved her on.

"My husband was an ambitious man. He had plans." She sighed heavily. "Lots of plans. He'd try one business idea, full of hope and ambition."

"I thought he was a liquor salesman?"

She laughed, but there was no humor in it. "That was just the last job he had. The last job he could get. He knew his booze. I'll give him that."

"Didn't he win some kind of award?"

She nodded. "Salesman of the Year for Illinois. It was a fluke – some idiot opened a bar and bought a year's worth of booze right at the end of the contest." She paused to get a pocket mirror out of her purse. "We flew to Spain on the company dime."

"I hear a but."

"Yeah. They bumped his sales target, and he missed it. Badly." She checked her face in the mirror, and when she was satisfied, she put the mirror back. "But that was his last job. He had a dozen jobs, maybe more, and various businesses, both on the side and as the main thing."

I had a feeling where this was going. Grandma wasn't in the Wolfburg because she had money. "What happened?"

"Lots of things *happened*. What didn't *happen* was the making of money." She glared at me. "Your grandfather could fuck up a store selling water in the desert." She hissed. "And selling water in the desert was probably the only business we didn't try."

"I'm sorry. I'm also not seeing how this is relevant."

"Young man, that's what I'm trying to tell you. I kept hoping Ollie would finally make it. That we'd finally get some damn money and stop living hand-to-mouth. *It never happened.*" She put her hand on my shoulder. "That's why I'm living in the poor house. I'm trying to spare you the pain of getting your hopes crushed."

"But..."

"But nothing. There's no gold. There never was. I don't know how she got the house. Hell, for all I know, she gave a banker a blow job." She waved her hand dismissively. "Get used to it. Plan your life accordingly."

Just then one of the nursing home people showed up at the reception desk, a cup of coffee in her hands. Grandma got up and went to the desk to sign in. As she did, she glanced at me. "Coming?

"Yes."

We walked down the hallway to Great Barb's room, got her in the wheelchair, and headed into the dining room. Dinner was chicken-fried steak with brown gravy, mashed potatoes, carrots, and a biscuit, all served on plastic plates delivered by staffers on plastic cafeteria trays. The food was as bland as the cinderblock walls and green carpet.

After the meal they rolled out desserts on a cart. I had the brownie, Great Barb and Grandma had the cherry pie. "Are you here for your school project?" Great Barb asked.

"That and to visit you," I said.

"Did I tell you about my brother Luidas' Tommy gun?" she said.

"No," I replied.

Oral History Project

Oral History Project by Patrick Kowalski, Eastville

High School, May 2, 1986. My oldest living relative, Great-Grandmother Barbara Pikus, told me this story while I was having dinner with her and my grandmother, Mary Balthus.

Your uncle Luidas [she means my great-uncle, her brother] was also working for Mr. Capone.

"I thought he had a heart condition," my grandma said.

"He did," Great Barb replied. She looked at me. "When he was a boy, he got a fever. Nearly killed him. Doctors said he'd never live to adulthood, and there was nothing they could do about it. Well, he made it to 1959 before it got him."

"But he was always talking about his heart," Grandma said.

"He was concerned," Great Barb replied. "Which is why he ran the still and didn't make deliveries." She continued with her story.

As I was saying, in 1959, his heart finally quit on him. About a week before he died, he asked me to come visit him. He was still living in his house on Strawberry Creek. I drove out to see him.

It was a nice spring day and I'd driven with the windows open. When I got there, he was in his bedroom with the windows closed and covers on. It was hot, but he was freezing, he said. I guess his heart wasn't pumping enough blood.

I was trying to figure out what to say to him when he said, "Don't bother. I look like shit, and I feel like shit that got stepped on."

"He knew he was dying," I said.

"Everybody knew he was dying," Great Barb said. She took a bite of her pie and chewed it carefully. "They do make good pie here. I'll give them that."

I suspected they bought their pies frozen from somewhere, but I didn't say anything. She swallowed and then continued talking.

"I already talked to Mroz," Luidas said, "I told him what I want for my funeral, and he's already got the coffin. Don't let him bill you for nothing."

"I won't

"Good." He pointed at the closet with a bony finger. "Open it up."

I did so and found a Chicago typewriter leaning against the corner of the closet.

"A what?" I asked.

"She means a Thompson submachine gun," Grandma said. "I've heard this story."

"And he hasn't," Great Barb said. "So either listen or go sit in the lobby."

"Yes, Mom."

Great Barb continued. I asked Luidas if it was loaded. "How the hell would I know?" he said. "Haven't used it for years."

I checked. It was, and there was a bullet in the chamber. I cleared it and dropped the drum, which was also full.

"You wanna close your mouth?" Grandma asked, smiling.

"How..." I said. She was talking about handling a machine gun as calmly as a toothbrush.

Great Barb chuckled. "It wasn't the first time I'd handled a Tommy gun." She took another bite of her pie, chewed it careful, and then continued her story. So I asked him, "What do you want me to do with it?"

"I don't care," he replied. "But my wife doesn't like it, and who knows about the kids."

Great Barb sighed, then continued.

His son, she said, referring to Luidas' son, had gotten into the drugs and, last we knew, had moved out to California. His daughter was, well, back then, we called her feeble-minded. I don't know what they'd call her today. We barely trusted her with a steak knife, so clearly, neither of them were going to want or need it.

There was an old and tattered horse blanket on the shelf in the closet, so I wrapped up the gun and drum in it and put it in my car. Two days later, Luidas passed. Mroz buried him.

[Here, she reminded us that she had a prepaid funeral with Mroz Funeral Home. She discussed briefly with her daughter what songs she'd like played at that funeral. She eventually continued.]

A couple of weeks later, I finally decided to sell the gun. I had even less need for a Tommy gun than did Luidas. O'Malley had a gun shop behind his house, so I took it to him.

It was a damp day – not raining hard, but sprinkling continuously. I walked in, and he was hand-loading shotgun shells at a workbench. O'Malley and his sons did a lot of trapshooting back then.

"Mr. O'Malley," I said. "You buy guns, right?"

"I do."

"I've got one I want to sell," I said. I was carrying the Tommy gun in the blanket.

"Well, let's see it."

I unwrapped the gun, and his eyes grew as big as saucers. "Where'd you get it?"

"Mr. Capone gave it to my brother Luidas in case he had problems. He's dead, and I don't have the kind of problems that can be solved by a Tommy gun."

"Does it shoot?"

"I have no idea," I said. "Last time I saw it fired was

before the war." I meant World War Two, of course.

"Well, I've got a range," O'Malley said.

He had an indoor range – a space tacked onto his shop about as wide as a one-car garage but longer. We took the gun into the range, stuffed cotton into our ears, and gave it a go.

"You shot it?" I asked.

"Once more, for old time's sake," Great Barb replied with a grin. "Funny gun. Not much recoil, but it wanted to twist to the right."

She stopped talking for a bit, a twinkle in her eye, then continued. "After we'd emptied the drum, a deal was struck, and I got three hundred dollars for the gun."

"I thought machine guns were illegal," I said.

"They are," Grandma replied.

"For a while in the 1920s, you could buy one," Great Barb said. "Then the law changed." She smiled. "Not that Capone bought this gun."

"How would you know that?" Grandma asked.

"It was engraved with 'property of Ohio National Guard' on it," Great Barb replied. "He either stole it or bribed a trooper to steal it."

"So what happened to the gun?" I asked. "After you sold it, I mean?"

"No idea," Great Barb replied. "O'Malley died in 1972, the same year I got locked up in here."

"Wow," I said.

"I'll get her back to her room," Grandma said. "Meet me in the lobby in a few."

"Okay?"

Patrick

I was getting tired of waiting and was going to go look

and see if Grandma had fallen in when she came walking into the lobby of the nursing home. "Well?" I asked.

"I'm sorry," she said. She pointed at the same set of chairs we'd sat in earlier.

"About what?" I asked as we sat down.

"I was too harsh on you. It's been a bad stretch for you."

No shit, I thought. "It has."

"I'm also sorry because I'm going to lay something more on you."

"What?"

"Your mom. She's, well, she's not strong."

Again, no shit. "I know."

"When you lose the house, she'll, well, she may try to hurt herself."

"Grandma!"

"She's done it before," Grandma said. I stared at her open-mouthed. "I tried to stop her from marrying that-Michael."

That idiot Michael, you meant.

"Why?"

"Why did I try to stop her?" *Sure.* I just nodded.

"I saw in Michael the same crap I saw in my husband. I wanted to spare her that pain." She was tearing up again. "I failed." She looked at me. "I won't fail again."

No, you're just going to lay down and quit. Your daughter, my mother, got that from you. "Okay."

"Good. Have you started looking for jobs?"

"I have," I lied. "It seems like you took a long time getting Great Barb settled."

"She insisted on singing me a song," Grandma replied.

"What kind of song?"

"One from my childhood," Grandma replied.

"Something I remember her singing to my brother when she was trying to get him toilet-trained."

That was weird.

CHAPTER 22

Vincent Bisceglie III

Vince stopped by the bank after school and checked with Mr. White. He was on the phone but handed Vince a couple of sheets of paper while he talked.

It was a fax from the title company, listing the history of the house. Vince sat down in the chair and puzzled through it. Some of it didn't make a lot of sense to Vince, but the history section was clear enough. The house was built by a guy named Hermann in 1920, sold to a B. Pikus in 1925, then sold in 1973 to the current owners, Jack and Linda Anderson.

Nobody named Gigante ever owned it. *So why is Vince Gigante sniffing around like a dog looking for a bone*? Vince decided he needed to talk to an old-timer.

Vince's grandmother, Teresa Bisceglie, lived in a small brick house on Cleveland Street. He rolled up to the house and rang the bell, hoping Grandma T hadn't decided that the sun was over the yardarm yet.

After a bit, she opened the door, looking reasonably sober. "Come on in," she said. "Happy hour has just started. Care for something?"

"Whatever you're having," Vince said. He'd been drinking wine at home occasionally, and that's what she had when she was at his house.

"Two Manhattans on the rocks, coming up," she said, walking in front of him to the kitchen.

Vince was a bit concerned to note that a Manhattan consisted of a lot of bourbon, something called vermouth, ice, and a cherry. He took a sip and found it was smoother than he thought it would be. Grandma T led him to the front room, where he sat down on one of the plastic-covered couches.

"I'm glad you're here," she said. "I hate drinking alone."

For somebody who hates drinking alone, you do a lot of it. "Glad to help."

"So what can I do for you?" she asked.

"I'm just visiting," Vince said.

"Don't try to BS me, son."

"Okay," Vince said. He was feeling a warmness in his stomach from the drink. "Are the Gigantes related to either the Hermanns or the Pikus families?"

"I never heard of Hermann," Grandma said. "And Pikus was a puttana."

"A what?"

"Prostitute. A cheap one, too."

Vince blinked back his surprise. Grandma was known to be blunt, but this...

"Why do you suddenly care about family trees?" she asked.

That was a good question, one which Vince hadn't prepared an answer. But one suddenly came to him. "I'm doing some research for a school project."

"Ah." She waved her hand dismissively. "Education these days. All these fancy-pants projects. In my day..."

Vince had heard the song his grandma was about to sing. "Unfortunately, I don't control the school."

"Nor do I," she replied. She waved her glass at him and then took a healthy sip. "So, family tree."

"Right," Vince said, glad to have avoided one of her hobby horses. "Gigantes and Pikus."

"Hell no. Pikus was a damn Lugan. Gigantes are good people."

'Good people' in Grandma-speak were almost always Italians. Grandma was funny – if you were Italian, then by George, you'd better marry an Italian. "I'm sorry?" he said, not paying attention to what she'd said.

"She owed my husband a lot of money," Grandma said. "Or rather, her no-good lug nut of a husband owed my husband a lot of money."

What Vince wanted to ask was why Gigante was nosing around a house that had no relation to him, but Grandma was unlikely to have that answer. Nor could he just bolt out. Besides, the Manhattan was kind of good. So what he said was, "What happened?"

"Her husband was working for Vincent. My Vincent, your grandfather. The man stole a lot of money from us."

"What did the police do?"

Grandma took an alarmingly large sip of her drink before continuing. "We couldn't involve the police."

Vince nodded. *I am in a cut-rate Godfather movie.* He struggled not to let out a nervous laugh. We'll call it the *God Stepson.*

His grandma continued with the story. "The bitch, she had the nerve to claim her husband left her and begged my Vincent for money." She cocked a finger. "Which he gave her, gladly, out of the goodness of his heart."

She took another big sip of her drink. The glass was getting alarmingly low. "Then she shows up at church, begging to pay off what she owed. Vincent told her some low-ball number, which she paid. The following week, she rolls into town as if she'd found an orchard full of money trees in bloom."

"And Grandpa?"

She shrugged. "He'd publicly said she owed him nothing. If he'd gone back on that, things would have been bad."

"How much money did she owe? Or rather her husband."

"I don't actually know," Grandma replied, looking out the window. "Your grandfather and I had an understanding."

"What understanding was that?"

"After the first time he hit me, I told him that if he ever hit me again, he'd better kill me or learn to sleep with one eye open because I'd cut his dick off."

Vince's jaw literally dropped. "Grandma!"

"Don't you grandma me!" she replied, glaring at him. "You're a man now and should learn these things." She looked back at the window. "Your grandfather laughed at me. He wasn't laughing when I handcuffed him to the bed in his sleep and woke him up by prodding him with a pair of hedge shears."

Vince didn't know what to say to that, so he said nothing. Grandma took another sip and then continued. "We had what those politicians in Washington would call a 'free and frank talk.' At the end of it, we had an understanding. I didn't ask about his money or his whores, and he didn't hit me or embarrass me."

Vince swore he could hear the theme music to *The Godfather* playing in the background. "But apparently, it was a lot? The money, I mean. For him to break the deal."

"Apparently." She took a sip. "Although the deal was he could volunteer information. I just couldn't ask."

Also, apparently, the Pikus family, whomever they were, and his family had a history. But if Gigante's numbers were accurate, there was a lot of money floating around. Go to Washington University as a man of leisure money. "Promises aside, why didn't he keep looking for the money."

"The puttana sent him to jail. Mann Act."

"What's a man act?"

She spelled Mann. "It's some stiff-collared politician's name. He made it illegal to 'transport a woman across state lines for debauchery' or some such." Grandma sighed. "I should have made sure our arrangement included vetting his whores."

"Whose whores?"

"Your grandfather's, silly!" she growled. She waved her nearly empty glass with vigor. "Who else are we talking about?"

"You assume I heard the story."

"No, I don't," she said, looking suddenly very old. "I was pregnant with Edward, and Vincent had 'business' in Indianapolis. He took some fifteen-year-old Greek girl from Timon with him. The cops got a tip and busted them in the hotel room."

Timons was a tiny town just south of Eastville and not a very high-class place. Grandma waved a nearly empty glass. "When the cops busted in, she played all innocent. Bitch was a punchboard and swore like a sailor in three languages."

There were a dozen questions swirling in Vince's head. He asked the first one that got to his mouth. "You think Pikus set him up?"

"Hell, yes!"

The next question that came to Vince's mind was, "Who's Edward?"

"Your father's older brother. He died when he was

four."

"I never even heard of him."

Grandma finished her drink. "It was a long time ago. Your grandfather got a sharp lawyer who cut a deal. Four years in the pen. Edward was born the day he went in and died two days before he got out." She looked at her glass. "Drink up. Want another?"

"I'm good," Vince said. He took a sip. "But how did Grandpa get a bank?" *And how did Pikus get the money*? "I mean, felons..."

"Technically, I owned the bank," Grandma replied. "I signed all the paperwork. Vincent told me where to sign, of course, but it was my name. Your dad didn't get it until he was twenty-one."

She got up and went into the kitchen, returning with another drink. Vince was getting a bit buzzed on his, and he'd had half of it. He was bigger than Grandma, too.

"We actually had a bar first," she said, sitting down. "All through the Depression. When the war started, they couldn't mine enough coal, so all of a sudden, everybody had money. We took over the falling-down storefront next to the bar and put in the furniture store."

"And the bank?"

"The bank started right after the war. They had the GI Bill, and all these guys were coming back from the war with money to get a house. We loaned them the money to buy a house and sold them the furniture to put in it."

"What happened to the bar?"

"Caught fire. Took out the furniture store, too. We used the insurance money to build the current place."

How convenient, Vince thought. All of this is interesting but doesn't tell me why Gigante is interested in that house. "So, who is Pikus related to?"

"She had two or three kids," Grandma said. "Only one who stayed around was her daughter Mary. She married one of the Balthus kids. They only had one kid, who married a Kowalski."

Vince was always amazed when Grandma or Aunt C. would rattle off that kind of history. *What did they do all day - memorize who begat whom?"* "Would they have had a son, Patrick?"

"Yes," Grandma said. She pointed her glass at him. "He's around your age."

And we're foreclosing on his house. "Thanks a lot," Vince said.

"Finish your drink," she replied.

He did and begged off having a second. He was getting a bit loopy just from one. It wasn't until he got into his car that it hit him. "Maybe the gold isn't Gigantes," he said to the steering wheel. "Maybe it's Kowalski's." He turned the ignition key. "Or maybe it's ours. Maybe Pikus stole it from us."

CHAPTER 23

John B. Hood

"We only lost a week," Kelly said, sitting in the construction trailer.

"A week we didn't have in the schedule," Hood replied while looking out the window. It was snowing again. Or maybe still, he thought. There was a reason he lived in Texas.

The phone rang, and Kelly went to answer it. They had lost a week while the cops slowly and methodically removed the two bodies under the slab. The bodies were basically skeletons with hair and had been stripped of identification. Hood didn't envy the cops trying to solve a 60-some-year-old murder that apparently nobody knew about.

The door to the trailer flew open, sending in a blast of cold, damp air. "We got another body!"

"For God's sake!" Hood said. "What the hell is this place – a cemetery?"

"I'll call the cops," Kelly said.

"When you're done, I'll call Rick," Hood added. He looked at the young construction worker. "Y'all should know what to do now."

"Yes sir," the man said.

———

This body, singular, had been found almost at quitting time.

The same two cops as before had shown up. Stocky Cop, real name Joe Longino, and Runner Cop, Tom Kehoe, had taken one look at the hole then up to the darkening sky.

"Put a tarp over it," Longino had said. "I'll get a uniform to sit on the site overnight." He gestured at the hole. "El Gigante ain't going anywhere."

Hood, who had come out to the hole, could see that this stiff had been in life a pretty heavy fellow, judging by his coat. "No, he's not. Neither is my construction project."

"Any more slabs to pull up?" Kehoe asked.

"Fortunately, no," Hood replied. "But I can't dig new foundations until y'all get clear."

"The forensics guys aren't any happier than you are," Kehoe said. "Not digging in this weather."

"I imagine not," Hood said.

———

A group consisting of two cops, Hood and Rick Webster, the historian, ended up at Tellio's Steakhouse. Rick was a regular – the bartender started making his drink as they walked in – and Hood decided that since his budget was already shot to hell, he might as well put another bullet in it and enjoy a decent meal. Besides, happy cops meant he could get back to work sooner, and unhappy cops were amazingly good at finding ways to delay a project.

Thus, Hood was buying. Rick and him were eating – the cops had just said they'd have a drink and a munchie, and they were getting back to their wives. It was a light weekday crowd, but the bar was a bit loud, so the group had taken a table in the main dining room.

"Any ID on the first bodies?" Rick had asked, looking over the menu at the cops.

"No," Kehoe said.

"Not surprised," Rick replied. "Drivers' licenses back

then were just typewritten paper."

"The wallets were gone," Longino replied, shoveling a few fried mushrooms onto a small plate. "Ditto rings and jewelry."

"Stripped, huh?" Hood said.

"Except for one pocket watch," Kehoe said. "Not a high-end one, but it had a picture of a woman on the inside cover."

"No name, I guess," Rick said.

"Hah," Longino replied. "We'd be so lucky."

"I assume they were murdered?" Rick asked.

"Multiple gunshots from a .45," Kehoe said.

"Chicago typewriter," Rick replied. To Hood's puzzled glance, he said, "Tommy gun."

"Ah." To the detectives, Hood said, "You don't have any missing persons from that era?"

"We've got a lot," Kehoe replied. "A lot."

"Back then," Rick offered, "skipping town was a lot easier than getting a divorce. Cheaper, too."

"Still is," Hood said. "Ask me how I know."

"Sorry," Rick replied, taking a sip of his bourbon.

"Don't be," Hood replied. "We're both from Texas. It was either a divorce or pistols. Divorce hurts less."

"There's a little hope," Kehoe said. "The lab-coat crew thinks they can lift fingerprints from the one of the John Does." He took a swallow of his beer. "He was wearing leather gloves. If they were in the system, we'll eventually get a name."

"It's been my experience," Longino said, a fork with a fried mushroom on it midway to his mouth, "that adult men who end up in shallow graves under slabs weren't choirboys when they were alive. All three of those stiffs were dirty. The question is, did they get caught and do we still have the paperwork on them?"

———————

When the two cops rolled up the next morning, Hood went out and offered them donuts.

"A bit stereotypical," Longino said.

"Well, I like donuts," Hood replied. "Besides, I saw this movie before. You're going to stand around while they dig. And before you asked, I offered them donuts, too. They declined on account of needing to keep the crime scene clear."

"I could always eat a donut," said Longino, the stocky cop. He tapped Kehoe on the stomach. "And you'll run it off anyway."

The group adjourned to the trailer, where Hood learned that Kehoe had run a marathon last year and was in training for another. Rick Webster pulled up to the lot and stepped inside the trailer.

"You bored?" Longino asked.

"Actually, yes," Rick replied. "I didn't want to retire, but it beat going on unemployment." He glanced at the box of donuts. "May I?"

"Sure," Hood said. "Help yourself to coffee as well. It's fresh."

After he did so, Rick asked, "Any news on our first set of bodies?"

"The lab got fingerprints off of one," Kehoe said. "From the inside of his leather gloves. Smirnov."

"Like the vodka?" Hood asked.

"Smirnov in Russian is like Smith in English," Kehoe said. "But we got a missing person, one Ivan Smirnov, from the right time period. A man who was also arrested for distributing booze."

"Which is how his fingerprints were in the system," Longino said, waving a Long John around. "Unfortunately, we got no ID on the other dude."

"An innocent?" Hood asked.

"Probably more like a 'hadn't got caught yet,'" Longino offered. "I'm guessing the two of them were running booze and got ambushed."

"This county was pretty rural back then," Rick offered. "But given that it's technically the south side, Capone thought he owned it." Rick shrugged. "Who was, in fact, in charge out here was up for grabs."

"Which is what we think happened," Kehoe said. "During the grabbing part of that, these two jamokes got caught in the crossfire."

"And Mister Large?" Hood asked.

"Would have been buried in 1954," Rick said.

"Probably unrelated," Longino said. "One of those accidents that you don't see in novels."

CHAPTER 24

Patrick

"So, what did your grandma learn?" VG asked. We were sitting in the bleachers waiting for the second half of the Monday night JV basketball game to start. I was in our highly geeky 'pep band' uniform, but since the pep band didn't go to break out instruments and warm up until the fourth quarter of the JV game, I had some time to kill.

"Ouch," I said, gesturing at the court. Our center had gotten knocked on his ass by an opposing player.

"She said ouch?" VG asked.

"No, I was talking about the game."

"The hell with the game. They're getting blown out."

Which was true. Our basketball teams that year were the 98-pound weaklings of the league.

"So?" VG asked.

"So nothing."

"Nothing?"

"She refused to ask. Insisted that the gold had never existed and that I was in denial."

"Denial's not just a river in Egypt."

"You're never going to get on SNL with that material."

"And you're never going to find that gold like this."

Out on the court, our center bricked his second free

throw. The kid had a great future as a mason. As a basketball player, not so much. I didn't say that out loud – I had spent my sophomore year warming the bench, so it wasn't like I was Larry Bird.

"Maybe there's no gold to find."

"And how did Grams explain buying the house?"

"She suggested that her mom had sex with somebody at the bank."

"Woah, harsh!"

"And she wasn't very subtle about it."

"Neither was my grandmother."

"Pardon?" I said, turning to glare at him.

VG held up his hands. "Dude, just the messenger."

"What did she say?"

"You promise not to hit me?"

"Sure."

"She called her a puttana."

"Which means?"

"Prostitute."

What the hell kind of family did I have? Running booze for Capone, blazing away with Tommy guns, and now Great Barb as a hooker? "Wonderful."

"Sorry, dude."

"Not your fault." Out on the court, our star point guard got faked out of his jock strap, and the other team scored a breakaway layup. "There was one thing."

"What?"

"When grandma put Great Barb to bed, Great Barb sang to her."

"What?"

"Sang. A song. In Lugan."

"What kind of song?"

I shrugged. "No habla Lugan," I replied.

"I know you 'no habla,' Pat," VG said sharply. "Your gram does. So what was the English translation?"

"Something about using the toilet."

"Huh?"

"You heard me. Using the toilet."

"You've got a weird family," VG said. "Why can't she just tell you?"

"She's senile," I said.

"She remembered the gold and the plane ride," VG offered.

"And sticking a gun into Mister Big's gut."

It wasn't until we were putting away our instruments after the varsity game (we lost, but at least it was close) that it dawned on me. Great Barb had said that she moved into town from Strawberry Creek to 'get a job.' She also said that she ended up taking in laundry and boarders. Maybe she really had been a hooker, and there was no gold. Even though it was late, I had to know. With a sick feeling in my stomach, I called Grandma. She answered on the fifth ring and sounded groggy.

"Was Great Barb a prostitute?" I asked.

"What? Who the hell is this?"

"Pat. Was she?"

There was some rustling on the other end, and I swore I heard another voice. "Do we have to have this conversation now?"

"Yes, damn it, we do. If you want me to stop looking for the gold, I need to know how she could buy a house."

"I'll call you right back." She hung up. I assume she went into the other room of her small apartment to use the other phone. My phone rang and I picked up before the first ring was done.

"Grandma?" I said.

"Definitely not a leprechaun," she said.

"Not funny."

"Cut me some slack. I'm old and tired..."

"And not alone."

"And that's none of your business. I'm more than old enough."

"Great Barb."

"I was just a kid," she started. "And she did take in legitimate boarders."

My stomach, which I didn't think could get any lower, took another dive. "*And* legitimate boarders."

"Yes. But she also had gentlemen guests."

"Who paid her." For sex, I left unsaid.

"She told us they gave her gifts."

Well, you probably wouldn't tell your small kids that mommy fucked for money. "Go on."

"There's nothing else to go on to. As I got older, and well, frankly, as she got older, the ratio of gentlemen callers to boarders fell. Then she started to take in laundry. In '38 or '39, Maple Corners Tent and Awning got a big Army contract, and she got hired on there. Then the war broke out. They added a second shift, and she was a foreman. The boarders moved out for various reasons."

I realized my eyes were watering. "Damn."

"She did what she had to do, I guess," Grandma said. "Tony and I never missed a meal and always had clothing."

"Does Mom know?"

"I sure as hell never told her. My mom was always coy about the deal, so I'd guess not."

"Thanks."

"This does not need to be in any school report."

"Hell no," I said.

I hung up, composed myself, and called VG. When he answered, I said, "She was turning tricks."

"Sorry, dude."

"No, it's okay," I lied. VG said something I didn't hear, so I asked him to repeat it.

"I said, that explains why there's gold left over."

"How do you figure there's still gold?"

"She didn't start hooking until she got into town, right?" VG said. "So, how did she get the house?"

"Slept with a banker?"

"Dude! Just how hot of a chick was she back then?"

"Dude, that's my great-grandmother you're talking about!"

"And that's one hundred and fifty grand of gold we're talking about."

True. "So you don't think she had sex to get the house?"

"That's an awful nice house, especially back then."

"So we're back at square one."

"Maybe not."

"How so?"

"Think about this," VG said. "Great Barb came into a lot of money. The Mob felt her husband owed them money. She had two small kids, and who knew who they'd blab to. She'd probably spent years hiding that money, even to herself. The song was her way of remembering where it was."

"Maybe?"

"Got any other ideas?"

"No. But how does this help us?"

He didn't know either. We chatted for a bit, then hung up. I got ready for bed. I was brushing my teeth when it hit me.

As it happens, one of my few memories of Great Barb's house was of the bathroom. They only had one, and it was small and dark, and the four-year-old me hadn't liked it.

I only had vague memories of that house, but I had been in a couple other old houses in town, including the one where VG's grandmother had lived. In that house, they'd added a bathroom by carving out space from an existing first-floor room. The result was a small and dark place.

A small and dark place that was added on. During the addition, could somebody build a hiding place for gold?

The next day, I ran into VG before the first period. I told him, "We need to get into that house."

"Why?"

"I think I know where to look for the gold."

"So now we're back in the gold hunt?"

"Why not?"

He shrugged. "So, Sherlock. Where is it?"

"It's in the bathroom." I explained my logic to him.

"Thin, dude," he replied when I was done.

"Dude, what's with the negative vibes?"

"Huh?"

"Never mind. Movie I saw on TV the other night." I wasn't sleeping worth a damn and had been watching a lot of late-night TV. "You're the one who said this was worth money."

"How do you plan on breaking in?"

"This is Eastville, remember?" I said. "People don't lock their doors."

"Some people do."

"Is your door locked right now?"

There was a long pause. "I don't actually know."

"Then let's at least try the knob."

"I wouldn't do that at my house," VG said.

"Why not?"

"Dad's got a gun."

"Then we need to figure out when they're not there."

———————

Our first problem was figuring out who actually lived in the house. I mean, I met a woman coming out of it, but I didn't know her. Yes, in a small town, we're all supposed to know everybody, but that's not always true. I mean, I knew the names of everybody in my class, but especially for the ones who I didn't hang out with, I didn't know exactly where they lived or what their parents looked like. That's just for kids at school. If they didn't have kids near my age, I might not know them at all.

I decided the easiest way to get their names, at least, was to look at their mail. I knew from when school was on break our mail was delivered right around noon. I also knew that the mail lady who delivered mail to us also handled Garfield Street. There was a Karkowski family who lived on Garfield and we occasionally got letters for them. Dad had talked to the mail lady about that one day in the summer, just before he got sick, and she had said she delivered to them before us. Ergo, 221 Garfield, got mail before noon.

Technically, Eastville High School has a closed campus lunch policy. We're not supposed to leave school before end-of-day dismissal unless we're sick or have other emergencies. But in my case, at least, nobody seemed to give a damn. So, when my lunch period came up, I headed out to the parking lot. Of course, that's the day that somebody decided to give a damn.

"And just where do you think you're going, Pat?" This was from Mr. Jones, who taught basic math and was standing at the door from the cafeteria to the parking lot.

"I left something in my car," I said, trying to be cool. I felt flushed, so I don't think I looked cool.

"What would that be?" Jones asked. His face was flushed as well, but that was pretty typical for him.

"A book for VG," I lied. "He lent it to me, and I was going to return it."

Jones was clearly not buying it. His basic math classes were full of stoners and tokers – the kind of people who really didn't want to be in school in the first place. He heard a lot of lame excuses. "What's the title?" he asked.

Well, shit. I certainly didn't have a book in my car. "Okay, you got me," I said. "I'm not going for a book. I'm going to see a lawyer. About my dad."

"I'm sorry about your dad, but why do you need to see a lawyer? Why isn't your mother going?"

"With Dad gone, she needs all the hours she can get at the IGA." This was true, although, in part, her being at the IGA meant she didn't need to deal with shit. I sighed heavily. "We're thinking about suing."

"Suing?"

"Malpractice. It took them forever to figure out what got Dad, and by then, it was too late."

Jones actually looked bashful. "I heard it was some weird blood thing."

I pressed the point. "And they think he got it from a blood transfusion."

"Darn." He glanced around. It was just us and other students in the area. "Go do what you've got to do." He held up a hand. "But in the future, get some kind of note or letter or something. I've got a boss, you know."

And tenure. "Thanks. I will."

I rolled out, feeling the cold air cooling the sweat on my face. I thought about that note. I did have a lawyer – the legal aid lady. Maybe I could get her to gin something up? I also decided to stash a book in my car for future use.

Garfield Street was a short drive from the high school, and given that it was well below freezing outside, the car didn't even have time to warm up before I was in front of the house. Despite the cold, my hands were sweaty, even without gloves. The last time I was that nervous was when I went to second base with Cindy Tomsky after the prom last year. Given that she'd slapped me, I hoped that this time, things would work out better.

I took a deep breath and exhaled, my breath creating a fog in the car. *It's just mail.* I got out quickly before I lost my nerve. There was a thin layer of snow on the ground, but their sidewalks were clear, which was good. Nobody was visible, although in my mind, behind every window lurked a little old lady calling the cops with one hand and snapping pictures of me with a telephoto lens in the other.

The mailbox was a plain black metal box, actually just like ours. It was the second cheapest mailbox K-Mart sold, a fact I'd discovered over the summer while working at K-Mart. The mailbox was right next to the front door. A little curved overhang covered the tiny stoop, but the sides were wide open.

Feeling a thousand eyes on me, I opened the mailbox. I had a bad moment when I thought it was empty, but there was stuff in it. I took it out and glanced over my shoulder then looked at my prize.

The first piece was an advertising flyer addressed to "Our Friends at 221 Garfield." The second was even more generic, a postcard addressed to "Local Postal Customer." Fortunately, the third piece was a bill from CIPS, the power company, to Jack and Linda Anderson. "Finally," I said, my breath coming out in a fog. I stuffed all three pieces back into the mailbox and walked to the car, trying not to break into a run.

CHAPTER 25

Patrick

Once back in the car, I fired it up and drove away. My original plan had been to go back to school, buy a burrito from the snack bar for lunch, and finish out the day. Somehow, I ended up in front of our house, four blocks away from Garfield and even farther from school.

I sat in the car for a minute or two with the engine running. I eventually decided that, since I was 'meeting a lawyer,' there was no reason to go back to school. I also was hungry, and we were on a clock. The next court hearing was set for Monday, February 24, two weeks and a weekend away from today.

Having made that executive decision, I shut the car off and went inside. I made myself a peanut butter and jelly sandwich with a glass of Kool-Aid and pulled out the phone book. As I ate, I looked up the Andersons. There were a ton of them, but only one, Anderson, Jack & Linda, with a Garfield Street address in Eastville.

After I washed up the plate and glass, I went to the answering machine and played the message I'd saved. It was from somebody calling for money for 'fallen cops.' I listened again to the recording, taking notes. There was no way I could get my voice as deep as the guy in the recording, but since that couldn't be helped, I just did it.

It took me three tries to finally dial the number. I was expecting anything from an immediate answer to an answering machine to threats to call the cops. What I was not expecting was for the phone to ring. It just rang, like, ten times.

I hung up, and went to the bathroom – well, trotted to the bathroom, as my nerves were getting to me. When I finished my business, I dialed again. Another ten rings with no answer.

Now I was stuck. They clearly weren't home at the moment. But my plan had been to talk to them and see if I could get some idea of when they would be home. Don't ask me how I was going to do that. But obviously, that wasn't going to work, and for all I knew, I'd roll up to the house just as soon as Jack Anderson, all six feet and 200 pounds of ex-NFL linebacker, came home from his day job of breaking people in half.

"A hundred and fifty gees is worth some risk," I said to the refrigerator. "Let's do it."

I headed back out to the car and drove the few blocks to Garfield. I thought about being stealthy and parking somewhere not obvious but decided that somebody walking down the sidewalk in the cold would be more obvious than a car. Besides, if the old biddy Neighborhood Watch crew had seen me, they'd seen me.

I climbed out of the car again and walked up to the front door. The day had started out clear but windy. Now, it was windy, and a sheet of gray clouds covered the sky. I walked up to the door and almost tried the handle before deciding to knock. If the old biddies were watching, maybe they'd think I was let in.

I counted thirty Mississippi aloud to myself in a

whisper, my breath creating a fog. After no answer, I tried the door. It was one of those handles with a lever you pressed down on with your thumb. I pressed, and the door opened. "Welcome to Eastville," I whispered.

Stepping inside quickly, I closed the door. I was in a very light and airy front room, with light-colored wood-paneled walls to my right and a built-in bookcase painted white to my right. This was not what I remembered. The house I remembered was dark, with dark wood and thin green carpet.

Moving into the house, the bookcase gave way to a door leading into a small room. There was no bed, just a lot of little kid's toys. In the original house, the front room had been separated from a second room by an arched entryway. There was no arch in this house, just a wooden beam along the ceiling.

"The bathroom should be off of that," I said to myself quietly, pointing to where I guess the dining room should have been. It wasn't a dining room anymore but instead held a pool table. I walked to the table and turned left, expecting to see a bathroom.

Instead, there was a small room laid out as an office with an adult-sized built-in table facing the window and a counter along the wall. Judging by the stuff on the table, the kids did their homework on it. A little further into the house, there was a staircase going upstairs, and under it was a bathroom.

But it was a half-bath! Just a toilet and a sink, and barely enough room for one person to use. No place to, like, take a bath or anything.

"Well, hell," I said quietly.

"Jack, are you home?" I heard a female voice from upstairs.

I felt like somebody had grabbed my stomach and squeezed it! Moving as fast as I dared, I hustled out the front door, carefully and quietly closing it behind me, then fast-walked to my car. I jumped into it, cursing my decision to not leave it running, and drove off, rubbernecking as best as I could to see if anybody was after me.

I was sitting on the couch at home when I heard a knock on the door. I jumped up, and my heart skipped a beat. I was sure it was the cops coming to arrest me. The knock came again, so I screwed up my courage and opened the door.

"I saw you get past Steamer," VG said. His face turned puzzled. "You okay?"

"I thought you were the cops," I said. I stood aside so he could come in.

"Why would Steamer send the cops after you?"

"Who?" I said.

"Steamer Jones. Math teacher at Eastville High?"

"I'm not worried about him," I said as VG took off his coat. "And why are you calling him Steamer?"

"It's a term my dad uses for drunks," VG said, half out of his coat.

"Jones is a drunk?"

VG stopped, coat halfway off, and looked at me. "Why do you think he brings in a thermos of coffee every day?"

"Because he doesn't like the coffee in the teacher's lounge?"

"Yeah," VG said, snickering. "It doesn't have vodka in it." He finished taking off his coat. "You missed another one of Three Stick's hilarious performances in English."

"Wonderful," I replied.

He turned and looked at me. "What's eating you?"

"I was in the Anderson house today."

"Who?"

"The house on Garfield Street," I said. "Owned by a Jack and Linda Anderson."

"You went in?" he said, his voice rising an octave.

"Yes. Remember – you told me we had to?"

His look suggested he hadn't been entirely serious. "And?"

"And they remodeled. Completely. Tore everything up. Oh, and Mrs. Anderson was at home."

"She was what?"

"At home!" I waved my arm emphatically. "I called, no answer. Twice, for ten rings! So I went over. She must have heard me because she called out asking if I was Jack."

"I bet she works nights."

"Oh?"

"Yeah," he replied, his hands in his pockets. "Actually, when we were there the other day, didn't she say she'd be late for her shift?"

"She did."

"So she probably works nights. And when she's home, she turns the ringer off on her phone."

"Because she's a light sleeper."

"Yep," VG said. He grinned at me. "And she didn't lock the door."

"Nope." I sighed.

"Did she see you?"

"I don't think so."

VG made a show of looking at the door. "No cops out there. How would they know anyway?"

"Maybe one of her neighbors saw me."

"Saw you do what? Did you kick the door down? Did you come out screaming and waving a severed head?"

I actually chuckled a little at that. "No."

"She didn't see you. All the neighbors saw was you going in and leaving."

"But they didn't see her open the door."

VG pointed at my door. "Did your neighbors see you open that door? No."

"So I'm probably not busted." I had been telling myself that for a couple of hours now, but it felt good to hear it from somebody else.

"Probably not." VG patted me on the shoulder. "But next time, call. I'll pull lookout for you."

"Won't be a next time."

"Why not?"

"Like I said, they remodeled the entire first floor! If there were gold hidden there, they'd have found it." I looked at the floor. "So now we're back to square one."

"No," VG said. "You need to pay Great Barb another visit." He patted my shoulder. "Then come out tomorrow to drink beer with me."

CHAPTER 26

Amy Burton, Land of Lincoln Legal Aid

I knocked on my boss's door. "Got a minute?" I asked.

My boss, Lee Song, looked up from his papers. He ran a hand through his thick black hair. "Sure."

"So, I'm working a foreclosure."

"I heard."

"It's weird. The loan was originated by b-Friendly Savings and Loans, but at least some of the paperwork says the note is owned by Fifth Street Mortgage."

"What's so weird about that? S and L's sell loans all the time."

"I've never heard of Fifth Street Mortgage."

Lee shrugged, his skinny shoulders wrinkling his suit coat. He always wore a coat in his office. "Tons of mortgage companies out there."

"Except they're listed with an Illinois address but don't appear in our business directory."

"Sort of weird. Maybe they're new and opened up after the directory was published."

"Maybe," I said. "But something's fishy about this. I mean, the assessed value of the house per the real estate tax bill is greater than what they owe." Assessed value for tax purposes was always low. It made the taxpayers feel better.

So, if the assessed value was higher than the principal, the real value of the house had to be way higher than the note.

He leaned back, clearly puzzled. "And unless the county assessor is an idiot..."

"Red County," I said.

"And she's not," he replied, "the owners should have more than enough equity to refinance."

"So why isn't the S and L offering that?" I asked.

He shrugged again. "Call them."

———————

That afternoon, I did call them, going through the switchboard to a Mr. Dan White. After I explained who I was, I asked him why they weren't willing to refinance.

"I can't answer that," he said.

"Aren't you the chief lender?" I said.

"I am. But my boss is handling this deal."

His boss was, I assumed, the owner of the company. "Can you transfer me to him?"

"He's not in right now."

"Can I leave a message?"

"I'll have him call you as soon as he gets in," he said. Then he hung up. The problem was he didn't have my phone number.

Something was definitely fishy. The problem was I didn't know if I could use it. At the end of the day, the Kowalskis had signed a note to pay money. I could make the payees jump through hoops, but eventually, they either got the money or the house.

Patrick

By dinnertime, I had calmed down from my breaking and entering escapade. Although, if you don't actually break anything, do they still call it breaking and entering? Is there such a thing as just "entering?" I put it out of my mind. Worrying about what had happened wasn't going to get me any gold.

But going to my grandmother was a non-starter, so I decided to ask Mom. We were sitting in the front room after dinner, watching *Dallas*, which she loved. When the commercial came on I meant to ask what happened to Great Barb's stuff. What came out was, "Why don't you and Grandma believe Great Barb?"

Mom snorted. "She's full of shit."

"Such as?"

"Such as in one story she lived in Kansas City."

"What's wrong with that? Back then, trains ran there every day. Still do, as far as I know."

"Remember the Volodkas?"

They were briefly our neighbors when I was little. They were also WWII refugees. DPs, we called them, although not to their faces. "Yes."

"Well, one day, we're talking with them, and they remembered being bombed. Great Barb said she'd been bombed, too, in London." Mom clucked. "She never left the US during WWII or after."

The show started back up, so the conversation ended. At the next commercial break, I asked, "What happened to Great Barb's stuff?"

"What stuff?" Mom said.

The trunk with the gold in it. You know, the one with all the locks on it. "Stuff. Furniture, that kind of thing."

"Well, a lot of it got sold."

Great. "Why?"

"She needed the money. We've never been wealthy people, and nursing homes aren't cheap."

"Did we keep anything?"

"Sure." She pointed at the dining room. "That glass curio case."

The case in question was a tall glass-walled cabinet full of various plates and stuff. Nice, but clearly not full of gold. "Anything else?"

Mom waved me off as it looked like the show was starting again. It was a false alarm, so I asked again.

"It would help if I knew what you were looking for," she said.

Gold. "I don't know. A trunk with papers and pictures or such."

"Great Barb is not a sentimental person, and neither is my mom."

"So nothing?"

"Just that big box in the basement."

Surely I hadn't been sleeping over the damn gold? "What big box?"

"The steamer trunk under your dad's workbench." Her voice caught at 'dad.'

"What's in it?"

"Papers, pictures. Nothing important."

"Why's it under the workbench?"

"It's really heavy." She shushed me as J. R. Ewing's face showed up on the TV.

False bottom?

————————

Mom went to bed right after the weather report on the late TV news. I don't know why she even stayed up that late – the weather guy spent several minutes repeating the shocking news that it was going to be cold for the next few days. Like that was news?

I waited until the news was over and Johnny Carson

had finished his monologue to head downstairs and look in the trunk. It wasn't much – a battered leather-covered box at the bottom shelf. Dad had stored paint cans on top, and they had created colorful rings on the leather.

"Maybe I should try to sell the lid as modern art," I said quietly after clearing off the last of the cans. It wasn't as heavy as I thought it would be, at least not as I slid it towards me.

The trunk had a pair of brass latches holding it closed. The little thumbpieces that were supposed to pop the latch didn't work. Either they were locked or stuck. One of Dad's big flat-head screwdrivers popped the latches open with minimal effort. I opened the box.

If I'd been expecting a glow like when Indiana Jones popped open some ancient tomb I'd been disappointed. The thing was barely half-full, containing mostly black-and-white pictures of people I didn't know. There were some books, in Lithuanian and English and a shoebox full of letters. I took all of that out and piled it on the floor next to the trunk.

I chuckled to myself when I found two framed photographs. One was a shot of her in front of the old airplane. It looked like it was the same shot as the one in the newspaper. There was also a picture of a young man, a studio shot, wearing an old-style suit. He looked a lot like the pilot in the first picture. Finally, at the bottom of the chest, there was a box with some white fabric in it.

"That's your grandmother's wedding dress," Mom said. I was sitting on the floor in front of the trunk, but I still jumped back. "I hope you washed your hands. That trunk was dusty."

"I did, actually."

"What were you looking for?"

"Gold. Great Barb told me she found gold and had lots

of it left. Enough to fix all our problems."

She looked sad. "Great Barb always told good stories. None of them were true. Like the airplane rides."

"I saw a picture of her in the newspaper!" I said, louder than I intended.

"Not that one. She said she flew to New York City. And San Francisco."

"Her brother was in the Navy in New York."

"How'd she pay for that? And why would she go to San Francisco?"

"Just because we never go anywhere doesn't mean she wouldn't," I said. "Riddle me this, Mom. How did a woman so broke that she threatened a mobster with a gun buy a house a year later?"

Mom shook her head. "She got an insurance settlement. Here, since you opened the chest, let me show you." She sat down next to me and rummaged around in the chest, eventually coming up with a manila envelope. "Here's her husband's death certificate," she said, pulling out a faded and fragile piece of paper. She handed it to me. "And here's the insurance letter."

The death certificate was a pre-printed form which had been filled in by hand. I looked at it. "This is the wrong date."

"Huh?"

"Her husband went missing in 1924. This says 1931."

"Who told you her husband went missing in 1924?"

"Grandma. She doesn't remember him, and she was born in '24."

Mom waved her hand dismissively. "So he skipped out. Back then, they didn't get divorced. They just left."

I looked at the insurance letter, another faded and fragile piece of paper, this time typed. "1931," I said, pointing to the date. I read aloud from the letter.

"Since you have finally obtained a death certificate by reason of disappearance, we are now in a position to pay this claim." I skimmed ahead. "Wow. A big five hundred dollars."

"That was a lot of money back then."

"Not enough to buy a house. And this is 1931. She bought the house in 1925." I went to the death certificate. The handwriting was a bit ornate for me, but I figured it out. "Cause of death: unknown. Reason for issuing certificate – missing and presumed dead since 1924."

"Are you sure she wasn't just renting the house?"

"The county lists her as the owner. I saw the records."

"She got a loan," my mom said, doubt in her voice.

"According to the county, she paid cash."

Mom took the papers back from me and looked at them as if I'd magically changed what was written on them. Her mouth opened several times as if she were going to say something, but she never did.

Finally, I asked, perhaps a bit heatedly, as Mom glared at me. "Why do you and Grandma always doubt what she tells you?" I pointed at the papers. "These back her story."

"She lies," Mom said, almost to herself. "She always called Michael her second husband."

"Maybe he was."

"And that she lived in Kansas City," Mom continued. "But how..."

The picture of the pilot, stiff in his old-style suit, was sitting on a pile of books. I picked it up. "Who's this guy?"

"I don't know."

There was a label on the back advertising the photographer. "Well, it was taken in Kansas City," I said, turning it around. I pointed at the shoebox of letters. "What are those?"

"Just old letters."

"Wanna bet that I find letters from this guy," I said, waving the picture at her, "in there?"

Mom didn't take me up on my bet, which was good for her. His name, the man in the picture, was Roger Dawson. He was a pilot from Kansas City, and apparently, it was love at first sight. According to the letters, he bought her a train ticket in late 1912, and she moved to Kansas City.

The next big find was a telegram from London dated in January 1915. Roger had been 'provisionally accepted' into the Royal Flying Corps, and they were buying him a steamship ticket to London. There was another letter, in Lithuanian, of which Mom could read a little. It was from Kansas City, which was the same in Lithuanian and English, and addressed to "Dear Mother." Also in the letter and in English was London and a ship's name.

At the back of the box was a picture of a very young and quite attractive woman posed in front of Big Ben. On the back was a date, June 1916, and the word "love from your daughter" in Lithuanian was written on the back.

Then, there was a telegram, even more fragile than the letters. Dated December 1916, from the British Expeditionary Force, it informed her that Lieutenant Dawson had died of an infection after surgery for appendicitis. The place of death was a town with a French name.

I practically crowed. "She was in Kansas City and London!"

"But the bombing," Mom weakly said.

Now, I was glad I'd stayed awake in history class. "The Germans bombed London in both world wars. In WWI, it was mostly by blimp, but they did drop bombs."

Mom stared at me for a bit. A couple of times, her mouth opened, but no words came out. Finally, she waved weakly at the trunk. "We just thought all of this was just stories. I mean, it's *Eastville*."

Then it hit me. That was the answer. All Mom and Grandma saw of Great Barb was an Eastville housewife. One with 'gentlemen callers' but just a plain local woman slowly getting old. They didn't believe her because they couldn't wrap their heads around the idea of somebody leaving town and coming back.

But that's what had happened. She'd run off with Roger Dawson, pilot, to KC and then London. When he died, she came back. At some point, she met Michael Pikus and then things progressed from there. "But now you believe her?" I asked.

Mom waved again at the trunk. "I guess so."

None of this got me any closer to the gold. But it did give me another reason to go talk to Great Barb. Maybe if I got her talking about Roger the Pilot, I could get her to talk about Mister Good Boots' gold.

CHAPTER 27

Patrick

Mike and Melody Richards, fraternal twins I'd known since kindergarten, were throwing a party. When the cat's away, the mice will play, and their parents were in Las Vegas. The party was in their parents' detached garage out in the back of the house. It was presumably easy to clean, and if things got rowdy, there was less to break.

It was also cold. A large portable kerosene heater was running in the center of the garage, which knocked some of the chill out, but I left my coat on. Mike, a serious jock, was guarding the fridge. I said hi to him and opened the fridge. My choices were cans of Coke or Old Style, and I took the latter.

I grabbed a lawn chair next to VG, who was sipping on his beer.

"It's fully krausened," VG said, making a show of holding up the can to his face.

"I think that's German for 'horse piss with alcohol,'" I said.

"But you can't beat the price," VG said. "Or the view."

He was looking at Melody Richards, who was rather nicely filling out her scoop-top T-shirt. It was black, of course, as were her pants, hair and fingernails.

When we were all little kids, Mike and Melody's parents had tended to dress them in very similar, if not matching, outfits. As if in rebellion, now the two dressed as opposite as possible. Mike, besides being a serious jock, was sporting a crew cut. He'd signed papers to join the Marines after high school and had started leading exercise sessions for other military-bound kids after school.

"Yeah, the view's okay." Three Sticks walked in, followed by his date, Candy, a mousy sophomore who was a cousin to Melody. That and the fact that we were both in the band and Melody was the drum majorette got us in. Three Sticks and Cindy went to get beers and started to mingle.

"Thanks for coming," Melody said, sliding up to us.

"Thanks for having us," I said.

"Yeah," VG added. "Say, where's the john?"

"Use the outhouse," Melody said.

"Really?" VG replied.

"No," she said, laughing. "In the house. Just don't move the doggy door."

"Thanks," VG said, getting up. "I'll be back," he said in what was supposed to be an Arnold Schwarzenegger voice. It wasn't very good.

While he was gone, I added my bag of Fritos to the meager collection of food sitting out on a workbench in the back of the garage. On VG's return, I said, "Everything come out all right?"

"Just fine," he replied.

"How was the doggie?"

"Doggies. Multiple. Little yappy walking furballs."

"We all have our crosses to bear."

"I'm glad we don't have to use an outhouse," VG said. "My wee-wee would get cold."

"Yeah, it is a bit frosty out."

"My grandma had an outhouse until 1949," VG said after taking a sip of his beer.

"She live out in the sticks?"

"No – the same house she lives in now."

I was puzzled about that. "But that's got plumbing."

"So it does," VG said. "And it always did. But grandpa was too cheap to pay the sewer bill, so no toilet."

"And in 1949, he hit the lottery?"

"No," VG said. "Somebody blew the outhouse up."

I gave him a startled look. "Blew it up? How?"

"Tossed a stick of dynamite down the hole," he said with a shit-eating grin, which was entirely appropriate for the conversation.

"Huh?"

"I've heard three versions of the story," VG said. "The version told when my grandparents are around was that high school kids were driving around at night blowing up outhouses for kicks."

"Why dynamite?"

VG shrugged. "Back then, it was easier to get, or so I'm told."

"And the other versions?"

"Well, one of them is that my dad was tired of using the outhouse, so he traded a bottle of his dad's homemade wine for the kids blowing up the outhouse. The other version is he traded the bottle for a stick and did it himself."

"Well, that's one way to get rid of an outhouse. But it's not like you can install a toilet instantly."

"I guess they used buckets for a while. But that's why you need to walk through the kitchen and the laundry room to get to the toilet."

I'd been in his grandparent's house. The bathroom was a little room off of the kitchen. Apparently it had been a large pantry until dynamite struck. Then they'd cut it in half. "So since they had to run a drain, they added the washer and dryer," I guessed.

"I'm told before that Grandma had to use the laundromat," VG said with a wink. "Which makes me wonder if Grandma might not have been in on the demolition."

"Yeah, I could see that," I said. I took a drag on my highly krausened beer.

"Why are you two talking about outhouses?" Three Sticks asked. I turned around to see him standing behind me, a beer in one hand and a pile of chips in the other.

"It just came up," I said as he walked around in front of us. "And I hate outhouses." My only experience with outhouses had been on a field trip to Forest Meadow, the county forest preserve. It had been a hot day but cloudy, which made the outhouse both smelly and dark. "I just can't see going out in the dark of night to piss."

"Supposedly, Grandpa's outhouse had electricity," VG said.

"How?" I asked.

"I guess they ran an extension cord from the eaves of the house to the outhouse. Supposedly also had an electric heater and a fan."

"A heater?" Three Sticks asked.

"So I'm told," VG said. "It was gone just before Dad went into the Army." VG shrugged. "Per Dad, it didn't do much because you had to turn it on when you went in."

"By the time you were done, it had probably just started to blow hot air," I said.

"Which is why he wasn't sad to see it get blown to bits."

"This conversation blows," Three Sticks said.

"Kinda," I agreed.

We went on to other topics, and Three Sticks wandered off to another conversation. Eventually, VG asked, "Any news on the package?"

"Last I talked to Great Barb, she was having one of her bad days. I said. "I don't know if she was making sense in Lugan, but she definitely wasn't making sense in English."

"That's no good."

I shrugged. "No, it's not."

"Hey, dude," VG said. "I'm just the junior partner on this deal. You're the one who's gonna end up living under an underpass."

"Don't remind me." I took another swig of beer and made a face.

"Somebody has to. Remind you, I mean."

"Heh. Just what exactly are you doing for that fifteen percent? Besides being a pain in my ass?"

VG held up a hand. "Sorry, dude."

I sighed. "Well, I do have another opportunity to work on the old people."

"Oh?"

"Yeah. We found a box of Great Barb's stuff in our basement."

"And?"

"And Michael Pikus was her second husband. She married a guy named Roger Dawson just before WWI. He ended up in the Air Force, and she went with him to London."

"Wow."

"Yeah. So I've got another reason to talk to Great Barb. Maybe if I get her wound up on the old days, she'll spill something."

"Maybe."

I drained my beer. "Want another?" I asked, waving the empty can at the fridge.

"Why not?" VG said. He drained his can.

It wasn't until I got home that night that it hit me. Maybe the reason Tony was scared of the toilet was because it was an outhouse.

Oral History Project

This interview took place on Sunday, February 16, 1986. It was shortly after I discovered a photograph and letters suggesting that Great Barb had been married to a pilot, Roger Dawson, during WWI. The interview opened with me showing her the picture I had found and asking her who it was.

That's my first husband, D. Roger Dawson. It wasn't until we said our marriage vows that I learned the "D" stood for Dwight, a name he hated. You've probably figured out he was the pilot of that plane that flew here in 1912.

[I asked if he was wealthy. She laughed.]

Hell no. He was broke, paying for flying by working on planes. He was flying that plane to a new owner in Indianapolis. He landed in Eastville in part because he'd gambled away the gas money in Decatur the night before.

No, Roger was always broke. That's why he had to get the Brits to wire money for a boat ticket. Steerage class, because the Brits were going broke fighting the war. He was going to go to England without me, but I refused to let him. We were just married!

So, I got to tag along. But when we got to London I had to get a job to help with expenses. I was a charwoman. That's what the Brits called a woman who cleaned office buildings and the like. It was honest work.

[She kind of drifted off, and I asked about life in

London.]

London was, well, it wasn't Eastville or even Kansas City where Roger lived. We got to London shortly before the Krauts started to bomb the city. Roger was scared to death for me. I worked evenings, so I was out and about when the Zepps came over.

There was a little park, no bigger than a postage stamp, right next to the office I cleaned. The Army parked an AA gun there. After the first night when that gun went off, the other girls and I took to carrying cotton balls with us. When the sirens went off, we'd pack our ears with the stuff.

It wasn't like in the second war – Zepps only came over occasionally. Lots of nights, it was quiet. [She chuckled.] One night, one of the soldiers came knocking on the office door. "Gotta use the loo, love," he told me. Fortunately, I'd figured out by then that loo meant toilet, so I let him in.

I think a couple of the girls were sweet on the men, so we ended up having a regular arrangement. They'd come in for bathroom breaks, and we'd run out a pot of tea for them. The men had it easy – on the front, men were living in mud and shit.

[She paused for a long time. I was starting to prompt her when she continued on her own.]

Then Roger died. Infection due to an emergency surgery. Happened a lot back then. I got the telegram just as I got back from buying his Christmas present.

I moped around for a few weeks. There was talk of introducing food rationing, and the Krauts were screaming about unrestricted U-boat attacks, so I decided to leave. Roger's family didn't like me – blamed me for Roger running off to war – so I came back here.

[end of oral history]

"How did you meet Michael?" I asked.

"The flu. They called it the Spanish Flu. We all got it in November 1918. We were so weak that we could barely stand. Michael was living with his cousin in a house down the road. When we didn't show up for church, he came over to check on us." She teared up. "I don't think I would have made it if he hadn't. Dad didn't."

"I'm sorry."

"I was too. It was just Mom and I, and Mom's hips were bad, so as she could barely walk in good health. I hired Michael to work for us." She smiled. "He couldn't speak a word of English and couldn't read either Lithuanian or English. I started teaching him. Things just went on from there."

"And the Capone thing?"

She shrugged. "People like to drink. Me included. I thought it was a stupid law."

I decided to just ask. "And the gold?"

"I gave it to Tony."

"I thought you said you kept some?" I said. I could feel my face fall.

"No, no, I gave it all to Tony."

"Your son Tony?"

She nodded. "He used to write me. But not anymore."

Great. Tony had the gold, and I bet he's dead. The nurse came in to take her to lunch. I said my goodbyes and left.

CHAPTER 28

Patrick

Between my leaving Great Barb's room and getting to my car, I decided to take one more shot at things. That meant a visit with Grandma, so I drove to the Wolfburg Hotel. Back in the day, it had been the nicest hotel in Maple Corners, but that was a long time ago. Now, it had been converted to cheap one-bedroom apartments, which was why my grandmother lived there.

I walked inside and was almost at the front elevator when I saw Grandma sitting in the lobby reading a book. I went over and said hi, then asked, "Why are you sitting here?"

"These chairs are more comfortable than in my room," she said, still reading. "Besides, I like the view."

The windows looked out onto a parking lot. "If you say so."

"What do I owe this visit to?" she said, looking up from her book.

"Questions," I said.

She gestured at the chair next to her. "Grab a seat."

I did, settling into the old wooden chair. It looked like something out of a 1930s detective movie and was probably original to the place. It was surprisingly comfortable.

"Ask away," she said.

"So if you weren't the hot baby of 1924," I said, "it had to be Tony."

"Yep," she said over her book. "He was hot as a kid, too. He could sweat in a snowstorm."

We sat for a bit. Grandma was like that sometimes – she didn't feel the need to talk just because you were with her. Again, over her book, she said, "Was that all you wanted to know?"

I swallowed hard. "No," I said, "so what happened to Tony?"

"He left Eastville."

"I kind of figured that."

"If you figured that, why are we talking?"

Why are you being so pissy about this? "Why did Great Barb give Tony all the gold?"

"Ha," she said, but it wasn't a humorous laugh. "What gold?"

"The gold she found. The gold she's been telling us about." I held up a hand. "And before you tell me she's full of shit, I've got proof she was married to a guy named Dwight Roger Dawson and lived in both Kansas City and London. Got bombed there and made friends with the crew of an anti-aircraft gun." I was getting mighty tired of this 'Great Barb lies' shit.

She sat down her book on a side table with exaggerated care. "We've been busy, haven't we?"

"Yes. Trying not to lose our damn house."

"I've lost a house." She waved airily around at the Wolfburg's lobby. "It's not as big of a deal as you think."

"You're not answering the question."

"I know for a fact that she did not give any significant amount of money to Tony."

"How?"

She looked around the lobby. Other than the guy behind the counter, who was on the other end of the room and looked old enough to have taken Great Barb to her high school prom, we were alone. "This needs some privacy," she said. "Let's go up to my room."

"Okay," I said, wondering who she thought was going to hear us or, for that matter, care what we said. She led me down a hallway past a barbershop to a back elevator. It was ancient and had a folding metal grate for a door. We climbed in, and she punched the black button for her floor and we went up, the electric motor whining.

She lived on the sixth floor, just off of the elevator. We went inside, and she shut the door behind her. Her apartment was really two rooms – a sitting area with a tiny kitchenette and a bedroom just big enough for a bed. The bathroom was just a toilet and tub – the sink was in a little hallway between the bathroom and the bedroom.

"Sit down," she said, pointing to a faded couch. I did.

She sat down across from me. "Tony was a poof," she said, her voice barely above a whisper.

"You mean gay?" I asked quietly. She shushed me. Apparently, I wasn't quiet enough. "We're in your room."

"The walls here are thin."

"Really?"

"Yes," she said. "Look, he was gay. Poof, queer, limp-wristed, whatever," she said, waving her hand in a chopping motion.

"So?"

"So he got caught doing the gay with some other man. This was just before we got into the war – 1939 or 1940."

"So?"

"So," she hissed, "Back then, you could go to jail for what they were doing." She made a sour face. "As far as I'm concerned, still should."

"Isn't that a bit harsh?" I said. "He's your brother."

"It's a sin, you know."

It was. I wasn't, like, in favor of being gay, but neither did I want them to go to jail. "So what happened?"

"He was concerned about either getting beat up or jail, so he left town. Hoped a freight and headed west. Ended up in San Francisco." Her coffee table had storage underneath it. She lifted up the top/lid, rummaged around for a bit, and produced a worn photo album.

"This is him," she said, showing me a page with a black-and-white photo. The man in it, wearing a US Navy sailor's uniform, was in his late twenties and bore a strong resemblance to Grandma. On the opposite page, there was a postcard from San Francisco – a painting of the Golden Gate Bridge.

"Is he still out there?"

Grandma shrugged. "I have no idea. My mom got the occasional letter or card from him. She flew out to see him in 1960. He's never been back, and I have no idea if she still gets stuff from him."

"Don't you get stuff from him?"

"I was the one who caught him being gay," she said, an angry look on her face. "With a man I thought I loved. I told both of them to get out of my life, or I'd shoot them."

I sat there like a fish out of water. What the hell do you say to that? She kicked her own brother out? "Did Great Barb know you – you did that?" I finally asked.

"No. Or at least I never told her. I don't know what Tony said." She gave me a cold look. "And she doesn't need to know from you."

"Fine," I said, more to move on than because I thought it was a good idea. "But if Great Barb flew out there..."

"After she visited, we still got the occasional letter. In several of them, he asked for money."

Which didn't mean she didn't give him the gold. He might have blown the money. I also had no idea what gold was worth in 1960. Maybe it wasn't as much back then as it was now? I tried to take another tack.

"Why was Tony scared of the toilet?" To her questioning look, I added, "Since we're on the topic of Uncle Tony."

"It was an outhouse," she said. "Hell, I didn't like it. Cold in winter, hot in summer, and you had to carry a candle out there at night."

"Thought so," I replied. "Then there is still hope."

She snorted. "If it even existed, somebody else found it long ago."

"I was worried about that when I saw the house on Garfield had been remodeled."

"And how exactly would you know that?" she asked sharply.

"I was in it recently."

"Playing Amway salesman?"

"No, the door was unlocked. Nobody answered the phone, so I went in."

Grandma shook her head. "If you get caught breaking and entering, you won't have to worry about a home. The State of Illinois will find a place with three hots and a cot for you. At taxpayer expense, no less."

And soap on a rope. I decided not to tell her that the house was occupied when I went in. "Then I won't get caught."

"Good. The old biddies around here gossip enough without me having to listen to them go on about my grandson, the felon."

"You are an old biddy, Grandma."

She swatted at me. "Hush now, you young

whippersnapper." She pointed at her book, which she had left on the counter that divided the tiny kitchenette from the living area. "I was just getting to the good part." She looked at the clock on her table. "And I've got a book club meeting in two hours."

"Then I'll leave you to it," I said, standing up. We hugged awkwardly, and I left.

When I got to my car and fired it up, the radio was on like usual. I turned it off and drove home in silence. By the time I got to my house, I had decided that there probably wasn't any gold. But if there was, it was in an abandoned outhouse.

CHAPTER 29

Vincent Bisceglie III

"Is there some reason you ordered a title search?" Vince's dad asked him. They were sitting in the front room waiting for his Mom to call them in for Sunday dinner.

"Mister White told you?" Vince asked.

"It *is* my bank. Besides, title searches cost money."

Vince glanced toward the dining room. His Mom and sister weren't visible – probably still in the kitchen cooking. "Money."

"Yes, money. Title searches cost money."

"No, you don't understand, Vince said, exasperated. "I was looking for money."

"What? Going to buy the house and flip it?"

"Kowalski's grandmother owned that house."

"You mean the Kowalskis we're foreclosing on?" Vince's dad waved his hand dismissively. "Whatever. They don't own it now."

"But they did."

Vince's dad gave him a questioning look. "I think I'm missing a few pieces of the puzzle here, son."

"The gold, or whatever her husband stole from Grandpa, might still be hidden there."

"The Kowalskis? What would they have stolen from

my dad?"

"Not the Kowalskis. Pikus. Barbara Pikus. She's..."

Vince's dad held up a hand. "Let's talk about this later."

"Why?"

"Because I said so," his dad growled. He screwed a smile on his face. "Now, let's eat. And what the ladies don't know they don't need to know, capisce?"

"Got it."

His dad got up and glanced over at the dining room. Vince followed his eyes and saw his sister bringing out a bowl of pasta. "After dinner, we talk," his dad said. "Downstairs."

"Okay."

After dinner, Vince followed his dad into the basement office and turned on the electric heat.

"Have a seat, son." Vince sat down opposite his dad's chair. "What makes you think that Pikus stole anything from us? Equally important, what makes you think this Kowalski kid knows shit from shinola about any of this?"

"Why else would Kowalski need to know the price of 600 ounces of gold?"

His dad shrugged. "He's doing a school project. He thinks he's found a leprechaun's pot of gold. Who knows?"

"Grandma told me Pikus and this family have a history."

"And how many Manhattans had she downed when she told you this?"

"Just one."

His dad bobbed his head from side to side. "For her, that's not a lot. So what do you think you know?"

"I talked to Grandma. She said that Pikus' husband went missing and had stolen a bunch of money from us. Then, his wife shows up and buys a house. Why they didn't call the cops was not explained."

"You idiot," his dad said, but with no heat. "They were running booze back when that was illegal. You can't call the cops on your fellow crooks."

Well, you *could*, Vince thought, as long as you had a good story. But they probably didn't have one. "She said Grandpa didn't talk to her about money and business, but if she knew about it, it had to be big."

"It was," his dad said. "And the bitch put dad in a spot where he couldn't publicly go after her."

"Something about church."

"Yeah." His dad shook his head. "Church was big to them. You could kill a man, but don't miss Sunday Mass."

Vince heard the violins warming up, getting ready to play the *Godfather* theme again. "But..."

"But nothing. If Big V's crew heard he wasn't taking care of the widow of one of their own, well, they might take care of Big V."

Vince had a pretty good idea that 'taking care' of Big V involved a shovel, a gun, a tarp, and an empty field somewhere. *Well, if we're going to go all gangster, let's go all gangster.* "So why didn't he go back at night or something?"

"In where?"

"The house. She had to hide it in the house, right?"

His dad looked surprised. "One minute you're Mister Clean, the next minute you're Al Capone himself."

"Dad..."

"He did," his dad said, raising a hand. "They did go in. Several times. He told me he even brought in a specialist from Chicago."

"A specialist?" Vince asked.

"Some guy who was an expert on hidden compartments and lock-picking. Supposedly he'd been in on several robberies of jewelry and shit from the homes of society types."

"So why didn't they just, I don't know, try to get Barbara to talk?"

His dad cocked his head at Vince. "What? Like somebody in a World War Two movie?"

"Maybe."

"I assume they tried," his dad said. "But I don't know for sure. The whole thing was something the Old Man didn't like to talk about. Whatever they did, it didn't work, apparently."

"You'd think if they'd grabbed one of her kids..."

"Out of the question," his dad said. "They had a deal with the sheriff. No kids or civilians were to be hurt."

An image of Marlon Brando saying, 'I'm gonna make him an offer he can't refuse' popped into Vince's head. He suppressed a hysterical giggle.

"What's so funny?"

"Nothing," Vince lied.

"And they couldn't find it. Then dad got sent to prison..."

"Heard that story. Banging an underaged hooker."

"She might have technically been underaged..."

Vince held up a hand. "Also heard that. Bottom line is he got caught with his dick in the wrong chick."

"That's my dad you're talking about!"

"I know," Vince said, too loudly. "I also know she was fifteen! Sis's age!"

"It was different back then."

It was still illegal. But then, so was running booze.

Something wasn't adding up, Vince thought, but he'd have to figure out what later. His dad said something, and Vince, who wasn't paying attention, asked, "Huh?"

"I said she's a stubborn old goat."

"Is?"

"She's still alive, I think."

That might be worth following up on. "So your dad was convinced the money wasn't in the house."

"Or that when she told him she'd spent all the money she had that she was telling the truth." His dad looked away. "Then dad went to prison, and when he got out, Capone was in jail, too, and the new bosses in Chicago didn't know us from Adam."

"So we had to go honest."

"Or open a tavern, which was as close to honest as he could." His dad looked at Vince. "But even if there was money in the house, it's gone."

"And you know this how?"

"Leo did a gut renovation of the place when the Andersons bought it."

"Leo, the same cousin who supposedly owns Fifth Street Mortgage?"

"The same," his dad said. He shrugged and added, "It's a small town."

"Maybe she put it in a bank?"

"Or on the fucking moon," his dad said. "All I know is that you're chasing a ghost."

"Pat Kowalski seems to think otherwise."

Vince's dad waved his hands as if washing them clean. "Fine. Go ghost-hunting."

"Just one question," Vince said. "Did they look in the outhouse?"

"Why would they?"

"I don't know, but Pat Kowalski is suddenly fascinated about the history of outhouses in Eastville."

His dad laughed. "Well, try not to get any shit on you."

Vince's alarm went off at two AM. He groggily rolled out of bed and got dressed as quietly as he could, then slipped out the back door of the house. It was clear, with a half-moon, but damn cold and damn windy. He shivered in his coat as he hustled to his car.

It was a short drive to the house on Garfield. Vince drove down the alley behind the house. He considered turning off his headlights but decided that nobody was up this early anyway. He pulled up behind the house, parking his car behind the shed in the back.

He left the car running but turned off his headlights. He'd stashed a bolt-cutter from Dad's workroom in the back seat of his car, which he retrieved, along with a flashlight. Tools in hand, he went around to the front of the shed.

This has to be where the outhouse was, he thought. It was the only outbuilding on the lot, and there was an old cement walkway, now partially obscured by the new deck, running from the back door of the house to the shed. He was concerned because the shed was a metal unit and clearly not original to the house.

"Those who dare, win," he said, his breath white in the moonlight. There was enough light from the street that he didn't need the flashlight to see the small and rusted lock on the door. It still took him three tries to cut the lock, largely because it was hard working in gloves.

But eventually, the lock came off, and he tossed the pieces of it aside. He opened the door, then glanced over his shoulder at the house. No motion or lights were visible. He stepped inside, closed the door behind him, and clicked on the flashlight.

The floor of the shed was plain old dirt, now frozen in the cold. There was no hole, no indication that there had ever been any hole, and no indication that the dirt had ever been disturbed.

"This was a bust," he said. He grabbed a couple of shovels and rakes to make it look like a theft and headed back to his car. He drove out to the town dump, where he would ditch his stolen merchandise.

CHAPTER 30

Vincent Bisceglie III

"Why do we have to move boxes today?" Vince asked as he rode with his father to the bank. The sky was lead-gray, and the wind was up.

"The bank is closed," his dad said. "President's Day."

"I know. That's why I don't have school."

"Do you really want to dodge customers while you're hauling a box of papers through the lobby?"

Vince didn't really care either way, so he shrugged.

"I don't," his dad said in the silence, "Which makes this a great day to move boxes. Besides," his dad said, patting him on the stomach, "you could use the exercise."

"So could you!"

"True," his dad said with a nod. "I'll help."

I'll believe that when I see it.

They pulled into the back lot of the bank. On business days, it was usually full, and employees had to park across the alley. Today, it was nearly empty. A white rental cargo van was parked right in front of the back door. Mr. White was standing beside it in a green parka. The parka was unzipped, revealing his sweater and open shirt collar. He was wearing jeans and smoking a cigarette.

"I don't think I've ever seen you without a tie," Vince

said when they got up to him.

Mr. White tossed the butt in the direction of the street before replying. "Files don't care about ties." He waved at the parking lot, and two other men got out of their cars. The group gathered around the van. Vince knew one of the guys, Tommy, who worked at the bank as a teller. Tommy introduced the other man, whose name Vince promptly forgot, as his older brother. Older Brother was between construction jobs and needed a little extra cash. The group then knocked on the glass door going into the lobby, and Al, the security guard, opened it for them.

"You're here today?" Vince asked of him as they walked in.

Al shrugged. He was a big man, old, a retired sheriff's deputy. He adjusted his belt, which strained against his gut, and he patted the small snub-nosed revolver he carried on it. "It's a job."

"That it is," Vince said, following the rest of the group upstairs. They went from the front office into the main office area, which was an open space with a number of desks. They called it the bullpen, and most of the support people for the bank worked in that area. Almost every desk had at least one cardboard box on it. There were other stacks of boxes in various nooks and crannies. All the boxes were printed on the outside with a cheesy wood grain. There was a white space on one end, in which various numbers and letters had been handwritten in black magic marker.

"Okay, team," Mr. White said, addressing Vince and the group. "Simple plan. All these bankers' boxes need to get downstairs and into the van. Make sure the side with the label," he slapped a nearby box which had some cryptic lettering hand-written on it, "is facing out. I'll be downstairs loading the van. Al will hold the door for us and handle any customer who's forgotten we're closed today. After we get all the boxes into the van, we drive to the storage facility."

The storage facility was a former tavern owned by Vince's family that they had converted to house records. Mr. White continued. "Then we unload and put up. At the storage facility, Mister B. will direct you, which is why you need the labels so he can see them. Once the van is empty, we'll pull all the stuff we can destroy from the archives, load it into the van, and I'll take it to Champaign for shredding. I hope to be on the Interstate by lunch. Let's get to it."

Vince grabbed a box, as did everybody else, and headed downstairs. His dad actually grabbed a box as well. Vince noted that his dad's box didn't go into the van but rather into the trunk of their car. A second box followed it, and his dad drove off.

While this was going on, Vince and the other peons worked like, well, peons. It was mindless grunt work, but Vince didn't have a say in the matter. After a bit, his dad returned but didn't move any more boxes. Rather, he retired to his office. Probably reading the paper, Vince thought, wiping sweat from his brow.

They were down to the last few boxes when Vince's dad called him into his office. Vince followed him into the office, which was a large room at the front of the bank with a wall of windows overlooking the street. His dad went to the large but plain wooden desk and opened a drawer. "I need you to sign something."

"Okay," Vince said. "What?"

"Contracts," his dad said, his head down as he shuffled papers. "Here's the first one."

"What is it?" Vince asked as his dad handed him a typewritten stack of paper held together by paper clips.

"Just sign where the note is," his dad said, looking

through another stack of papers. He nodded at this desk set. "Pen in the desk set."

"I know where the pen is, Dad," Vince said. There was a wood-and-brass nameplate and pen stand at the front of the desk. Vince and his mom, well, really his mom, had bought it for Dad as a Father's Day gift.

"And the little Post-it thingie shows you where to sign."

"I can see that, Dad. What am I signing?"

His dad finally looked up. "Just sign the Goddamned thing. Christ, I taught you how to wipe your ass. Trust me."

It would have been much more convincing had Vince not seen a look of concern on his father's face. He sat down in a guest chair in front of the desk, found a more-or-less paper-free corner, and pulled out the gold pen from the pen stand next to his dad's brass desk nameplate. He signed where the note indicated.

His dad handed him two more pieces of paper, which Vince also signed. All these papers went back into the desk. Vince was opening his mouth to again ask what this was about when Mr. White knocked on the doorframe of the open office door. "You ready?"

"Yes. We'll be right down," his dad said. "I'll get the lights up here and turn the thermostat down."

Vince clopped down the stairs. He was hot from the manual labor, so he went outside to the parking lot and stood next to the van to cool off. Mr. White had gone ahead of him and was standing next to the presumably locked van. He pulled out his pack of cigarettes and offered one to Vince.

"I don't smoke," Vince said.

"Good for you," Mr. White replied. "Getting to be an expensive habit." Unbidden, he added, "Tommy's taking a leak. When he gets done, we'll go."

"Why'd you tell Dad I asked for a title search?" Vince said.

"I didn't. He asked me why I had ordered one." Mr. White took a drag on his cigarette. "We're not doing a lot of home loans at the moment, so it kind of stood out."

"Why not? I mean, why aren't we lending?"

"The government won't let us."

"They can do that?"

Mr. White laughed. "They can." His smile faded. "Just before they shut us down."

"Are they really going to do that?"

"Unless somebody shits a million dollars or so, yes."

Well, there didn't appear to be *that* much gold to get. "How soon?"

"Probably early April." He waved a hand at the building. "They've already got a regulator stationed here full-time. Some guy from Indy. He's sitting where Bob used to be."

Couldn't they at least wait until graduation? Then he wouldn't have to look at his friends and explain why the bank went tits up.

Vince looked at the van. He pointed at his dad's car. "Why did my dad put some boxes in his car?"

"What boxes?" Mr. White said.

"I saw two boxes..."

"I didn't."

Vince started to say something smart-ass but caught himself. "Got it."

"Yep."

"So, hypothetically, if my dad did put stuff in his car, why would he?"

"Maybe he's taking some personal stuff home?"

"And why would he do that? I mean, we own the

bank."

Mr. White took a drag on his cigarette before answering. "If, or rather when, the government seizes the bank, everything owned by the bank is subject to seizure."

"Everything?"

"Yep."

"But personal stuff..."

Mr. White looked contemplative. "Strictly personal stuff? No, that you keep." He waved his cigarette at his dad's Cadillac. "But a lot of the stuff you 'own' is technically bank property. Like that car. And once the government gets their hands on the place, they're not going to let us take out anything bigger than a paperclip until we can prove it's not bank property."

"That sucks."

Mr. White shrugged. "Yes, it does." He waved at the bank building. "If you've got anything, I'd get it out."

"I don't got nothing."

"Good."

Vince's dad came out of the bank.

"Tommy fall in or what?" Mr. White asked.

"We forgot the boxes behind the teller line," his dad said. "They're loading them on a hand cart."

"Which we'll want when we get to the storage place," Mr. White said. He reached into his pocket to get the key.

"Yep," his dad replied as Mr. White unlocked the van.

Tommy came out of the building pushing a two-wheeled hand cart with three boxes on it. Tommy rolled over to the van, and Vince unloaded the cart.

"One more cart," Tommy said as he walked away.

"Good day for a move," Mr. White said.

"Yep," his dad said. He glanced up at the slate-gray sky. "If the snow holds off."

"It will," Mr. White said. He gestured at a rolled-up newspaper sticking out of Vince's dad's pocket. "What's the news?"

His dad shrugged. "The eggheads are still trying to figure out why that space shuttle thingie blew up."

Vince winced at that – his whole class had been watching the launch on TV.

"Waste of money if you ask me," Mr. White said. "The space program, I mean."

"Yeah," his dad agreed. "But the government will piss the money away on something else."

Tommy rolled up with another hand cart load of boxes. "This is the last of it," he said.

Vince and Tommy loaded the boxes and cart into the van. Just as they finished, the air was suddenly full of frozen pellets of sleet. Vince hustled to his dad's car and got into the passenger's seat.

"Good thing we've got an overhang at the warehouse," his dad said, starting the car.

———————

By the time they were done unloading the van at the warehouse, the street was getting seriously slick, and Mr. White decided to make the destruction run some other day. Still, a bank holiday was also a school holiday, so after the boxes got moved, Vince had the rest of the day off. He climbed into his dad's car.

"What was in those boxes?" Vince asked.

"You packed them," his dad said.

"No, I mean the two that went into the trunk of this car."

His dad turned the ignition key. "Papers."

"What kind of papers?" As his dad reached for the gearshift, Vince added, "Mr. White told me that the government will take this car."

His dad had just put the car in reverse. He put it back into park before answering. "If the bank fails, yes. This is technically a bank-owned vehicle."

"And the papers? The ones you hauled away?"

"What do you want to do for lunch?" his dad asked, putting the car in reverse again. This time, he also eased off the brake, and they started rolling.

"I take it we're not talking about paper?"

"I'm hungry," his dad said.

We're not talking about papers. "I could eat."

They were on their own today – Mom and his sister were both out of town visiting one of her relatives. I hope they checked the weather before they left, Vince thought, watching the sleet fall in sheets. The Interstate will be slicker than snot.

"Log cabin?" His dad asked. It was a small restaurant at the edge of town.

"Works for me," Vince replied. It was his dad's favorite place in town. Not that there were a lot of choices. "Question," Vince said. "How could I find out what other places the Pikus family might have owned?"

His dad turned on the windshield wipers and put the car in drive, having backed out onto the street. "Why?"

"Gold. Remember? We talked about this."

His dad chuckled. "Usually, if you're looking for gold, you find the end of the rainbow. That's where the leprechaun puts it."

"Not funny, Dad."

"I thought it was." Something in Vince's tone made his dad's smile fade. "I know you think you're going to save the family or something, but even if there is some buried treasure, we have no claim on it."

"Neither do they."

"Well..."

"No, bullshit," Vince said, feeling heat on his face. "You told me they stole a bunch of money from us. That's the only way they could end up with gold." If his dad didn't like Vince's language, he didn't say anything about it.

They had come to a stop sign where the side street hit a main road. His dad looked around Vince to see if anybody was coming. The road was clear, and the car rolled out into the street. Vince felt the ass end of the car slip around a bit on the sleet-covered road.

"Weather like this reminds me of the time I had to save my dad's life." His dad tapped the dashboard nervously.

"Save his life?"

His dad waved at the weather. "It was pissing ice like this, and he'd walked to the tavern. When he didn't come back after closing, Mom sent me out to find him. Good thing she did. He was passed out in somebody's yard. His coat was open, and he was half-frozen when I found him. I don't think he would have made it to morning. As it was, he was sick for a week." His dad frowned as the big Cadillac fishtailed again on the road. "It was also the time he told me about the first time he killed a man."

"Grandpa killed a man?"

"Several," his dad said, nodding as if in agreement with himself. "More than one, I think." The car pulled to a stop at the town's one stoplight.

Vince felt his head spin. What the hell kind of family did he have? "How? Why?"

"How's easy. He shot them."

"But..."

The light turned green, and the car started moving again, fishtailing a bit as it did. "Grandpa worked for Capone."

"I thought he just sold moonshine?"

His dad chuckled, but there was no humor. "Making booze would be too much like real work for my dad. No, he didn't *make* anything."

"So what did he do?"

"Mostly crack skulls. He ran the crew and told them what to do. They actually did stuff."

"What kind of stuff?"

"Whatever stuff needed to be done. Run booze, run broads, run numbers, make book, make loans, and if anybody got out of line, 'discipline' them." He sighed. "And on the side, steal anything not nailed down real good."

They rode in silence for a minute or two, then pulled into the parking lot of the Log Cabin Restaurant. It was a real log cabin, albeit one that was a modern kit building.

"So, tell the story," Vince said. "About that night."

His dad turned off the car but made no move to get out. He twisted in his seat to look at Vince. "Like I said. My dad got drunk one night. Well, he got drunk most nights but this night..."

"He ended up passing out."

"Yep." His dad looked out into the parking lot. There I was, barely fourteen, bundling my drunk-ass dad into our car to drive him home."

"You had a license at fourteen?"

"Hell no. But at two in the morning, nobody was out to check."

"Then he just told you he'd killed a man?"

"No, first he pulled out a gun." His dad looked at him and mimicked, pulling something out of his coat pocket. "I asked him why he was carrying it."

"And he said?"

His dad shrugged. "Protection, he said. Then he said it didn't protect him from the ghosts."

"What ghosts?"

"Exactly what I asked him. Well, I stopped the car and took the gun from him first. If he was too drunk to walk, he was way too drunk to wave a revolver around. Then I asked him."

The car was quiet except for the sound of sleet hitting the metal roof. Finally, his dad continued. "The Old Man said when he'd first robbed a man, way back when he was younger than you and still living out East, he'd pulled a gun. Just to scare the guy, he said."

"And the guy didn't scare?"

"No. The guy went for his own gun. So dad shot him." He shook his head. "It was a stickup, and the Old Man was after the other guy's wallet. You want to hear the best part?"

"I guess so."

"The guy? The guy he shot? He had five dollars in his pocket." His dad looked away. "My Old Man killed a man for five dollars."

Vince didn't know what to say to that. Finally, he said, "Maybe Grandpa really needed the money?"

His dad laughed or maybe coughed. Vince couldn't tell. "The Old Man *always* needed money."

Vince waited for the explanation. It came a second later. "My Old Man loved to gamble. Horses, cards, dice – you named it, he did it." Vince's dad shook his head. "He sucked at it. Mom said the best way to pick a winning bet was to bet the opposite of what Dad did. He always owed a bookie or two."

"So anyway," Vince's dad continued, unbuckling his seatbelt, "There are two morals to the story. The first moral is just because you don't *want* to hurt somebody doesn't mean they won't get hurt. The second moral is what you do will haunt you the rest of your life."

Vince unbuckled his seatbelt. As he did, his dad put his hand on Vince's shoulder.

"I know you mean well. I know you really want to go to college in Saint Louis. But you've got to understand something."

Vince looked at his dad. His face was a mask of emotion. "What?"

"You're eighteen. You do anything, they charge you as an adult. That means your life is ruined."

"Dad..."

"Don't you 'Dad' me!" His dad yelled. He took a deep breath. "I mean it. After jail, you're a felon. Branded as a crook for *life*." A tear leaked from his dad's eye. "And living with the consequences of your evil forever. I saw what it did to my Old Man. It was tearing him apart."

"Okay," Vince said uncomfortably.

"Your word you won't."

"I swear."

His dad smiled and wiped his face. "Good. Let's go eat."

They got home from lunch, his dad's Cadillac sliding the whole way to find a message on the answering machine. His dad played it. Mom was staying over another night. "I hope you like leftovers," his dad said.

This is definitely better than leftovers, Vince thought, forking the last of his chicken lemon. Vince's grandmother had called shortly after they'd gotten home, concerned about his mother driving home in the sleet. She'd ended up by offering to cook dinner for 'her boys.' Vince smiled. It had been an offer they couldn't refuse.

"Great, Mama," Vince's dad said. He glanced at Vince.

"You got a hollow leg?"

"Hey, I was carrying boxes all day!"

To Grandma's quizzical look, his dad said, "We were moving papers to the archive."

"Ah." She got up. "Coffee?"

"Yes, please," they both said. His dad elbowed Vince, so he got up. "Let me help with the dishes."

"Just scrape them off and put them on the counter," his grandma replied. "I'll wash them afterwards."

"Okay," Vince said. He followed her into her kitchen with its big yellow refrigerator and yellow double oven carrying some plates. There wasn't much food left on the plates to scrape off, so his job was over quickly.

"Looks like it quit sleeting," his grandmother said as she poured water into the coffeemaker.

"Roads are probably still slick," Vince said.

"Lousy time to move out."

"Move out?"

His grandmother pointed out of the window. "The Stevenson's. They're moving somewhere."

Then it hit him. "You said that the Pikus woman 'rolled into town.' When we talked."

"Yes," she replied in a quiet tone.

"Rolled in from where?"

"Strawberry Creek. Should have stayed there. It's a trashy place for trashy people."

"She had a house down there?"

"I'm sure I don't know," his grandmother replied snootily. She paused. "Actually, I do. It was near the arch."

"What arch?"

She waved her hand. "The rock arch. Never mind, the coffee's ready."

Now I need to find out what 'arch' she's talking about.

CHAPTER 31

Patrick

There was no school on Monday, so I decided to pay Great Barb a visit. The court hearing was just over a week away – time to get serious. She was sitting up in bed, looking at a TV with the sound off. "Hi, Great Barb," I said. It took her a long time to respond to me.

"Antonio?" she said.

I thought about saying yes but decided that would be mean. "No, it's Patrick."

"Oh. Who?"

"Patrick. Ruth's son." She didn't say anything, just nodded. "How are you today?" I asked.

"I called my lawyer," she said.

"Your lawyer?"

"I called him to post bail." She waved her hands vaguely. "I want out of jail."

"You're not in jail, Barbara. This is a nursing home. They take care of you here."

"They can call it what they want," she said with venom, "but I recognize a poor farm when I see one."

The county used to have a Poor Farm, which had been converted to a nursing home for, well, poor people, but she was at a private facility. I decided not to argue with her. "Were you thinking of Tony?"

"He used to send letters," she said. "Some of them are in the drawer." She pointed at the plain laminated bedside table. "You can read them."

I went to the table, and sure enough, there were a stack of open envelopes with letters inside. I sat down and glanced through them. They were all from an address in San Francisco and, at a brief glance, had nothing of great importance to say. I noticed that the most recent letter was from early last year. *So much for Grandma saying that Tony had disappeared.*

I decided to read the latest letter in more detail. In it, Tony Pikus-Morgan, as he signed it, asked why Great Barb hadn't replied to his last two letters and wondered if she was okay. "Didn't you write him back?" I asked, waving the letter at her.

"I had Mary write him a letter," she replied. "My handwriting has gotten so bad."

I had a feeling I knew exactly what had happened to that letter. "Do you mind if I write him?" I asked.

"No. He's your uncle."

Actually, great-uncle, but close enough. I carefully put the letter in a back pocket of my jeans. "When did you last see him?"

"Years ago. Just before I got locked up." She sighed. "He hated to come back here. Too many bad memories. We met in St. Louis."

I had heard of the great trip to St. Louis. I would have been two years old when this happened, but it had been a staple of family stories. Great Barb had driven herself to St. Louis and not told anybody. We're positive she got lost at least once on the way there. On the way back, she forgot to check her gas gauge and had ran out on the Interstate.

A trucker had picked her up and taken her to a truck

stop, where he called my grandma who came and picked her up. The family told Great Barb that her car had gotten stolen. In fact, it had been towed by the cops, and when they got it out of the impound yard, they sold it.

"And how was the visit?" I asked.

"We stayed in a fancy hotel downtown," she said. "Tony has a good job and he paid for everything. He's gotten very big, you know. Not like his father."

"That's nice."

"He was still a hot person," she continued. "His face was always red."

"Mary told me that. She also told me that he didn't like the outhouse."

"What outhouse?"

"The one you toilet-trained him on. On Garfield Street."

She chuckled. "I bought that house specifically because it had indoor plumbing. Your mom wouldn't go to the outhouse at night, so when we moved, indoor plumbing was a must."

By 'my mom,' she meant my grandma. "She said Tony was scared."

Great Barb laughed. "No, Tony wasn't scared. He wasn't scared of anything. Twice, he jumped out of his bedroom window onto a bail of hay." She raised a wizened finger, which shook like a leaf. "Now, your mom was scared. Of the outhouse, of the flush toilet, of mice and bats and broomsticks."

Well, either Great Barb or Grandma Mary was confused. At this point in the proceedings, I really didn't care. None of this was getting me any closer to the gold. If it was real, of course. If not, well, I was sure GI Jack could get me into somebody's army.

One of the nurses came in and said to me, "It's time for

her dinner. Are you joining us tonight?"

"No, thanks," I said. I kissed Great Barb on the forehead. "I'll write Tony for you."

That night, I read Tony's letter to Great Barb more carefully. He talked about his 'partner' Charlie Morgan and announced he was thinking about retiring from the bank. The rest of the letter was the kind of stuff you write when you talk to somebody very occasionally.

There was one odd line, though. He asked if she had finally sold the busted-down house on Strawberry Creek. I decided to ask Grandma Mary about that. In the meantime, I wrote a letter to Tony, introducing myself and telling him what I suspected had happened to the previous replies.

"I don't know what this town is coming to," Pat's mom said as she walked into the door.

"What now?" I asked, looking up from my textbook. I was in the front room waiting for the meatloaf I had made to finish cooking. I love cookies, and Mom always worked and didn't have time to make them, so she had taught me how to bake. This had morphed into me cooking a lot of the meals at the house.

"Somebody broke into a shed. Here in Eastville."

"Oh. Where?"

"On Garfield."

I gasped and turned it into a cough. "When?"

"Last night," she replied. "They were talking about it at work." She finished taking off her coat. "The chief was in the store and told us about it."

I wasn't sure that was what cops were supposed to do, but it is a small town. After dinner, I went to my room and called VG. "Did you decide to go gold-hunting without me?"

"No. What made you think that?"

"Somebody broke into the shed at Great Barb's old house."

"Not I. Probably some kid."

"On a Monday night?"

"Not everybody worries about being on time to school." VG laughed. "Hell, why am I telling this to you? You're the great cat burglar who's missed more class this month than half the potheads combined!"

He did have a point, which I admitted.

As it happened, I had an excellent opportunity to talk to Grandma at length. We had a meeting with the legal aid lawyer in Champaign, and Grandma offered to drive. Her car, an Oldsmobile, was much nicer than mine.

We were on the Interstate, and Grandma had just set the cruise control when I started. I had been trying to figure out what to say since I got in her car. Telling her I'd read Tony's letter seemed to be a bad idea. Telling her I'd just mailed a reply seemed even worse.

"Whatever happened to the house on Strawberry Creek?" I asked.

"Why do you care?" She chuckled at the windshield. "And no, we went through the house pretty thoroughly. No pot of gold to be found."

"I was just curious," I lied. "But I do have a report to write, and actually, a picture of the house might be nice to add to that report."

"It burnt down years ago."

"Before or after she sold it?"

Grandma stole a glance at me. "Why would you think we sold it?"

"Well, she didn't live in it. Not after 1925."

"Luidas did."

"Her brother didn't have his own house?"

"He did. A few years after we moved to town, the Great Depression happened. His house was mortgaged to the hilt. Hers' wasn't. He ended up in her house."

"And when he died?"

She sighed. "I couldn't get that hard-headed woman to sell the place. She wanted to keep it as a 'weekend house.' I finally got her to rent it out."

"Who'd want to rent a house with no running water?"

"Luidas had built an addition in the late 1930s. He added a bathroom."

Fortunately she hadn't caught on to my fixation about indoor plumbing. "So what happened?"

Another sigh. "What's with the 20 questions?"

"Oral history project, remember?" I waved at the Interstate. "And we've got some time to kill."

"The place caught fire three or four years ago. I'm sure it had something to do with the electrical. Luidas had it done when he did the addition. Knowing him, he paid whoever did it in beer instead of money."

"So we still own the house and land?"

She sighed. "Not anymore."

"We sold it?"

"Ha."

"What do you mean, ha?" I asked.

"I tried to sell it," she replied, irritation in her voice. "Before and after the house burnt down. Nobody wanted it." She clucked her tongue. "Not surprisingly. It was a shitty little house in the middle of nowhere."

"So what happened?"

"The county seized it."

"Because?"

"Because, my nosy grandson, that's what happens when you don't pay your real estate tax."

Great. The county bought it, tore it down and some construction worker found our gold.

"You ignoring me now?" Grandma asked.

"Just thinking of something else." Yeah, my gold being gone.

"What did you say?"

"I'd like to see where it is. For my report." And to see where an outhouse might be.

"We'll drive by on the way home."

CHAPTER 32

Amy Burton, Land of Lincoln Legal Aid

My Wednesday had gotten off to a shitty start. The answering service called me (I was the on-call attorney) with Mrs. King's latest soap opera. Her husband had gotten himself drunk, gotten into a fight, lost the fight, and then got tossed in the county jail. Every time I thought he couldn't get any stupider, he went and proved me wrong.

We don't handle criminal cases – that's what the Public Defender does – but Mrs. King couldn't wrap her head around that. Much of being an adult seemed to baffle her. Our answering service, which we kept primarily in case of early morning evictions or other landlord nastiness, heard 'emergency' from her and so called me.

Mrs. King didn't answer her phone, so I went to the jail at four in the morning to find her perched on one of their hard plastic chairs in the waiting area. She'd called in from a payphone and hadn't left a number.

There really wasn't much I could do, and there wasn't anything anybody could do until the bail hearing at nine AM. I eventually got her calmed down and got hold of the Public Defender's office. They owed me for another deal, so I was able to get a pledge of somebody to be with King at the bail hearing.

Not that it would help much. King was a regular at the jail and well on his way to finding a favorite cell. We do our best to help everybody at Legal Aid, but some people just aren't ready to be helped.

By the time all of this was wrapped up, it was six AM, way too late to go back to bed. I'd heard about a new donut shop. It was my turn to buy donuts for the Thursday morning staff meeting, so I decided to give them a try.

The donut shop was in a new strip mall on the corner of Fifth and Green, running along Fifth. It was four units, only two of which were occupied, namely the donut shop on one end and a copy shop. Just what a college town needed – another place to make copies. The donut place didn't open until six thirty, which meant I had fifteen minutes or so to kill.

I had taken the file for the Kowalski foreclosure home with me the night before, and they were my first meeting of the morning at nine-thirty, so the file was in my briefcase. I pulled it out and looked at my notes.

I saw that the mortgage was recorded to Fifth Street Mortgage, but all the foreclosure paperwork was from B-Friendly S & L. I had made a note to ask at the next hearing for an assignment document from Fifth Street giving B-Friendly legal authority to foreclose.

What jumped out at me was the address listed for Fifth Street. It was 656 South Fifth Street, #102. The strip mall was 650-656 South Fifth Street. Each of the storefronts had their own street address. I did not see any mortgage companies in the strip mall.

I did see a copy shop which had the number 656 above the door. As I watched, somebody in jeans and a bomber jacket climbed out of an ancient VW Bug and went to open the front door. I got out of my car and went to the copy shop. The person I had seen proved to be a woman who, judging from her wardrobe and hairstyle, was still stuck in the Sixties. No, there was no mortgage company there. Yes, one could rent a mailbox. Yes, your address would be 656 South Fifth Street, plus the number of your box. Box numbers started at 100.

———————

"Say what?" This was from the kid, Patrick Kowalski, who was a bit brash.

"Fifth Street Mortgage is probably a front," I said, leaning back into my ill-padded chair. We were sitting in my tiny office, furnished in the cheapest cubicle-style office furniture we could find. The Kowalski kid and his grandmother, Mary Balthus, were sitting in front of me on a pair of stackable plastic guest chairs. The kid's mother was AWOL. Apparently, Mrs. King wasn't the only woman who had adulting issues.

"What does that mean?" Balthus asked.

"If I'm right," I said, "it means that B-Friendly is trying to move assets out of the S and L and into some other entity that they control."

"And why is that a problem?" she asked.

"Well, first off, since Fifth owns the mortgage, legally, B-Friendly needs written permission from them to do anything except take your payments." Actually, they needed a servicing agreement to even do that, but I was trying to keep it simple. "More importantly, given that Fifth is a front, I suspect that the deal is chock full of conflicts of interest. A bank examiner would find that very interesting."

"So does that mean we can keep the house?" the kid asked.

"Unfortunately, not automatically. It does mean that they may be willing to cut a deal to avoid having this out in the open."

"Well, what does stop this?" the kid asked.

You're about to get your first lesson in adulting, I thought. "Unfortunately, the only *guaranteed* way to stop a foreclosure at this point is to pay all the money that you owe."

"Not just get current?" Balthus asked.

"Unfortunately not. The loan is written such that if you get 120 days behind, you owe the entire remaining balance." They were over 150 days – no way I was going to get that overlooked. We try our best, but there's only so much we can do.

"So if we suddenly get the money, I should run straight to B-Friendly?" the kid asked.

"If you win the lottery or otherwise get the money," I said, "do *not* under any circumstances just run into B-Friendly. Call me first."

"Why?" he asked.

"We want to get a legal release," I said. "We want them to sign a document saying that they no longer have any claims against the house. We then take that document to the courthouse and get the mortgage on your house cleared."

"But if we pay..." Balthus said.

"Trust me," I said. "You want all your I's dotted and your T's crossed on this. *Especially* if they're up to something fishy. As soon as you hit the lottery, call me." I reached over and handed her a card. "If it's after hours, tell the answering service it's an emergency and leave a number. I'll call you back as soon as I can."

"We will," the kid said.

"You got a hot tip on a pony?" I asked, trying to keep it light.

"Something like that," the kid said.

He seemed serious. "Okay, then. Well, until your ship comes in, let's go over the rest of this."

CHAPTER 33

John B. Hood

"Fancy meeting you here," Hood said as he walked into the bar. Rick Webster was sitting on a corner, accompanied by a black-haired woman of his same age.

"Happy hump day," Rick replied, making a toast with his drink. "Belly up to the bar."

"I will," Hood said, doing so. "Unfortunately, we're working Saturday, so that makes tomorrow hump day. All these bodies are putting us behind."

"That sucks," Rick said. He took another drink. "At least they gave me something to do."

"And I'm glad," said his companion.

"John, meet my wife, Helen," Rick said. They shook hands, then the bartender came over, and Hood ordered a drink.

"How so?" Hood said. "Giving you something to do, I mean?"

"So the missing persons report for Smirnov lists as a contact person one Ludmilla Smirnov. She gave a phone number of Oak Lawn 3344 and an address that's now the parking lot of a Holiday Inn."

"Things do change in sixty-some years," Hood said. The bartender sat his Scotch down in front of him, and Hood took a sip. "And so?"

"And so they hired me as a consultant to track down Smirnov's next of kin for five hundred dollars."

"Which is way too cheap," Helen said.

"That was the maximum they could pay, so I took it," Rick said. "It ought to at least cover expenses."

"So, you're a Consulting Detective now," Hood said.

"More an underpaid flunky, but yes, the good taxpayers of this county, of which I am one, are tossing money at me."

"Any luck so far?"

"On Smirnov? Actually, yes."

Hood took another sip of his Scotch. "Go on."

Rick, who'd had a head start, finished his drink and put the empty glass on the far edge of the bar. He gave the bartender the universal hand signal for another one. "Found the wife," he said, a satisfied look on his face.

"She's still alive?"

"And kicking. She was barely seventeen when she married Ivan and had just turned eighteen the day before he died."

"You got a date of death?"

"He didn't come home the night of December 23, 1924, so we're assuming that's the date, give or take a day."

"Did you talk to her?"

"Yep. Met her at her house, which she's still in. She's still driving to the hairdresser's, church, and the grocery store." Rick chuckled. "She's a character. Remarried, had three kids, now has a herd of grandkids who call her babushka."

"They call her a headscarf?"

Helen laughed. "No, Americans call the headscarf that old Russian grandmothers wear a babushka. The word is actually Russian for old woman."

"Oh. So now what?"

"They claimed the body and are burying it."

"And the guy buried with him?"

Rick's second drink arrived, which he used to wash down a fried mushroom. "No name, but some useful details."

"He's from downstate," Helen said.

"I assume you mean southern Illinois?" Hood said.

"Yes," Rick said. "Apparently, Ivan wrecked his truck, and some, in Ludmilla's words, 'hunky' from downstate was assigned to use his truck to make their deliveries."

"So the hunky was in the wrong place at the wrong time."

"Looks that way." The hostess came over and told the Websters that their table was ready. As he was getting up to leave, Rick said, "There'll be an article in Sunday's *Tribune* about the missing man."

"Hey," Hood said, "any word on the third skeleton?"

"That's going to be tough," Rick said as his wife headed to the table. "They're trying the same leather glove trick they did with Smirnov but I guess they're having problems with getting a good print. Rick grabbed the plate of fried mushrooms. "Hopefully, they'll get something. I get paid by the body."

Patrick

After the meeting with the lawyer in Champaign, we drove back, detouring to go by the place on Strawberry Creek. The wind was picking up, causing Grandma's Oldsmobile to rock a bit. The skies were gray with low clouds. When we got there we stopped and got out to walk around. I could see why nobody had wanted to buy the place.

Other than the sign announcing the property was coming up for auction, it didn't look like anybody had done anything around there for years. The tiny front yard, a little strip ten feet wide from the road to the busted concrete stoop, was full of waist-high weeds, dried and brown from winter.

The rest of the house was a pile of half-burnt lumber, which had some dried weeds poking up through them. A recent thaw was melting the snow in town, but here in the creek valley, it was still cold. The house, even with the addition, couldn't have been that big.

"Four rooms," Grandma said. "Front room, kitchen, two tiny bedrooms. Luidas enclosed the back porch for a bathroom and another sitting room. That was it."

The lot was wooded, trees bare this time of year. "How far back does our property go?" I asked, pointing to the backyard.

"Until it hits the bluff," she replied. "Some of these houses had coal mines going straight into the bluff."

"We weren't so lucky?"

"No."

"I bet we're not on city water or sewer," I said.

"Ha," Grandma laughed. "Of course not." She pointed at a utility pole with a line drooping off of it. "And every heavy wind or snow, you lose power."

"The taxes couldn't have been that high," I said. I waved at the potholed asphalt road. "Look what you're getting."

"Neither was the rent I could get," she said. "Not a lot of people want to live out here." She stamped her feet in the cold. "And when I stopped getting rent, well."

"Insurance?"

"Stopped paying the bill."

"What is it with us and not paying people?" I asked.

"It's called being poor, dear," she replied. She waved at the auction sign. "Since we can't sell it, let the county have it back."

I noticed the date of the auction. Tuesday, February 25 – the same day as our next court hearing. *If there is anything to find here, I need to find it soon.* I shivered. It was cold down in the hollow. "I've seen enough."

"What about pictures?"

"I'll get some later." I turned to go back to the car. "Now that I know where it is."

"Hungry?"

"I could eat."

We climbed into her car and headed back to Maple Corners. I was coming back, but I needed to call VG first and have him come with. I didn't want to be wandering around in the woods alone, especially if I was looking for a literal shit-hole.

CHAPTER 34

Vincent Bisceglie III

Vince was getting frustrated. He'd had two reports to get done, plus a redo of his damn oral presentation for Parker. He'd had no time to breathe, let alone look for a stone arch.

Then, on Thursday, he got a breather. As part of the morning announcements, he learned that PE was canceled for all periods. Students were directed to go to the library instead. *For once, I'm not going to be hot and sweaty during lunch.*

When Vince filed into the library, he made a beeline for the local history section. After a few minutes of not finding anything about a local arch, he said the hell with it and went to ask the librarian.

Miss Hopkins was on duty. She was brand-new, just out of college, and a real hottie. This meant he had to wait a couple of minutes to talk to her while a football player tried to hit on her. Finally, he got up to ask his question.

"Do you know anything about a rock arch around Eastville?"

She frowned. "Not really, no. Why?"

"I'm doing an extra credit report for history."

"Oh." She smiled. "A lot of seniors are suddenly scrambling for extra credit."

But I'm scrambling for extra gold. "Cleaning up transcripts for college."

"Might be a bit late for that."

"Maybe," Vince allowed. "So, do you know anything?"

"Down in Strawberry Creek, there used to be a small outcropping of sandstone. One of the tributaries of the main creek cut an arch through the stone."

I kind of figured that. "Used to be?"

"Yeah. Back in the '50s, the arch collapsed. Some people claimed blasting from a nearby mine weakened it." She shrugged. "In any event, it's gone now."

"Where was it?"

Another shrug. "No idea. I'm not from around here, and last time I was down in Strawberry Creek, I got lost."

"Where was what?" Vince glanced over his shoulder to see Diane Lee, the biggest toker in his class, standing behind him with some books in her hand.

How the hell would she know? Girl's usually so high God would need a radio telescope to find her.

"The old stone arch," Miss Hopkins said.

"Oh, that. It's on North Creek Road about midway between Rose's Tavern and the AME Church." Diane looked at Vince. "County's ripping out what's left to widen the road."

Well, she may be higher than a jet airliner, but she is a Creeker. "Cool, thanks."

Vince stepped away from the desk and went to find a county map since he had no idea where either of those two landmarks were. He only had the vaguest idea of where North Creek Road was. Fortunately, the map had that labeled. Just as the bell for the next period rang, he'd found the road on the map, and it looked to be only about five or six miles long.

He put the map back and started to follow the crowd to lunch. As he walked, he decided that he'd just drive down the road in question on Saturday. He had three points of reference – a church, a tavern, and some road construction. How hard could it be?

He reached this decision as he walked into the cafeteria. Today's main meal was meatloaf smothered in canned brown gravy. Edible at best, he thought, taking a bite after having sat down at his usual place.

"Hey, Three Sticks," VG said, plopping down across from him. Pat Kowalski was right behind him and heading to a spot to VG's right.

"Hey," Vince replied. *When I go to Washington University, I'll finally be able to get people to use my real name.* "Anybody know why PE was canceled?"

"Yeah," Pat Kowalski said. "Water leak."

"Huh?"

"A pipe burst," Pat said. "Dumped a bunch of water on an electrical panel. The gym's a mess."

"What about the game tonight? When are they going to make it up?" VG asked while carefully buttering his white bread. *The man was meticulous about his butter.*

"Cancelled," Pat replied.

"They got a makeup date?" VG asked.

"Don't know," Pat replied. "Not that it matters when we get our asses kicked."

"Well, it does matter for band," Vince said.

"I'm sure when the powers that be know, they'll tell us," Pat said.

"Did you see the *Chicago Tribune* today?" VG asked. *Besides covering his bread, he's obsessed with Chicago.*

"No, why?" Pat asked.

"There's an article about a body that got found in Chicago."

"Lots of bodies get found in Chicago," Vince said.

"This one was dumped in December 1924," VG said. "And had a picture of Pat's great-grandmother in his pocket."

"No shit?" Pat said.

"Sure looked like it to me," VG replied.

"I'll be damned," Pat said. "What else did the article say?"

"Just that he got shot with a Chicago-area moonshiner, and they didn't know who he was."

"They wrote an article about some old body?" Vince said.

"They want people to contact the DuPage Sheriff's Office if they recognize the picture," VG said. "So they can put a name on him."

"I guess I've got another letter to write," Pat said. "But not tonight."

"Write it in study hall," VG said. "Mr. Patterson has stamps."

Why Patterson had stamps, or for that matter why VG knew or cared he had stamps, mattered not to Vince. What did matter is why wouldn't Pat Kowalski, a member of a pep band that wasn't playing, have time to write a letter after school?

"The game's cancelled," Vince said. "What else do you have to do tonight?"

"I've got other plans," Pat said, winking at VG. "And so do you."

"So do I?" VG asked. Then he nodded. "Yes, I guess I do have plans tonight."

What, you two dating? Vince took another bite of his meatloaf and nearly choked. *Fuck me – they're making a move on the gold!*

"You okay?" Pat asked.

"Yeah, fine," Vince said. "I found the one grain of

pepper in the whole loaf." *They know where the old Pikus house is. Hell, they could just fucking ask somebody without having to play detective.*

It made perfect sense, Vince thought while ignoring the conversation. Both their parents thought they would be at a basketball game, so there'd be no need to gin up an excuse.

Nor do I need an excuse. Mom and Dad will think I'm at the game. Vince looked at the two of them. *But they know where the damn place is while I've got to find it. It's a race now.*

Something in the conversation caught his attention. "What did you say?" he asked of Pat.

"I said that Mr. Olsen thinks he can get me into Illinois State as a history major."

Why in the hell would anybody want to pay money to study history? "I thought..." Vince blurted out.

"Thought what, Three Sticks?" VG asked, a mock innocent look on his face.

"I thought with your dad's problems, you didn't have the money to go to school," Vince said, feeling embarrassed.

"I believe I've got that solved," Pat said, winking at VG.

Fuck me again! That family makes church mice look like Donald Trump! I'll be damned if he goes to college and I don't! He put his hand to his face, realizing he was flushing.

Vince spent the rest of the afternoon pondering. The first problem, as he saw it, was figuring out where on the damn place the gold was. 500 gold coins would fit in a coffee can. Clearly, the Scooby Gang thought they knew where to look. The second problem was turning gold into cash. *But if I don't have the gold I don't need to worry about that.*

When the bell rang for the start of the last period of the day, Vince had his plan. It was a plan he could never tell his dad about, but it was a plan. It was simple and foolproof.

I'll be there before they are. When they find the gold, I'll pull a gun, scare them, and take the gold. He smiled to himself. *Pat and VG will piss their pants when I show up. Nobody will get hurt.*

CHAPTER 35

Pat

"Why couldn't we do this in the daylight?" VG asked me, waving his flashlight around.

"Did you see that road?" I asked. "We're right on top of it."

"So?"

"So, we don't own this property anymore. The county does. What if some bored County Mountie were to cruise by and wonder what the hell two kids were up to? Now stop waving that light around like you're signaling for help, and let's find this outhouse."

He mumbled something under his breath but held the light down. The old homestead in Strawberry Creek was as dark as the crack on a well digger's ass and much colder. I truthfully didn't think we had much to worry about from the Sheriff's Department, but I didn't want to press my luck. What really worried me was falling into something like a well or the outhouse.

I stopped, and VG bumped into me, his flashlight hitting me in the kidney. "Watch where you're going!" I said.

"I would if I could see shit," he replied.

"Use your flashlight!"

"You told me to keep it down!"

I stifled a curse. Never ask VG for a sandwich and step on it unless you wanted his shoeprint on the top of your bread.

"How sure are you of this?" VG asked.

"Not very." I wiped my nose, which was running because of the cold. *Why couldn't they have foreclosed on us in the spring when we didn't have to worry about frostbite?* "Remember, this gold-hunt was your idea."

At that, we heard something move in the bushes. We both swept our flashlights around, in my case forgetting to worry about being seen from the road. At first, nothing, then something large and brown jumped out in front of us and took off. VG yelped, and I jumped a foot before I realized we'd startled a deer.

"Damn!" VG said. "What was that?"

"Just a deer."

"What's he doing out here?"

"Deer stuff. Probably sleeping. And I think it was a she."

"How can you tell?"

"No horns, idiot."

"I think you mean antlers."

I sighed, my breath a cloud in the cold. "Whatever. Let's keep looking. The sooner we find it, the sooner we can get warm."

We headed back into the lot. When we got to the first row of large trees, I stopped.

"Let's keep going," VG said.

"Let's think for a second," I said. I waved my light back towards the wreck of the house. "They had to walk out here at least once a day, right? And Grandma said her brother added on to the house in the back, right?"

"So?"

"So, how far would you want to walk in the cold if you

had to take a dump?"

"Not very far."

I waved my light into the trees ahead of us. "Those trees look pretty old to me. The outhouse can't be that far into the woods."

"Makes sense. I'm still not seeing a house."

"It's got to be along this tree line. You stay put, and I'll go left."

"Why do you want to split up?"

I gritted my teeth. "I'm looking for a fucking hole in the dark. What if I find it by falling into it?"

"Ah. That's why you wanted the rope."

I nodded, which he probably couldn't see. "Exactly. Now, stay put. If you hear me yell, come carefully. I'll try and shine my light up so you can see me."

"Got it."

I went left along the line of trees, looking for an outhouse. I went along for what felt like forever but was probably only 30 yards away when I hit the moss-covered remains of a split-rail fence. I decided that surely it would be closer to the house than that, so I doubled back.

When I got to where VG was standing, I had him stay put again, and this time, I went right, stopping when I hit another fence. This one was barbed wire and in decent shape, which I determined by hitting it. Fortunately, my coat prevented the rusty barb from getting into my skin. I also noticed a paper sign nailed to a tree just past the fence which said, "No Hunting." Apparently, it was the neighbor's fence line.

"Well?" VG asked when I returned.

"Looks like a bust." I stood there for a second. "It's got to be here somewhere!"

"Maybe her brother found the gold when he added

onto the house," VG offered.

"And not tell Great Barb?"

"She didn't tell him."

"True." *Or maybe she had just forgotten about it.* My hands were cold, even with my gloves, so I sat the flashlight down and shoved them into my pockets.

"We should go," VG said.

"Let me think for a minute."

"We could think in your car. With the heat on."

We could. I'd parked the car a little ways down the road – far enough from the house that it wasn't obvious where we were. I bent down to pick up my flashlight and noticed that it was pointing at a clump of brush. A gust of wind moved the brush, but something was stopping the brush from going all the way back. "I might have found something."

"Where?"

I stood up and shined my light at the brush. "Behind those weeds."

We walked over there. What I'd seen weren't actually weeds but rather some kind of thorn bush.

"Wild roses," VG said.

"Whatever they are, be careful," I said, trying to find a way to not get stuck with a thorn. I found a stick, which I used to push the brush back found myself looking at a wall made of wood faded to gray. By feel and the flashlights, we determined that the wall was only four feet or so long.

"The building must have collapsed," I said.

"You did say they got plumbing back before WWII," VG said. "They didn't need it anymore."

So, in the typical manner of our family, rather than properly tear it down, we just let it fall down. "Guess so."

"We're going to need to cut this shit back," VG said, referring to the bushes. He wiped his nose with a finger. It was amazingly cold and damp down here in the hollows.

"Yep."

"Back to the car for tools."

I looked at the lot. There was a faint impression of what was once a gravel driveway. "I think I can get the car up that and behind the house. Then we could use the car's headlights to work."

"What about being seen from the road?"

It was a good point. On the other hand, nobody had driven up or down the road since we'd been there. Still... "We'll have to make sure what's left of the main house blocks our lights."

"Okay."

We went back to the car and drove it in. I then sent VG out to the county road as my spotter. We were able to get the car situated such that you couldn't see it from the road as long as I didn't have the high beams on. I left the car running and climbed out, then popped the hatch to get our tools.

"I hear something," VG said. We'd been working for maybe thirty minutes and had only gotten about half of the thorn bush out of the way.

"Probably another deer," I said, picking up a shovel. "These woods are full of them."

"Are you sure?" he replied.

"Christ, quit being such a baby." It was the third time he'd stopped because he heard something.

"Shit!" VG said, raising his flashlight. I looked where he was pointing.

"I'm no deer," Three Sticks said, walking out of the woods.

"Three Sticks! What the hell are you doing here?" I asked.

He raised his hand up and pointed it at me. I thought for a second he was holding a pipe. Then I realized it was a gun.

"That's my gold, Patrick," Three Sticks said. "And please, call me Vince."

"The hell it is!" I replied. "Wait. How do you know about the gold?" I poked VG in the arm. "What did you tell him?"

"Nothing! I swear!"

"VG didn't tell me anything," Three Sticks said. "But I found his note in a library book. I've been following you two clowns around for days."

"Following?" I said. I felt like I was standing beside myself.

"You got a hearing problem?" Three Sticks said. "Following," he continued. "Watching you two chase around like dogs in heat." He stomped his feet. "And now that you've found the gold, I'm going to take it."

"Look, Three Sticks," VG said.

"Vince, damn it!"

"Look, Vince," VG said, "we haven't found anything."

"You will," Three Sticks replied. "Keep digging."

"It's my gold," I said. "I'm cutting VG in for a piece for helping. Maybe..."

"Maybe you two quit farting around and get back to work." He waved the gun at the outhouse. "Get on it."

I tossed my shovel on the ground. "I said, it's my gold." I was trying for tough, and I think it came out whiny, but damn it, it was *my* gold. "And it surely isn't yours."

"That, Patrick," Three Sticks said, "Is where you're wrong. See, it is my gold. Your great-whatever robbed my grandfather, then his putana of a wife got him sent to jail."

"Says you," I replied, wondering where he'd gotten

that particular line of bullshit from. Not that it really mattered.

"Says me," he replied with a shrug. "And this fine gun made by Mister Ruger." He waved the gun expansively in the air, and for the first time, it dawned on me he'd really been pointing it at me.

There was an air of unreality to the whole thing. I mean, I'd known Three Sticks my whole damn life! I mean, we weren't best buds, but we'd been in the same damn kindergarten class! Just this afternoon, we'd eaten lunch together!

Three Sticks continued, acting as if he had all the time in the world. "But here's the other thing. You don't own this property. So legally, that there gold belongs to whoever finds it."

I didn't think Three Stick's legal analysis was worth shit, but before I could say anything, VG said, "The county owns this land. Says so on the auction sign. You going to give this to the county?"

"Were you?" Three Sticks asked. We didn't say anything. "Didn't think so. Nice thing about stealing from thieves is they don't call the cops."

"We're not thieves," I said.

"Last time. Do you or any of your relatives own any part of this piece of shit?"

Our silence was the answer. Nobody said anything for a minute. Finally, Three Sticks said, "Start digging."

"Are you really going to shoot us?" VG asked in a shaky voice. On the one hand, I thought VG really needed to keep up with current events. On the other hand, VG's voice sounded like I felt.

"If I have to, yes. Don't make me."

"You really want armed robbery and murder on your head?" I asked.

"Want?" he replied, again waving that damn gun around. "No." The gun went back to being pointed at me. "I'd feel real bad about it. Not as bad as you would, but bad."

Three Sticks was about ten feet away. I shuffled a little to my right while looking at VG. "We could rush him," I said as quietly as possible.

"Speak up," Three Sticks said, apparently seeing my breath.

"Nothing," I replied. I looked at VG. "On..."

VG turned and ran away! He just ran into the woods!

Three Sticks took two big steps towards me, then stopped and held his hand out to block me. "Don't even think about it!"

I wasn't thinking about anything except what a pussy VG was. We could hear him thrashing around in the trees, the leaves crunching under his feet. The sounds quickly faded.

"And I would have bet that you'd be the runner, Patrick," Three Sticks finally said.

"Guess you were wrong," I said. "He's going to call the cops, you know."

"Maybe," Three Sticks said. "If he doesn't get lost in the woods. Woods he's running deeper into."

VG had taken off away from Three Sticks, which meant away from the road. "Can you take that risk?"

"Yes. Can you take the risk of me shooting you?"

I glared at him for a minute, then looked at my shoes. "Are you going to help dig?" I finally asked.

"There's two kinds of people," he said. "Those with guns and those that dig. You dig."

CHAPTER 36

Pat

After a while, I wasn't worried about the cold, having worked up a sweat demolishing the old shithouse. As I worked, I felt dizzy and sick to my stomach. *All of this work for some lard-ass to waltz in and take the money? And then his dad's bank takes my house?* But since that lard-ass had brought a gun and VG was off in the woods somewhere getting eaten by a bear (well, more likely a coyote in Illinois), it looked like that was what was going to happen.

It turned out that the wall I had found was the only one still standing, and it was basically propped up by a tree branch which had grown over what I guess would have been the throne.

In short, it took me a lot of work to get to the point where I was looking at what had been the floor. At some point, linoleum had been put down on the floor. It was green with moss but still holding together.

"I need a break," I said.

"A short one," Three Sticks replied. "Very short."

"Listening for cop cars?" I said, trying to sound hopeful.

"If the cops were coming, they'd been here by now," Three Sticks said.

"Explain to me, just for shits and giggles, why you

think this gold, if there is any, belongs to you."

"Like I told you, that Pikus asshole stole from my grandfather," Three Sticks said. "Your grandfather."

"Pikus would be my great-grandfather."

"Whatever. Like I sat down and drew your damn family tree."

"And he disappeared."

"So did my grandfather. In the Fifties." A shrug. "They just got tired of their Old Ladies and went out for cigarettes."

"Well, the timeline matters because why would he hide the gold here and then disappear?"

"Look, Patrick, ask me if I care." He stomped his feet on the ground. "Break time is over."

"Yes, boss," I said. I pointed at the moss-covered linoleum. "Got a saw?"

"For what?"

"This floor. What do you want me to cut it with?"

"Fuck do I care? Hell, just lift the whole floor up."

"Sure," I said doubtfully. I stuck my shovel under the lip of the floor and started prying. A good chunk of the floor came up. The linoleum was acting like a skin, holding large chunks of rotten and termite-holed wood to it as we pried. The floor came up quickly as if I was rolling up a carpet.

The outhouse was in a tiny depression, maybe a foot lower than where I'd parked the car. I'd also piled the bushes, lumber, and general junk between the car's headlights and whatever was under the floor. It meant that whatever had been under the floor was now in shadow.

"Okay, now I do need your help."

"For what?"

"For maybe shining a fucking light on the fucking ground so I can see your fucking gold!"

His lips curled into a smile. "Since you ask so nicely."

He shined his light down. Removing the floor had exposed the dirt. A piece of rusty metal, like the top of a box, was clearly visible. With my hands, I tried to scoop the dirt away.

The ground was frozen so that wasn't happening, but VG had brought a garden trowel. When he'd run away like a little girl, he'd dropped it. I crawled over on my hands and knees to where it lay and crawled back. It didn't take long to get enough of the box free.

I picked up the box. It was heavy – a lot heavier than I thought – and almost as soon as I got it off the ground, the bottom fell out.

As did a shitload of gold coins.

"Son of a bitch," Three Sticks breathed.

I sat back down on my haunches. "She was right."

We both stayed frozen for a minute, watching the gold shimmer in the light from Three Stick's flashlight. Finally, he said, "Enjoy the view because that's all you're gonna get."

"We could split it," I said. "Fifty-fifty. Right here, right now."

"And we both just go on our merry ways?"

"Why not?" I pointed at the gold with both hands. "That's two hundred thousand dollars. Maybe more."

"I thought you had a deal with VG?"

I waved my hands. "You see him anywhere?"

"No."

"So our deal's off." I pointed at the gold. "What do you say?"

"I say nice try, Patrick, but I'm taking all of it."

So much for that idea. "Well, given that the box is busted, you got a bag, Mister Criminal Mastermind?"

"No. But I'm sure you do."

"It's in the car," I said, making to get up.

"No, maybe I should get it," he said.

And maybe I should do what VG did and take off running. Two hours ago, I'd have bet everything that Three Sticks wouldn't kill a fly. Now, I was wondering if I was going to end up in the hole I'd just exposed.

"Everybody just freeze!" My grandmother yelled.

Three Sticks and I looked towards my car, where her voice had come from. We were blinded by the glare from the headlights and couldn't see her.

"What the hell are you doing here?" I called out.

"Talk later!" she replied. "You with the gun – drop it!"

"What are you going to do, hit me with your purse?" Three Sticks yelled.

A gun barked from the direction of the car and a board sticking up between me and Three Sticks jumped back. Clearly, Grandma had shot it, and I was too surprised to react. I didn't even know she had a gun! "Answer your question?" she yelled.

Three Sticks raised the pistol and turned to his right, crouching down maybe a foot as he did so. He fired at the car, hitting one of the headlights and knocking it out. Grandma fired as well. If she hit something I didn't see what.

I threw the box in my hands at Three Sticks and scrambled to my knees. It was light, and he batted it away without flinching. Three Sticks was looking in the direction of the car, trying to block some of the glare from the headlights with his hand. If it had been me, I'd have been flat on the ground by now, but he was still standing up.

As I got up to my knees, my hand came across a pry bar, which I threw at him, hitting the arm holding the gun. He yelped but didn't drop the gun. He did drop the flashlight and put his now free hand on his arm. He was clearly trying to figure out what to do next, and as the gears slowly turned in his head, I got to my feet. I lunged at him awkwardly, half-tripping on some rotten boards. As I fell, I pushed him to his right with my hands.

I should have tried to break my fall, but instead, I fell flat on my face. As I scrambled up, the pry bar came into my hand, and I swung it blindly. It connected with something, making a muffled thump, and he grunted. Something metallic fell and hit another board.

The gun. I grabbed it while dodging his foot as he tried to step on my hand. Still rolling around on the ground like a drunk, I scrambled back a foot or two.

"Now, who's got the gun?" my grandma yelled.

"You're not dead?" Three Sticks yelled back to her, an annoyed look on his face.

"You're a shit shot and didn't hit me!" she yelled back.

Three Sticks looked at me. I was holding the gun in both hands, and I think I had two fingers on the trigger. I'd never shot a gun before, so I really hoped that it was ready to fire.

"Now..." Three Sticks said.

"Shut up!" Grandma yelled. "Everybody just shut up and stop!"

Three Sticks glanced at me. He was holding his arm and his side. "Okay."

"Pat, you okay?" Grandma asked.

"I'm fine," I replied.

"Good," she said.

"Look, Pat," Three Sticks said. "We were talking about a deal..."

"And if you say one more word, I'm going to blow your dick right off," Grandma said. "Got it?"

"Yes, ma'am," Three Sticks said.

"Good. Where's your car?"

He gestured with his head behind him. "Down the road behind me."

"Okay," she said. "When I tell you, and not before, you're going to bend down and carefully pick up your flashlight."

"It's busted," Three Sticks said.

"Here," I said, taking one hand off of the gun and tossing a flashlight at his feet.

"Okay," Grandma said. "Pick up the flashlight."

He bent down and did so, then stood up.

"Now," Grandma continued. "When I tell you, and not before, you're going to turn around and move as fast as you can to your car. Don't stop, don't look back, and whatever you do, don't come closer to me or mine. Got it?" He nodded, which Grandma apparently didn't see, so she shouted her question again.

"I got it!" Three Sticks said.

"Good. Now, turn and run away!"

He glared at me, then did as he was told. We listened to the rustle of leaves fade as he ran.

I started to cry. "I thought he was going to shoot me!"

"He might have," Grandma said. "It would have taken him a while to work up to it. Pat, put the gun down, please. VG, you can come out now."

"Yes ma'am," VG said. They both came over to where I was.

"That's a lot of gold," Grandma said.

"I told you so," I replied.

"You did," she said.

"How did you find me?" I asked.

"Worry about that later," Grandma said. I noticed that she was carrying a big black revolver. "We need to get the gold and be gone before that wanna-be gangster gets his courage back." She held out her hand to me. "I'll take that gun, please."

As she said that, VG plopped down next to the gold and started shoving fistfuls of coins into a gym bag.

Once we got the gold and our tools in the car, VG and I took my car and followed my grandmother's car to her place at the Wolfburg.

"I thought you'd abandoned me," I said to VG once we were on the county road.

"I wouldn't do that," he said. After a long pause, he added, "Yeah, I did think about it."

"So what happened?"

"I ran into the woods and circled back to the road. When I got there, I ran to that tavern we'd passed."

"Rose's?"

"Yes."

"To call the cops?"

"Well, at first, yes," VG said. "But as I ran, it dawned on me that Three Sticks was right."

"How so?"

"Well, I mean, they'd definitely arrest him," VG said. "Cops take a dim view of people pointing guns at other people, even if they're only a .22."

"A .22? He was sticking me up with a fucking .22?"

"Yeah, a Ruger target pistol. Nice gun – we used it a couple of times in Scouts." VG tapped me on the shoulder. "And if he'd shot you in the head, you'd die just as bad as if he'd hit you with a .45. Mob hit men use .22s all the time – they're easy to silence."

"Glad to know that," I said, not really meaning it. "But you didn't call the cops. Why not?"

"I figured," VG said, "that they'd arrest Three Sticks

all right. Then they'd want to know what we were up to out there. And if you'd found the gold by the time they rolled up, they'd take it."

"Maybe."

"No, for sure. Now, maybe you'd figure out a way to get it back with lawyers and shit, but that might take months. Maybe years."

And in the meantime, we'd lose the house. "So you decided to call my grandma."

"Yeah."

"Why her?"

VG's coat rustled, which I assume was him shrugging. "Who else would come running to help?"

"True. I didn't know you knew her number."

"I didn't. I Burnt through two bucks of quarters on the pay phone talking to 411."

"Thanks."

"Are we adding that to my finders fee?"

"No," I said with a laugh. "Fifteen percent is plenty."

"Next time I'll make sure it's finders fee *plus* expenses," VG said with mock sadness.

"There will be no next time. I'm done with treasure-hunting."

When we got to the Wolfburg, we pulled into the parking lot, and Grandma took a space next to us. We all got out of our cars. She pointed at my car. "Leave it here. We'll ride in mine."

"Where?"

"Indianapolis. I know a pawn shop that will buy our gold."

"We'll go tomorrow?" VG asked.

"No, we go tonight," she said. "The sooner that gold's converted into money in the bank, the safer everybody will be."

"Where's Three Stick's gun?" VG asked.

"Who?" Grandma said, and then she waved her hand. "Never mind. It's in the car on the front passenger's floor. You know how to safe it?"

"Yes ma'am," VG said.

"Go get it." As he walked off, she looked at me. "You need to use the bathroom?"

"I do."

"We all should probably make a pit stop." VG returned with the gun. He pulled something at the bottom of the grip, and a black rectangle fell out. He handed that to Grandma and then pulled a tab on the back of the tube, causing a bullet to fall out.

"Safe," he said, showing the gun to Grandma.

"Agreed. Pick up the bullet, and let's go inside. I can get a baggy for the gun."

We went up to her unit, did our things, and headed back downstairs. When we got to her car, she handed me the keys. "You drive. Your eyes are better at night. I'll navigate."

————————————

It was a two-hour drive to Indy. I could have made it quicker, but Grandma insisted I drive the speed limit. "Last thing we need is to get pulled over with gold and guns," she said. "The cops will think we're Bonnie and Clyde."

I thought that was unlikely, but I followed her instructions. As we drove, VG, in the back seat, counted the gold. 599 gold coins. It was a lot. After he finished he announced he was taking a nap.

"I understand you two young men have a deal," Grandma said after VG started to softly snore.

"You do?" I asked.

"VG made sure I was aware of it. Told me twice."

"Before or after he told you where I was?"

"After."

"And?"

"And, are you planning on keeping it?"

"I was."

She clucked her tongue. "Boy, I sure wouldn't."

"He did come back for me."

"I know. Fifteen percent is just a lot." She sighed. "Oh well, it's your money."

We ended up in a strip mall just on the edge of downtown Indianapolis. Grandma had me park under a streetlight in the nearly empty parking lot. The pawn shop had most of the mall, but the end unit closest to us was a diner, which we learned opened at five AM.

"Two hours until breakfast," Grandma said. "Anybody got an alarm clock?"

"My watch has an alarm," VG, who had woken up when I pulled off the Interstate, said from the back.

"Is it loud enough to wake you up?" she asked.

"Yes."

"Set it to five. We're going to breakfast then. In the meantime, nap-time."

VG's alarm worked as advertised, and when we woke up – too soon, frankly, but better than no sleep – the restaurant was just opening. "Okay," Grandma said. She opened the glovebox of her car and produced a small black gun with a wooden handle. She handed it to me. "That's a .38 snub-nose revolver. Put it in your coat pocket."

"I've never shot a gun," I said.

"We'll fix that later," she said. "In the meantime, don't pull it out unless I do. Or I'm dead. In either case, point and pull the trigger hard. You've got five shots."

"Only five?" I said.

"If you need more, either you can't hit shit, or you're shooting at a vampire." She winked at me. "In either case, one more bullet won't help." She looked over at VG. "You bring the gold."

"We can't leave it here?" he asked. "And what about a gun for me?"

"If we have a problem, your job is to take the gold and run. As for leaving it in the car, I'd hate for somebody to steal it with the car."

"Okay," he said. We went inside and had a leisurely breakfast with lots of coffee, killing time until 7 AM when the pawn shop opened.

When it did, we went inside, where she was greeted as Mrs. Bathus by a small and bald black guy. She had VG show him the inside of the gym bag, and he led us to an office behind the counter.

The office was plain – white drywall, a cheap desk, and mismatched chairs. VG brought out the gold. We counted. He tested a couple with some chemicals and a scale, then pulled out a newspaper, a calculator, and a scratchpad.

"599 gold coins," he finally said. "as of today's spot price, $212,046."

"We'll take a cashier's check," Grandma said.

"Two-twelve is what I can sell them at," the man replied. "I gotta make a profit."

"Two-twelve is the minimum you can sell them for," she replied. "Collectors..."

"Want coins that are cleaned and graded," he said. "Which costs money."

"Tell you what," Grandma said. "Two hundred even." She spread her hands over the gold. "Surely you can clean, grade, and make a profit on twelve grand?"

He chuckled. "You drive a hard bargain."

"Not really."

"Sold, or rather, bought."

"Two checks?" VG said.

"You, young sir," Grandma said, "will get your cut after we get this in the bank."

The man went into a back room and came back a bit later with papers and a check. "You need to certify this isn't stolen," he said.

"My mom found it. Don't know how it got to where she found it."

"When?"

"1925."

"That's good enough," the man said.

After we finally finished all the paperwork, we drove to a bank nearby. Grandma helped me open up a checking account, out of which I cut VG's check for thirty grand. Grandma asked the clerk, "Can I make a phone call? Long distance, I'm afraid."

He frowned, then looked down at his papers. Apparently, 200 grand made us big enough shots that they could spare a call. She called our lawyer, and we set up a meeting for later that day. After she hung up, we had the bank cut another cashier's check for $51,403, the exact amount we owed on the house.

"Now, back home," she said, once we got the check. "Pat, can you find your way back? I need a nap."

"Sure can," I said.

CHAPTER 37

Vincent Bisceglie III

Some old biddy took my gold!
It was two AM, and Vince was standing in the basement bathroom shivering. The basement had a back door that led to the outside, making it easier to sneak into. Besides, his clothes were caked with mud, both from hiding while Pat and VG played Indiana Jones and from falling on his ass twice while running away from the old lady.

He winced as he lifted his shirt. He looked at his reflection in the tiny bathroom mirror. There was a nice red welt on his stomach, the size and shape of a crowbar. It matched nicely with the other welt on his left arm. He tossed the shirt on the pile of the other clothes.

My gun. When Pat had hit him hard enough to cause him to wet his pants, he'd dropped the gun. His dad kept most of the guns in the house locked in the gun safe, except one .38 in the bedroom and Vince's .22 Ruger target pistol. That usually resided in a cabinet in the basement, mostly because his dad didn't want Vince to have the combination to the gun safe.

Now Pat's got the gun. What the fuck am I going to tell Dad?

He looked down at his clothes. *What am I going to tell*

Mom? He absently patted his skivvies, then jerked his hand away. They were wet with piss.

I can't run the washing machine now. It will wake somebody up.

"What the hell?"

Vince jerked and turned to see his dad in a housecoat with a revolver in his hand looking at him. "Why is everybody pointing Goddamned guns at me?" Vince said.

His dad lowered the gun. "What everybody?" Vince didn't answer. He watched his father's eyes scan down to see the pile of muddy clothing. "In my case," his dad said, "I thought I heard an elephant rooting around down here."

"Sorry," Vince said.

His dad looked at him, anger in his eyes. "Do you want to tell me what the fuck is going on here?"

No, not really. "I was out..."

"No shit. Out digging for coal?"

There's just no way out of this. "Gold."

"Oh Jesus," his dad said. "What have you done?"

"Nothing!" He held his hands up. "I mean nothing! By the time I got there, they were running away with a big box in their hands!"

His dad looked down at the pile of clothes, then at the red mark on Vince's chest. "Really?"

"Really." Vince pointed at the clothing. "I fell chasing after them. Hard. It was dark, and I hit a tree."

"And your skivvies?"

"I hit the tree really hard. And it was cold out."

"If you're..."

"I swear!"

His dad looked at him, then the clothing. "Put all of the dirty stuff in a basket and go to bed."

"Mom?"

"She took a pill. She'll be out until morning."

Amy Burton, Land of Lincoln Legal Aid

The call came in around ten AM. It was the Balthus woman, calling long distance from Indianapolis. "We got the money," she said.

"How?" I asked, more out of reflex than need. There are things about one's clients that it's better we don't know.

"Found the end of a rainbow," she said. "Does it matter?"

"I guess not," I replied. "Do we need a cash counter?" This I did need to know – cash transactions have to be reported.

"No. We have a cashier's check for $51,403. Payable to B-Squared slash Fifth Street Mortgage."

My eyebrows went up at that. Most of my clients are hard-working but not sophisticated. Getting a check payable to both entities was something they'd never think of.

"You know," I said, "they may want to charge additional interest and late fees."

"That's why I've got a Philadelphia lawyer," she replied. "I'm sure you can persuade them to take the check."

I decided to take the term 'Philadelphia lawyer' as a compliment, given Mrs. Balthus' age. "Probably. Still, bring a checkbook."

"I will, or rather Pat will. They're starter checks, if that matters."

"I'm sure the bank will take them."

"Good. We're heading back home. I'd like to wrap this up today if possible. Could you call the bank and see if we could meet this afternoon?"

Nothing like a rush job to get the blood pumping. Still, I had a standard release form for stuff like this. One of our paralegals could fill in the blanks for me in no time. Besides, we usually lost foreclosure cases. It would be nice to notch up a win. "I'll see what I can do."

"Great. If we're not home, please leave a message. Oh, and by the way, we probably have a few bucks to spare to pay for your services."

"Land of Lincoln Legal Aid always appreciates the help." We said our goodbyes and hung up.

After I hung up, I pulled the Kowalski's file and hand-filled out the appropriate details on a blank release of mortgage form. When I finished, I had Debbie, one of our paralegals, type a clean copy for review. While she was cranking that out, I called Tom Ford, the attorney for the bank.

After two transfers and some obnoxious on-hold music, I finally got put through to Tom. "Mr. Ford," I said. "I'm Amy Burton, lawyer for the Kowalski foreclosure."

"Since when can they afford a lawyer?" he asked.

"I'm with Land of Lincoln Legal Aid."

"Look, Miss Burton," (I could hear the 'Miss') "we're a bank, not a charity. I'm sure you've got a sob story..."

"Actually, they have a cashier's check for fifty-one thousand." There was a long silence on the line, long enough for me to say, "Did we get disconnected?"

"No, I'm here. Where did those people get the money?"

"They were vague on the subject. They did say they wanted to get this matter closed today. Are you available this afternoon?"

Another long silence. Finally, he said, "I need to check with my client, but I am."

"Good. In the interest of time, what's your fax number? I'd like to send over a draft of the release paperwork for your review."

"Release paperwork?"

"Surely you don't think I'm just going to hand over a check without getting a release?"

The silence suggested he did think so. I was forming the impression that Ford was used to using his law degree to bully people who couldn't afford lawyers. I smiled, thinking of how much I enjoyed shoving stuff up the asses of petty tyrants and bullies.

"Fine," he said. "Do you have a pen?"

"I do." He rattled off a number, which I took down as Debbie walked in with the clean copy. We hung up, and I faxed over the documents.

About an hour later, Ford called back. "They owe us additional interest since we started proceedings," he said. "And legal fees."

"Given that they're prepared to hand you a cashier's check for the total amount listed in the court documents now," I replied, "surely you can waive that? Or would you rather tell the judge at next week's hearing that you balked and wasted her time over a few bucks of accrued interest?"

There was a heavy sigh. "Does two-thirty today work? At the bank in Eastville."

"It works for me," I said. "My clients implied that they were in transit, so I won't know for sure until noon. Unless you hear otherwise from me, please plan on two-thirty. Where exactly is the bank?"

"You know where Eastville is?"

"Yes."

"The bank's on the main drag. Next to the public library."

"I can find it. I'll see you then. I assume you're okay with the release paperwork." I was talking to dial tone.

"And a pleasure doing business with you," I said as I hung up. I dialed the Kowalski's number and left a message on their machine. I was just going out to lunch when Pat Kowalski called me back, confirming the appointment.

Vincent Bisceglie III

Vince had planned to blow off school the next day, but his dad had practically dragged him out of bed and made him go. "Hero in the night, hero in the morning too," he'd said, a shitty grin on his face. At school, Pat and VG were nowhere to be found.

Vince was walking past the principal's office to his afternoon class when he saw his dad come walking into the building. "The Pollak found something," his dad said. He pointed at the principal's office. "Come on, I need to sign you out."

"Why?"

"You stuck your nose in this, so now you get to see the end."

CHAPTER 38

Pat Kowalski

Ms. Burton asked to meet with us at the library before we went to see the bank. She looked at our check and showed us the paperwork we wanted to get signed. As we were doing all of that, she accidentally kicked Grandma's purse. Th big revolver made a metallic clinking as it hit her keys inside the purse.

"Mrs. Balthus," Burton said, "you know that carrying concealed weapons is illegal in this state."

"I've heard," Grandma replied.

"Just so we're clear," the lawyer said. She resumed going over the paperwork. At Grandma's suggestion, I'd left the pistol she'd given me in her glovebox. Three Stick's pistol, unloaded, was with me in a baggy in my backpack.

At two-fifteen on the dot, we all stood up and walked next door to the bank. Burton told one of the people sitting at a desk in the lobby we were there to see Mr. Bisceglie. He said we were expected, and he led us through a security door and upstairs into a large office with a big picture window overlooking the street. Mr. Bisceglie, AKA Three Stick's dad, was sitting behind a wooden desk big enough to land planes on. Tom Ford was standing behind him to his right, my left and Three Sticks was on the opposite side of his dad.

"Quite a party," Grandma said. She pointed at a painting on the side wall. "Mister Big." Then to Mr. Bisceglie. "Little Big." To Three Sticks. "Baby Big."

Something clicked in me. The guy over the fireplace was one of Capone's men! He was the dude that Great Barb had shoved a gun into his gut! I looked at Three Sticks. And apparently, he'd gotten at least part of that story, given what he'd said last night.

"Let's get right to it, shall we?" Ford said.

"Let's," our lawyer replied, settling into a chair in front of the desk. She opened a briefcase. "I assume you reviewed what I faxed over?"

"I did," Ford replied. "We still want interest..."

"And I want to date Tom Selleck," our lawyer said. "We don't always get what we want."

"We'll waive the interest due the bank," Mr. Bisceglie said, flapping a hand. "But the big problem is getting Fifth Street to waive what's due them."

"Please, sir, I'm not stupid," the lawyer said. "I know Fifth Street is a front."

"I don't know what you think you know..." Ford said.

"I know their mailing address is a copy shop in Urbana," she replied. I think she kind of enjoyed cutting Ford off. "I also pulled the corporate documents. One Tom Ford is listed as having filed them." She nodded at Three Sticks. "One Vincent Bisceglie III is listed as President." She looked at Three Sticks. "Are you even old enough?"

"I'm eighteen," he said in a high voice. Clearly, he had no idea he was in charge of anything.

"Perhaps..." Mr. Bisceglie said.

"Perhaps we should just cut the crap," Grandma said. She would have said more, but the lawyer put a hand on her lap.

"What my client is trying to say in her folksy way is that we have two choices here." She held up a finger. "One. We settle now, today, with a cashier's check drawn on an Indianapolis bank. We can even wait while you call and verify the check." A second finger. "Two. We have a court hearing Monday in which *somebody* gets to explain not only why they're wasting the court's time but why a high school senior is running a mortgage company out of a copy shop in Urbana." She put her hands on her lap. "I, for one, am indifferent as to which option we choose."

Mr. Bisceglie looked like he'd taken a big bite out of a shit sandwich, and Ford looked like he was going to explode. Three Sticks looked as if he were lost in space. I had to look down to hide my grin.

"Is that...?" Three Sticks said.

"Shut up," Ford growled.

"We're always glad to help keep people in their houses," Mr. Bisceglie said, holding a hand in the air. "Which bank did you say the check was drawn on?"

The lawyer told him and we waited while Bisceglie himself called to verify the funds. It was a quick call, and when he finished, he said, "Okay. Let's do this."

Our lawyer produced a manila file folder with papers in it. We all signed, and she notarized them. Once that was done, she said, "Thank you for your time." To me, she said, "I'll go file this copy with the county. You keep that for your records."

"We done?" Ford said. He still looked ready to blow.

"Not quite," Grandma said. "We have something of Baby V's." She nodded at me, and I took out the baggy with the gun from my backpack.

"This is for Three Sticks," I said, holding the gun in the baggy by the barrel. The bullets were loose in the bag and drooped down by my hand.

"Just leave it on the desk," Mr. Bisceglie said, "and get out of my bank. I recommend you close your accounts out."

"We will," Grandma said. "Right now."

We got up and went to the lobby, where I closed out our account, all sixty-three dollars of it. I took it in cash and put it in my pocket.

"Make sure you tell your mom before she writes any checks," Grandma said as we left.

"I think I'm writing the checks for now."

Vincent Bisceglie III

"What was that about me running a mortgage company?" Vince said as soon as the Kowalskis were out of the office. "Does that have anything to do with the papers I signed?"

"What do you think, you nitwit?" Ford growled. "We needed somebody to front the damn thing!"

"Tom," Vince's dad said in a quiet voice. "My son and I need a moment in private."

He left without saying a word, although he closed the door a lot harder than it needed to be. Vince and his dad both stared at the gun in its baggy on the desk for a moment. His dad finally picked it up and counted the bullets.

"I count nine," he said, his voice dangerously low. "The gun holds ten."

"It went off."

He stood up a lot faster than Vince thought he could and grabbed Vince by the shoulders. He pushed hard, hard enough to nearly take Vince off of his feet, and kept pushing until his shoulders hit the wall. "Do you want to try that again?"

Vince, tears in his eyes, told his dad the truth. His dad let go of his son. "Baby V, did nothing I tell you sink in?"

"I hate that name!" Vince cried. "My name is Vincent! Vince! Hell, even Vinnie! But I'm not a baby!"

His dad moved as if to strike his son but stopped. He let go. "Vince. So you want to be called Vince now."

"I've always wanted to be called Vince!"

"Okay, Vince," his dad said, his voice dripping with disdain. "I'll ask again. Why, when I specifically told you not to, did you decide to wave a gun around?"

You didn't specifically tell me not to wave a gun around. He looked at his dad and decided that quibbling was not a good idea. *You also didn't tell me that I was being set up as a frontman for something.* "I have to get out of this town. I *have* to."

"By putting a bullet into a kid's head?"

"He wasn't..."

"Bullshit. You didn't get those bruises by falling down."

I might have had to bust a cap out there. Vince looked down. "I was wrong," he choked out. He didn't quite agree with that statement, but it had to be said.

"Thank you. Thank you for saying what was obvious."

"Now what?"

"Now what what?"

"For me." Vince gestured at the closed door. "For them. For us."

"For them? They get to keep that house free and clear until they default on the real estate tax." His dad walked back to his desk.

"Can't we call the cops? I mean, they don't own that property. Where the gold was?"

His dad rounded on him. "And we do?"

"No."

"No." His dad pointed at the door. "So you're damn lucky *they* didn't call the cops on you for armed fucking robbery!" His dad resumed his stroll towards his desk. "As for you, John Fucking Dillinger, holding people up with a .22 target pistol, I don't know." He pointed at the gun on the desk. "I sure know where *that's* going to go. Under lock and key." His dad sat down heavily. "Now, I suggest you leave before I lose my temper."

"About this Fifth Street Mortgage..." Vince said.

His dad glared at him and pointed at the door. Vince left. He didn't know what hurt more – getting hit by Pat, watching that old biddy and her cheap lawyer stick it to the family, being used as a patsy, or his dad's anger and contempt at him.

CHAPTER 39

Amy Burton, Land of Lincoln Legal Aid

It was Friday afternoon, and I was just thinking about happy hour when the phone in my office rang. I picked it up.

"You bitch!" the man on the other end said. He ran on in a similar vein for a bit.

"A pleasure talking to you, Mr. Bisceglie," I said when he ran down.

"A regulator's got his head so far up my ass I can taste his Brylcreem," Bisceglie said. The image caused me to chuckle. "Wants to know all about Fifth Street. I thought we had a deal!"

"I'm sorry if you misunderstood me," I said, a smile on my face. "I merely meant that *you* wouldn't have to explain yourself to the judge at the hearing. As an officer of the court, I am bound to bring violations of law to the attention of the authorities."

His reply was unprintable and intemperate, so I hung up. I put on my coat, closing the office door as I did. Then I went into my briefcase and pulled out my Walther PPK, which I tucked in an outside coat pocket. A girl can't be too careful, and it's always better to be judged by twelve than carried by six.

Pat

"It's early," I said. "And cold."

"So, move to Florida," my Grandma said.

It was Saturday morning, and we were at the old slag heap outside of town. The hill rose a good hundred feet above the flat plain. It's red dirt and rocks were bare, even in summer. Whatever the rock was that they'd dug out of the old coal mine, nothing would grow in it.

"You got something to shoot at?" Grandma asked.

"Yes." Mom had snagged a couple of cardboard fruit boxes from the IGA. I set them out in front of the hill, weighting them down from the wind with loose rocks. I came back to find Grandma had put a trio of pistols on a towel on the hood of her Oldsmobile.

"This is Great Barb's gun," she said, holding up a black gun with a longer barrel. "It's a Model 1892 revolver with a four-inch barrel. Holds six .38 special bullets."

"Surely it wasn't made back then?" I said.

Grandma smiled. "Probably. It was my mother's, and she got it off of Mister Good Boots."

I looked at it dubiously. "Are we sure it won't blow up?"

"It didn't blow up when I shot it at Baby Vincent."

So you got lucky once, I thought. Aloud, I said, "So that's why it looks familiar."

"Yep," she said with a smile. "We'll start with this and work our way to the smaller guns."

"Why?"

"This one is heavy and doesn't kick much. Those snubbies bounce around a bit."

We shot through a box of bullets between all three guns. When we finished, she pointed at the snub-noses. "Which one do you want?"

"Mom won't let me have a gun."

"So don't tell her."

I picked the one with a plastic handle. "I'll take this."

"Okay. Now, we need to get you a passport photo."

"Why?"

"The state says you need a permit to own a gun." She patted my shoulder. "Don't worry, it's like ten bucks for the card."

"Okay." She checked that the other guns were unloaded and shoved them into a small bag. "We'll clean them at your place," she said as we climbed into her car.

Once we were on the road, I said, "We got a letter from the DuPage County Sheriff's Office."

"Oh?"

"They want to talk to Great Barb. They think they found your father's body."

"I'll be damned," she said.

"You should call them. Set something up.""I will."

The meeting was set up for Wednesday afternoon. I got to the nursing home first and was glad to see that Great Barb was having one of her good days.

"I got a letter from your son Tony," I told her.

"Good," she said, brightening visibly. "Read it for me. I can't find my glasses."

I truthfully think her eyesight had gotten so bad that she couldn't read even with glasses, but I was glad she asked me to read it. It allowed me to edit out the part about how Tony was upset at his sister's hiding his letters.

The letter itself wasn't very interesting. Tony, who was living with a 'long-term partner' named Joe, had just retired. They lived a fairly quiet life in San Francisco, and apparently, he had no intention of coming back. When I finished, Great Barb asked me to reply and send her love. I said yes, just as Mary and the cop from Chicago walked in.

"I'm Tom Kehoe," he said, introducing himself. He was nearly bald and built like a runner.

"Barbara Pikus," she said, taking his offered hand.

Officer Kehoe told us about the body in Bell's Burger Barn and how it had been found. He finished by saying what was obvious, that other than foul play, they had no information.

"Did you find a third body in the barn?" Great Barb asked when he finished. "A big, heavy man?"

"We did," Kehoe said, perking up.

"Mom?" Grandma said.

Great Barb waved her off with a feeble hand. "He's your shooter of 1924. Name of Vincent Bisceglie Senior."

"What?" Grandma and I both said.

"You heard me," Great Barb replied.

"How do you know that?" Kehoe asked. "And how do you spell that?" He added, reaching in his pocket for a notebook.

I spelled it for the cop. It was a reflex.

"Not another word, Mom," Grandma said. "I'll get you a lawyer."

"I put him there. Shot him with a .38."

"She's senile," Grandma said, her hand on Kehoe's shoulder. "She saw a movie..."

"No, I'm not senile," Great Barb said. To Kehoe. "That fat fuck killed my husband. So I did him."

Kehoe shrugged off Grandma's hand and moved to another page in his notebook. "Please go on."

"So it would have been in the early 1950s," Great Barb said. "Summer. Hot. I was at home when a man knocked at the door." She looked at me. "I don't know what the right term is nowadays, but back then, we called them colored."

"This colored man have a name?" Kehoe asked.

"Moses Rawlings." Great Barb leaned back in her bed. "He was very sick. Said the cancer had gotten him, and he wanted to get right with God before he met him in person." She looked at her daughter. "As do I."

"Go on," Kehoe said.

"He told me that he'd buried my husband. Back then, he was just getting started in the construction business, and he needed a truck and some money. Times were hard, and being colored didn't help. No bank would give him the time of day."

She wound down for a second but perked up with a visible effort. "But Bisceglie would. Mister Big, we called him. My husband worked for him, and they both worked for Mr. Capone." She used the Italian pronunciation, saying the final E.

"Al Capone?" Kehoe said.

"Yes. Mister Big was his downstate man. He was also a gambler and really bad at picking ponies."

"But your husband worked for him?" Kehoe said.

"Which made it easier, I think," Great Barb said. "For Big to set it up." She shrugged. "But that's a guess."

I was sitting there with my mouth open in shock. She knew this all these years?

Kehoe held up his hand with the pen in it. "For who to set what up?"

"Mom," Grandma said.

"Mister Big killed my husband," Great Barb said. "In an ambush. There was another fellow with my husband, but I don't know his name."

"We identified that body," Kehoe said, writing. He

waved his hand. "Please go on."

"Like I said, Big ambushed the two men in Chicago. he wanted their money and figured he could make it look like they skipped town with the cash." She shrugged weakly. "Or even if their bodies turned up, Capone would think a rival gang shot them."

"And how did this Moses fellow know all of this?" Kehoe asked.

"He was there. He worked construction and was pouring the slab they ended up underneath."

As the cop wrote, Grandma said, "Why did you believe all of that?"

Great Barb smiled. "I suspected that Big knew more than he let on when my husband disappeared. Then I got word that Big was short on payments to Capone and was blaming Michael. I loved my husband, but he simply wasn't smart enough to cheat Capone. Now Big, he was just smart enough to try."

"And with your husband missing, it looked like he'd skipped town with Capone's cash," Kehoe said. He nodded to himself. "Apparently, it worked."

"It did," Great Barb said. "I got concerned over time that Big would try to repeat that with me as the victim, so when he and his floozy-of-the-month took the train to Indy for a little party in the hotel room, I called the FBI."

"That was you?" Grandma asked.

"Why the FBI?" Kehoe asked.

"Big's floozy was all of fifteen," Great Barb said. She chuckled. "And a real piece of work. Made a nice bit of money playing Daddy's-little-girl for her clients."

I wasn't sure I wanted to know how Great Barb knew that. The whole thing was creeping me out a lot.

"Mann Act," Kehoe said.

"Yes," Great Barb said. "He got a stint in jail. Got out after Capone went to Alcatraz."

"Let's get back to Moses," Kehoe said.

"Is this the black man who fixed the roof?" My grandmother asked, looking stunned.

"No, that was his son," Great Barb said. "His dad said he owed us something." To Kehoe, she said, "Moses had tracked us down by the registration on Michael's truck. So he told me what had happened and where Michael was buried."

"Why didn't you go to the police?" I asked. Blurted, more like it.

"Illinois wasn't as bad as some states, but the word of a poor colored man against a rich white man?" Great Barb shook her head. "We'd have gotten tossed out of the police station on our ears."

"So you killed this Bisceglie fellow?" Kehoe asked.

"Yes," Great Barb said. "I had Moses call Big. Said they were remodeling and going to add a basement. Moses needed help to move the bodies."

"And Big bought it," Kehoe said.

"He did," Great Barb replied. "And I was waiting for him. I shot him with that old gun I used to keep in my bedside table." She looked at Grandma. "When you were little."

"I remember," Grandma said, looking especially pale.

"What happened to the gun?" Kehoe asked.

"I tossed it in the river," Great Barb said. "Or a pond. I can't remember. So long ago. This was before the Interstate, you know."

Kehoe stood up. "I need to call my boss."

"Surely you're not going to arrest her?" I said. "She's old!"

"And she just confessed to murder," Kehoe replied.

"I did?" Great Barb said. She started singing in

Lithuanian.

"What's she saying?" Kehoe asked.

"It's a nursery rhyme," Grandma said. "She frequently forgets her English."

Kehoe shook his head. "I need to find a phone." He walked out, notepad in hand.

Great Barb and Grandma talked in Lithuanian for a bit, and then Great Barb closed her eyes.

"She said she loves you," Grandma said.

Something didn't look right about Great Barb. I got up and went to her bedside. "She's not breathing!"

"I know," Grandma said.

I ran outside and grabbed the first nurse I could find, frantic to get some help. They came very slowly and just looked at her.

"Do something!" I shouted. By now, Kehoe was back in the room.

"She has a DNR," one of the nurses said.

"A what?" Kehoe and I asked.

"Do Not Resuscitate," Grandma said. "It means that when she stops breathing, it's over."

Grandma sounded calm, but I saw the tears in her eyes. I had to wipe my eyes, too. We stood there for a minute, just looking at her body. Finally, one of the nurses quietly asked us to step outside so they could "do what was necessary."

In the hallway, Kehoe said, "I'm sorry for your loss."

"Thanks," Grandma said, looking at the closed door to the room we'd just left. "It was a long time coming. She was ready."

I was not at all ready for another funeral. I was getting too damn good at them.

"About her husband," Grandma said. "How do we claim the body?"

"I actually don't know," Kehoe replied. "I was coming back in here to give her the Miranda warning." He shook his head.

"Well, that won't be necessary," Grandma said.

"No, it won't," Kehoe said, glancing at the closed door. "I need to go get some more quarters and call my boss back."

CHAPTER 40

Pat

We decided to have a double funeral – Great Barb and her husband. We had to delay for a week to get her husband's body – her second husband's body - downstate, but as Grandma said, Barb wasn't going anywhere. Michael's coffin was closed, of course. Grandma found a picture of him, which we put on the top of the coffin.

Her son Tony came in, shivering in the February cold. He had become a round man, bald, with a white Santa Claus beard. Grandma and him didn't say much to each other. There was no forgiveness in either of their hearts.

After the visitation and before the trip to the cemetery, Stephanie Mroz gave the family a moment alone with the coffins. I found myself standing next to Grandma in front of her open coffin. "She looks good," I said, mostly because that's what everybody seemed to say.

"Here," Grandma said, elbowing me. Her purse was open, and I could see the big black revolver she'd shot at Three Sticks. The revolver was in a plastic baggie.

"Here what?"

"Put it in the casket."

"Why?"

"This is the gun from the nightstand."

It took me a minute to realize that it was also the gun that had been used to shoot Mr. Big. "Why? She's dead, case closed."

"I don't want my mom's name dragged through the mud in the newspapers," she said. "Without the gun, all they've got is the ramblings of a senile old woman."

I didn't think anybody was going to run to the newspapers over a thirty-year-old murder, but I did owe Grandma a favor. I reached into her purse.

"Baggie and all," Grandma said. "I wiped it down good and unloaded it."

"Got it." I took the gun out of her purse, trying to hide it from anybody looking our way, and shoved it as deeply as I could inside the coffin. After I did that, I stepped back.

"Lock it up," Grandma said to Stephanie, who nodded and closed up the coffin.

"Dust to dust," Grandma said.

Vincent Bisceglie III

"I'm not going to go to jail, Miss Hamilton, am I?" Vince asked. He was sitting in an office in Maple Corners.

Debra Hamilton, Vince's newly acquired lawyer, didn't bother to hide her smile. "You should consider yourself the luckiest person in the county."

Vince didn't feel lucky and said so. Hamilton's smile faded. "Normally in this county, when one adult shoots a gun at another adult, they at least charge them with assault with a deadly weapon."

"But I didn't hit her!"

"Not for lack of trying, at least in the eyes of the law," she replied. "But since none of the three eyewitnesses who saw you blazing away bothered to call the cops, you're in the clear."

"They couldn't..."

"Of course, they could," Hamilton said. "Right after they got home and stashed the gold under Grandma Six-Shooter's mattress." Hamilton made a show of checking her meticulously painted nails. "But they didn't." She looked up at Vince. "For now. At any time, any one of them could get a notion to call the cops on you."

"But, if they wait, wouldn't there be questions?"

Hamilton waved her hand dismissively. "Your Honor, I was scared," she said in a simpering tone. "No, petrified, Your Honor, *petrified* with fear that Vince would hunt me and my family down. I've only now found the courage to come forward." She glared at Vince. "You got your one shot at being a gangster," she said in a normal tone of voice. "If you decide to wave your gun around again, find another lawyer."

Vince stared at her for a moment. "Got it," he finally said. "About the bank...?"

"What about the bank?"

The problem with the bank was why Vince had ended up with Hamilton in the first place. A week ago, on a Friday night, they'd arrested his dad and Tom Ford as they were seizing the bank. Ford had told him to 'find yourself a good lawyer, kid' as they were leading him out in handcuffs.

Not knowing what else to do, he grabbed a phone book and went to the Yellow Pages. Hamilton had been the first person to answer the phone. Since then, he'd told her everything.

"You know," Vince said irritably. "Fifth Street Mortgage."

"Again, luckiest man in the county," Hamilton replied. "Or, in this case, most clueless."

"Hey!"

"Hey is for horses," she replied curtly. "And your cluelessness is what will keep you out of jail. It's obvious you had no idea what you were signing." She leaned back in her chair. "So the District Attorney isn't charging you."

"He shouldn't," Vince said. "My dad plays golf with him."

"You're thinking of Fisher, the State Attorney. Bank fraud is a Federal beef, so your dad's golfing buddy's got jack-all to do with anything."

Vince felt a wave of relief wash over him. "Thank you."

"Don't thank me yet," she said. "You haven't seen my bill."

"About that," Vince said.

"We'll set up a payment plan," she said.

Great. I'll pay you out of my McDonald's wages while I go to Junior College part-time. You'll be old and gray by the time I'm done paying.

They went over some other legal mumbo-jumbo, and Vince left. He'd had to buy a car since the car he was driving was somehow owned by the bank, which now meant the government. He'd gotten a used Vega with one busted headlight.

Pat

I got an A on the oral history project. I decided to leave the gold out of it. That and the revenge murder. I also decided to leave Three Sticks, I mean 'Vince's' gun out. His dad got hauled off to the pokey, and the bank got closed, so he was having a shitty-enough time of it.

Grandma had persuaded Mom to stiff the hospital. "Can't get blood from a turnip," she'd said. She was good at just not paying people.

Since VG got 15%, which was $30,000, I decided that Grandma earned 15% for preventing 'Vince' from putting a cap in my ass. Mom really didn't earn her 15%, unless you count things like toilet-training me. Grandma suggested that I should count that.

After those checks, a thousand to Land of Lincoln Legal Aid, and paying off the house, I was left with $57,597. As Grandma said, it did not relieve me of the need to make a living.

It was, however, more than enough to cover four years at Illinois State. This was especially true since I showed no income and was able to get student aid.

I also traded in the Vega for a nice new red Pontiac Sunbird. I needed wheels to get to Bloomington, after all.

I just wish Dad was around to see me.

*** The End ***

Acknowledgements

My four previous books are all science fiction novels. This book came about because my dad, Mike Gerrib, said that mysteries sold better and that I should write one. I wasn't interested, but he taught me how to use a spoon, so I figured I owed it to him. (Yes, I know this is technically not a mystery, but it's close enough.) Since I'm thanking Dad, I also need to thank my mom, Martha Gerrib as well.

I want to thank the volunteers who run the Westville, IL, Depot and Historical Museum. One of the items they discovered was what they believe to be the first mention of Westville in the wider world – a one-paragraph report in the *New York Times* about a railroad strike blocking the tracks. This became Chapter One of the book.

That chapter was written in the summer of 2018 in the Geneva Public Library. I was participating in a writing jam with Don Hunt, the leader of my writer's group. I would like to thank him as well as Wren Roberts, Lauren Cidell, Jason Evans, and our two former members, Dex Greenbright and Phil Steadman. Their reviews and commentary made this a better book.

I want to send a shout-out to some former coworkers of mine: Gary McGlauchlin, Rick Webster, Tom Longino, and Joe Kehoe. Lastly, I want to thank you, the reader. I hope you enjoyed this book.

Chris Gerrib
Darien, IL September 30, 2024

Chris Gerrib has wanted to be a writer since he was a child riding his bicycle to the library in the small Central Illinois town where he grew up. Since then, he has spent a tour in the US Navy, got an MBA, and now has a day job with a multi-national software company as a project manager. For fun, he plays golf, travels, and is a voracious reader. He lives in the Chicago suburbs and is active in his local Rotary Club. He's had four science fiction novels published. Strawberry Gold is his first suspense thriller.

www.ingramcontent.com/pod-product-compliance
Lightning Source LLC
Chambersburg PA
CBHW050718180626
46814CB00002B/494